MW00413677

Jed Power

The **Boss**
of
Hampton
Beach

a Dan Marlowe novel

Dark Jetty Publishing

Published by
Dark Jetty Publishing
4 Essex Center Drive #3906
Peabody, MA 01961

Cover Artist:
Brandon Swann

ISBN 978-0-9858617-1-1

Acknowledgement

The author would like to thank his editor, Louisa Swann, for her excellent work, encouragement and patience, without which "Boss" would not have come this far.

This Book Is Dedicated To My Wife,

Candy.

Chapter One

CAPTAIN BILL MCGEE always said he wanted his ashes scattered off the coast of Hampton Beach. He'd never said anything about dying there and certainly not tonight. After all, he was in the prime of his life.

Still, that life had been a struggle recently, just like it was for every other party boat operator along the New Hampshire seacoast. The boom times of the 80's were long over. Now it was the 90's, and instead of having his charter boats overflowing with hopeful fishermen every morning when they left Hampton Harbor, he was lucky if the tubs were half full. Ditto for his whale watch and Wednesday night fireworks cruises.

Yeah, money was tight, real tight, and it had slowly dawned on him if he wasn't creative, he'd lose the whole shebang–the business, the boats, his house, everything. The worst, by far, would be losing the business that had been in his family for three generations. That's what he'd been thinking about–worrying about, really–for the past few months.

So when the well-dressed Hispanic had approached him with a proposition, it was like the man was reading McGee's mind. Even though he wasn't happy with the idea (in fact, it scared him to death), he didn't hesitate in giving the man an answer right then and there. He didn't even have to sleep on it. Yeah, he'd do it. For the right price. The man agreed to his price and told McGee not to worry. It'd be as easy as a bluefish run.

McGee had to admit everything had gone okay so far. He'd taken one of his best and oldest crew members, Harry, a guy who'd keep his mouth shut for a nice piece of change, and gone exactly where the Hispanic sent him– three miles out beyond the Isle of Shoals. The weather stayed good, calm seas and no moon. And the boat they were meeting had even shown up almost on time. When they'd gotten close enough to the larger vessel, somebody tossed the duffel bags one at a time over the side. McGee had caught them as best he could in the dark with the boat lurching. He'd passed them on to Harry, who'd stashed the bags below.

And so far, that had been that. It looked like everything was going to be all right. Easy money–real easy money.

At least so far.

Now they were on their way back from the pickup spot. McGee at the wheel, his grizzled face all screwed up, peered through the front cabin window as they came up to the mouth of Hampton Harbor. A long, rock jetty jutted out from the beach on their starboard side. Dead ahead loomed the Hampton Bridge. It was a drawbridge, but he was using the smallest of his boats tonight. Between the size of his boat and low tide he could pass beneath the bridge without the hassle of having it raised. In a few minutes they'd be in the harbor. A few more minutes and they'd tie up at his dock and be home free.

Not soon enough, McGee thought. He took his hands off the wheel and scrubbed at his sweaty palms. His heart was going at a good clip, too. He'd need more than a few cold ones when this was over.

He was thinking about how good those beers would make him feel when he heard an outboard motor starting up. Christ, it sounded like another boat was right on top of them. He tried to calm himself–sound tended to carry across the water on clear nights. A craft could be a lot further away than it sounded. At least that's what he was hoping.

"Harry, see what the hell that is." McGee scanned the darkness, seeing nothing but the black outline of the jetty and the lights of a few homes off to port.

He could hear Harry scrambling around the back of the boat. It sounded like the other craft was already in the boat with them, a fact he didn't like one bit. The Hispanic had said he'd meet McGee when they tied up at the dock in the harbor. Could he have changed his plans and decided to hook up with them out here, just to keep McGee honest?

There was a loud thump against the starboard side of the boat. McGee glanced over his shoulder and shoved the throttle forward, wishing that he was already under that damn bridge and back at his dock drinking cold beer.

"Harry, what the hell's going on?" he yelled, not surprised at the shakiness in his voice.

"Jesus, it's a . . . ahhh . . ." Something banged hard, followed by shuffling and more banging. McGee let go of the wheel and spun around. He grabbed a metal fish gaffe and held it shoulder high.

Two figures moved toward him from the back of the boat. As they got closer he could see that they both wore masks and that his hook wasn't going to scare anybody, because both men had pistols pointed directly at him. The first of the men was tall and powerfully built. The second man didn't look as threatening, although he didn't have to with that gun in his fist.

"Throw it over to the side, fuckhead," the big man said.

McGee tossed the hook to his left. Then he held his breath, thinking of every terrible thing that might happen to him in the next few minutes. He didn't have long to think. The big man walked right up to him and started swinging that gun for the side of his head . . .

. . . and that was the last thing Captain Bill McGee ever saw.

Chapter 2

DAN MARLOWE had heard all about Bill McGee and his crewman, Harry Something or other. He'd heard little else since the news broke yesterday morning. Working where he did, all people did was talk. In between that, a little eating, and a lot of drinking.

He batted his lips just as much as anyone else on the beach. How the two men were found dead, both shot in the head, sprawled in McGee's boat. The boat had cracked up on the jetty at the south end of the beach sometime during the night, and the police supposedly didn't have a lead.

According to the news there were no known enemies or hints of anything shady. That didn't keep Dan's customers at the High Tide Restaurant and Saloon from speculating on possible motives. Everything had been tossed around–drugs, gambling debts, fooling with the wrong woman, and other theories so out there they weren't worth repeating.

The incident was as hot a topic of bar conversation as Dan could remember. After all, double murders weren't everyday occurrences at Happy Hampton Beach. So Dan engaged in the conversation as much as any of the customers, except when it veered toward names. He stayed away from dropping names, thank you. He'd been in the bar and restaurant business long enough to know it didn't pay to bad-mouth people, especially local people, and especially when you didn't know what the hell you were talking about.

And most of these people, including Dan, didn't know their facts from their fiction. Still, it was part of his job, chatting customers up. He was interested, so it was easy, so he did. Just made sure to keep away from any name dropping.

Besides, it wouldn't last. Not even a double murder was likely to hold a bar crowd's attention for too long. Sooner or later the newspapers, radio, and TV would stop flogging the case, and then some other topic would become hot. That's when most people would slowly forget about McGee and his buddy and the fact they'd been shot in the head. Dan would, too. After all, people had their own problems to think about.   And so did he. Brother, did he.

That's what Dan was trying not to think about now–his own problems.   Easier to think about two guys getting their heads blown off a few blocks away than the unpleasant things going on in his life. Sure, McGee and his buddy had lost their lives, but at least they probably hadn't suffered long. Dan had lost his family and his restaurant. That tormented him every day.

He stood behind the foot end of the L-shaped mahogany bar of the High Tide Restaurant, hands resting on the polished surface like he was having a manicure, staring out the big front picture window. Outside was Ocean Boulevard, the main thoroughfare through Hampton Beach. Just beyond the boulevard was the municipal parking lot, the beach, and then nothing but Atlantic Ocean. The ocean looked as black as he felt today.

It was nine o'clock on a summer morning and the humidity was already building. Dan frowned. No good dwelling on circumstances he couldn't control. He came around the bar and flicked on the switches that controlled the two large wall air conditioners just like he did every summer morning.

Same routine every day, opening the bar and getting it ready for the day's customers. If it was going to be a hot one, turn on the A/C; if not, open the windows. Then he'd do all the other little things that had to be done to get the bar ready for business. He'd do them one right after the other, the same way every day. In fact, he figured he could do them with a bag over his head. He'd been doing it that long–back when he'd owned the Tide and still now when he no longer did.

The routine used to be how he made sure everything

stayed in order. Now the routine kept him sane.

He was the second one in every morning, right after Shamrock, the Irish dishwasher and the High Tide's jack-of-all-trades. Shamrock came in at the ungodly hour of around 4 a.m. Dan wasn't sure exactly. After all, he didn't have to pay the man anymore. The only thing the new owner cared about was that no matter what crazy time he got in, Shamrock got all his work done. And he did. Always. The man was a workhorse. He'd clean the floors, do the rugs, empty all the trash, shovel snow in the winter, and do any of the handyman jobs that were always popping up. Then he'd do a shift, sometimes two, on the dishwasher.

And when they needed someone to go through one of the trap doors in the floor that led into the dark, dirty crawl space beneath the building, who'd they get?

Certainly not Dan–he definitely wasn't paid enough to go down into that pest hole. Even the plumbers didn't want to go down there. Shamrock was the man. He didn't think anything of jumping in with whatever the hell crawled around down there.

Yeah, Shamrock did everything, and he'd been around quite a while now. He'd worked for Dan when he'd owned the business and stayed on with the new owner, just like Dan had. Most days when Dan came to work the first thing he'd hear was Shamrock greeting him with that County Cork brogue of his. Not this morning though; he wasn't there. But Dan could tell he had been and that he'd probably be back soon. He could see the mop and bucket down at the kitchen end of the bar and the vacuum sitting in the middle of the dining room floor. The Irishman had most likely gone for coffee and donuts, Dan figured. Hell, the little guy lived on coffee and donuts. He'd be back. Shamrock spent more time in the High Tide than the beer barrels.

It wasn't long before Dan looked up from the chrome beer chest he was restocking and there was Shamrock, looking just like a guy named Shamrock should, coming through the swinging doors from the kitchen, a box of donuts in his hands. He put the box down on a small bar table. "Will ya have a donut with me, Danny Boy?"

"No, thanks, Shamrock. I already ate."

Dan didn't stop to chat. He slid ashtrays out along the bar, made sure they were evenly spaced, then grabbed a large green bucket from under the bar and went back through the kitchen to the ice chest to fill it. He brought the filled bucket back behind the bar and dumped the ice into one of the bar sinks, making enough trips to fill both sinks, one at each end of the bar. All the while keeping an eye on the little Irishman.

Something was up with Shamrock. He usually had a big smile on that rosy mug of his. But not today. And talk? With Shamrock around no one had to worry about a lull in the conversation. But right now he wasn't making a peep. He leaned against the shoulder-high wooden divider that separated the bar area from the restaurant section of the establishment, nibbled on one of his donuts, and peered at the fish tank on top of the divider.

It wasn't until Dan was in the middle of slicing his lemons, limes, and oranges on a chopping block on the bar that Shamrock finally started talking. And he whispered it more than actually said it. "Danny, would you be knowin' how much they get for that cocaine powder nowadays?"

Normally that question would have made Dan a little leery, but coming from Shamrock it was downright out of the blue. He would've guessed the Irishman didn't even know what the stuff was, or at least, had never seen it.

Dan's heart picked up its beat. "Why?"

"For the love of Jesus, Danny Boy. I'm just curious. That's all. Nothin' more." The Irishman's voice was shaky and he couldn't meet Dan's gaze.

Even though he'd known Shamrock quite a while and knew he was ok, Dan's defenses went up as automatically as if he'd been asked the same question by a new bar customer. "I really . . . hmmm . . . don't know anything about that stuff, Shamrock." And even as he said it, he knew it wouldn't go over. Not even with Shamrock.

And he was right; it didn't.

"But Danny Boy, you must know something." Shamrock's voice cracked.

And there it was–Shamrock bringing up what most of

the beach people knew: Dan Marlowe had a drug problem. The key word was "had." That was all in the past.

So why would Shamrock, of all people, bring the past up now?

Maybe he was just curious. Or was there something more?

Dan didn't know, but he wasn't about to talk about something he'd rather forget. "I don't know anything about that stuff."

He must've sounded harder than he'd meant to, because the Irishman started to get real antsy and nervous. His face reddened.

"I . . . I got things to do in the kitchen." Shamrock grabbed his box of donuts and walked off through the swinging doors.

Dan kept working on the fruit. Something was going on with Shamrock, though Dan didn't have a clue what had gotten under the Irishman's skin. Had Shamrock heard some gossip that he couldn't resist following up? Or was he just trying to bust Dan's balls?

Both scenarios were unlikely. Shamrock didn't have a mean bone in his body. Besides, the little guy had been around during Dan's bad times. He might not have known all the gory details, but he had to know the gist of Dan's story.

Putting the past in a box didn't make Dan feel any better. His heart was beating triple time, his palms were sweaty, and he was starting to think about . . . well, thinking about things he didn't want to think about. Things that weren't good to think about. Things he could force himself to forget about for a little while, until . . . bang! Something would happen and the memories would flood his mind. Not good memories. Damn bad ones, as a matter of fact.

Dan walked to the end of the bar and stared out the front window at the Atlantic Ocean, hoping the ocean would work its soothing magic and help him forget. It had worked before. And it did today too.

Eventually.

Chapter 3

DOMINIC CARPUCCI was in the office of his Lynnfield, Massachusetts, home and he was none too happy. In fact, he was pissed off. Real pissed off. So pissed off he wanted to jump right over the big oak desk he was sitting behind and strangle Jorge Rivera, the man sitting on the other side of the desk. But he knew that didn't make any sense because it wasn't the kid's fault what had him so bullshit. No, it was just that Dominic wanted to take his pent-up anger out on someone. Anyone. Had to get hold of himself, though. After all, Jorge was his right-hand man. And besides, even though Dominic hated to admit it, the kid might be able to kick his ass. Still, even with the age difference, it'd probably be an interesting fight. Very bloody, for sure.

Dominic was short, hard, and built like a beer barrel. When he got his hands on someone they were in serious trouble. He'd proven that countless times growing up on the streets. Still the kid was about twenty years younger and a good half foot taller than Dominic. Solid, too. Not like a barrel–more like a middleweight fighter. If they were just a little closer in age, it would be a good go. But even a hardhead like Dominic had to admit time took its toll. The kid didn't even have a gray hair in his head. All black, the lucky bastard. Dominic smiled for a second before starting back in again on the same thing he'd been railing about now for the last twenty-four hours.

"I wanna know who ripped off those fuckin' hundred keys and I wanna know yesterday," Dominic bellowed. Jorge didn't even blink, just sat there cool and calm as ever. Why shouldn't the kid be calm? After all, it wasn't his stuff that'd been swiped. It was his, Dominic Carpucci's. Nobody took anything from Dominic Carpucci and got away with it. Never had, never would. Especially not now. Not when he was counting big on this load. "Whattaya dead? Ya gonna just sit there, or ya gonna tell me ya got something for me?"

Jorge Rivera brushed his expensive slacks and spoke in perfect English. "I've got my people in Lawrence checking there. And in Lowell. And also the whole seacoast right up to Portland. I have feelers out in Boston too. Anyone tries to unload anything big, I'll hear about it."

That didn't make Dominic feel much better. "What if they take it down the Apple? What if they do that? Take it down there or somewhere else? Then what? Huh? I wanna know where the fuck my product is. The longer that shit is out there, the harder it'll be to get it all back." He was shouting again and he could feel his face getting hot and he didn't give a shit. "When I get those motherfuckers I'm gonna pop their fuckin' heads off."

Jorge, still cool, said, "We're going to have to find out first who did the rip."

Dominic glared. That was another thing he and the kid had been throwing back and forth and they still weren't any closer to an idea. "Like I said already, who the hell could it have been? Not the Colombians. We give 'em too much business. Besides, I got a lot of it on the arm, so it wouldn't make any sense for them to rip off what's really still their load anyway. Not that they ain't gonna want their money, cause they are. Once that boat captain you recruited picked it up, it was my responsibility. That's the way it goes. You know that as good as me."

Dominic drummed his thick fingers on the desk. "That leaves our end. And the only people that knew were me, you, and our dead Captain Gilligan. I didn't swipe it, and I'm pretty sure you didn't do it either. And our dead captain didn't off himself. What about his brother? Ya told me the captain was gonna use his brother. According to my sources, the other stiff on the scow was one of the captain's employees. I'm thinking maybe our Captain Gilligan was set up by his own damn brother.

Whattaya think of that, kid? How's it sound?"

For an instant Jorge looked like maybe he didn't like something Dominic had said, but then the expression was gone. "I don't know the brother. If he'd have the balls to whack two guys like that."

Dominic let out a snort. "Where a few million bucks is concerned? Don't kid yourself. You and I both know people do it for a lot less. He saw a chance to make a big score and he took it, that's all. Don't take no genius to kill two sailor boys and make off with some duffel bags, especially when ya know where and when they're gonna be. Man, if that bastard boat captain wasn't already dead, I'd kill him myself."

Jorge looked squarely back at Dominic. "Maybe you're right, Boss."

"Bet your ass I'm right. Now go grab that asshole's brother. And while you're at it, get your people all over that fuckin' beach just in case we're missing the mark. Stay on top of it. I think we got a good chance of getting my product back, brother or not. If it turns out local amateurs pulled the heist, they won't have any good outs for that much stuff. They'll probably screw up trying to unload it. So I wanna know if anyone even moves a gram up there. Now get going. Shake some trees, break some heads if ya have to. I want that shit back yesterday."

Jorge stood up. "We'll find it, Boss. Don't worry." He turned and walked out of the room.

Don't worry. Right. Dominic slammed his fist on the

desk. This whole fiasco was really bothering him. He didn't have a good feeling about this at all. And not even being called "Boss" was helping that. In fact, that was another thing that was starting to bother him lately–people calling him Boss. Kind of sounded like chalk on a blackboard all of a sudden. Like maybe they knew how he felt, and they were saying it now just to rub it in. Sure, he was the boss, the boss of his crew. No doubt about that. And yeah, that's what he'd always wanted to be–a Boss. Mr. Big. The Man.

But now, today, he had to ask himself what kind of a boss gets ripped off like this? And without a clue yet where the hell the product was? Of all the scams he'd done through the years it had to be this load they grabbed–*the* load. The load that was going to get him out of all this hustling, once and for all. Yeah, what kind of a boss loses that kind of load. No boss he'd ever known, that was for sure. And definitely not his old boss, the one he used to answer to, way back when he himself was called "Dom," "Dominic," or just plain "Kid."

Twenty-five years ago, Filthy Phil Garrola had made the decision to jump on the cocaine express. It'd been just the two of them that day–just Dominic and Filthy Phil. He'd even had black hair back then, a full head of it. Not Phil though. Bald as a baby.

Phil had spoken to him in that deep guttural voice he had. "Dom, you been workin' for me a long time now, no?" His thick hairy forearms rested on the brown table in front of him as he stared at Dominic sitting on the opposite side.

"Five years, Boss," Dominic had answered, nodding his head proudly. It was 1970 and his hair was cut stylishly long. He wore jeans and a mod sport coat that was tailored to show off the muscles he'd worked so hard to build.

"Five years," Phil said solemnly. "Five years and ya done a lot for me, kid. Ya watched over my books, handled some tough collections, and best of all ya kept your mouth shut. Ain't caused me no problems either. I like that, Dom, and I like you. Ya ain't like the other young punks out there. They either wanna get high all the time or they wanna move up too fast or both. These young guys today, they think they're too good to have to pay their dues like the rest of us. That makes 'em greedy, and worse, unreliable. But you, kid, you're different. You're old school. Ya been good. And I want ya to know I appreciate it."

Dominic held up his hands in protest. "No need, Boss."

"Ah, but there is a need, kid," Phil said, his voice turning graver. "I know you're ambitious. Ya'd like to make more money. Ain't nothin' wrong with that. Long as you're doin' it the right way. And you can, kid. You'd like that, wouldn't you? More money?"

Dominic smiled. "Everybody'd like to be makin' more money, Boss. But I'm satisfied."

"Sure ya are, kid. But I think ya deserve more money. And to tell ya the truth, so do I. I don't wanna be hustlin' forever. I wanna be able to afford to get outta this someday before I'm too old to enjoy it. And the only way I know to be able to do that is to make a lot of dough fast." Phil looked slyly across the table at Dominic. "And I got a way," he added softly.

"What's that, Boss?" Dominic asked, fighting to keep the excitement from registering in his voice. This could be it, he knew instinctively. What he'd been working for these past five years. Something big. Something that would *make* him.

Filthy Phil gave Dominic a wide crocodile smile. "It's a way where your bein' reliable is gonna pay off. I know ya never tried to rip me off, and like I said, I like how ya always kept your mouth shut. And for what I got planned that's the type of person I need. Someone like you, kid."

"Whattaya got planned, Boss?" Dominic asked, struggling to keep his voice calm. This was it. He wasn't sure what Phil was going to propose but he knew it was going to take him up the ladder. Make him a bigger man than he was. And that was what he wanted. What he'd been working for.

Phil reached into the inside pocket of his gaudy sport coat and pulled out a clear plastic sandwich bag. He dropped the baggie on the table between them. "This, kid. This is what I got in mind."

Dominic reached over, lifted the baggie, and let it roll open. He could feel his hand shaking slightly. He moved his nose over the open bag, sniffed twice, then looked up at Phil and said, "Coke?"

Phil's voice hardened. "Yeah, coke, kid. And nothin'-and I mean nothin'-about this is to ever leave this room. Not only are the cops down on this stuff, some of the boys don't want anyone gettin' involved with it either. Say it brings too much heat, period. And a couple of others got their own little setups and they don't want any competition. Whatever, we can't step on any toes. So for these reasons, nobody can ever hear about this little talk of ours. I don't want it ever comin' back to haunt me. Ya got it? If ya understand this, then we can continue."

Dominic placed the baggie back gently on the table. "I got it, Boss. You never have to worry about me."

"Good," Phil said, nodding his big head. "Now here's what I'm gonna propose, kid. First of all, I know ya been movin' a little grass here and there." Dominic shifted uncomfortably in his chair. Phil continued, "And I don't mind that. Ya been makin' a little extra on the side. Grass? That's okay. 'Bout as serious as booze was back in the twenties. Besides, ya kept it away from my thing and that's good. And anyhow, I ain't interested in grass–too bulky. But this," Phil nodded toward the baggie of coke on the table. "This stuff. It's gonna get big, believe me. I talked to some people who know the score. Gonna be a lot of money in it soon. A lot of heavy heat too. Ya follow me so far, kid?"

"I follow you, Boss," Dominic answered. His gaze

shifted back and forth between Phil and the coke on the table.

"Okay," Phil said. He put his elbows on the table and folded his hands under his chin. "Now what I wanna know is–do ya think ya can get rid of any of this stuff?"

Dominic had no idea, but he wasn't about to tell Phil that. Dominic's people–the few he had–were just small-time pot dealers. Could they move cocaine? Was there even any demand for the stuff? He wasn't sure. But what to tell Phil? This was his big chance; he could feel it. If he told the old man the wrong thing, he'd blow it. Phil'd just find someone else to move the coke for him. Maybe bullshit him? Tell him that he could sell a lot and hope that's how it turned out? Or tell him the truth–that his outs were just small-time pot people, a couple of burned-out hippies, some blacks, some spics. Either way, he had to take the shot. "I'll have to do a little research, Boss. Talk to my people."

Phil waved the idea away. "Don't bother. I'll tell ya what they'd say. They'd say they can't do nothin' with it. You'd just be wastin' your time, kid. Here's what ya do. Take that bag and go see each of your people. Let 'em sniff a little. Go back a second and third time if ya have to, let 'em sniff more. Believe me, it won't take no longer than that and your phone'll be ringing off the hook with them wantin' more. I know guys in the Apple and guys on the West Coast went the same route. Now they're makin' more dough than they know what to do with. I'm tellin' ya, kid, it's the comin' thing. Lotta potential, but a lotta risk."

How the hell could this old guinea know the coming thing in the drug business when he wouldn't know what end of a joint to put between his fat lips? Still. Dominic glanced at the coke again. Not many things made him nervous, but this stuff did. This was heavy. Real heavy.

"They might be afraid of it, Boss," he said.

"No might about it. They will be afraid of it. But not for long, believe me. The guys I know had the same problem. Their people were scared to death of it at first. Funny stuff though. After a while they couldn't get enough of it. Then they started movin' more and more. It snowballed. I'm tellin' ya, kid, their business took off like a rocket. And it can for us too. It's just gettin' going around here. We're right on the ground floor."

"What's it gonna cost me?" Dominic asked, tipping his head toward the coke.

"Zilch," Phil answered, palms up. "That's the best part for you, kid. I'll get it. I got a top connection. The best stuff. Like I said, in the beginning we'll give out some for free. Uncut. You don't put up a dime. I put up the money and get the product. You're gonna be in charge of distribution. Once it starts to move, we figure out a price structure and how much we're gonna cut it. Then we split the profits–seventy-five me, twenty-five you. How's that sound, kid?"

Dominic wasn't sure how it sounded, but he wanted to move up and he wasn't going to refuse anything that might take him there. "Sounds good, Boss. I'll do the best I can."

Phil reached over and patted the back of Dominic's hand. "I know ya will, kid. I know ya will."

"When do we start?" Dominic asked, and he noticed there was a slight quiver in his voice. He hoped the old man didn't notice it too.

"Today," Phil said. "There's your sample." He pushed the baggie closer to Dominic. "Ya take it around, do like I said. Give 'em a little on the house. Leave 'em a little even. Tell 'em ya can get all they want. I don't care if it's just a gram or an ounce. They'll build up; I'm tellin' ya." Phil was silent for a minute and Dominic could feel the older man's eyes burning into him. "This is the one, Dominic. It's gonna make us both rich. We just gotta play it cool and handle it right."

The old man had been spot on. They'd caught the cocaine explosion when it hit Boston right on the ground floor. Rode that elevator to the top. And it had gotten both of them exactly what they'd wanted. So far.

Filthy Phil Garrola was in his twilight years now, retired in Florida with a penthouse, a yacht, and lots of dough stashed. Not to mention the nice chunk of change Dominic sent him every month as his cut of the business he'd let Dominic take over when he retired. The split wasn't seventy-five/twenty-five anymore either. They'd long ago renegotiated that in Dominic's favor, but still, the old man got fat, steady envelopes for doing nothing.

Yeah, the old man had had his turn. And what a turn. Dominic could picture the old fart on the bridge of his yacht, bald head, shades, and lime-green polyester Bermudas high up on his big belly, with some sweet young cupcake hanging all over him. Nobody in a million years would ever believe that old man had made his pile as one of the pioneers of the cocaine trade.

But Dominic knew he'd gotten what he'd wanted too–to be the Boss. Just like Filthy Phil. And the money that came with the title wasn't anything to sneeze at either. Only problem, he had something Phil hadn't had back in the day–expenses. Not to say Phil hadn't had any expenses back then. But everything cost more today, now that the "War on Drugs" was in high gear. Christ, back then there had been few problems and the old man had just raked it in.

Today everything was different. Just when it seemed to Dominic that he almost had enough to get out of the racket and live the high life like the old man, something would happen that cost him plenty. Either someone was getting popped and lawyers and bail had to be taken care of, or a load was stolen or seized. It was always something happening at the most inopportune times.

That was part of the reason he was sick of the whole shebang. Every day the life Phil lived in Florida looked better and better. Lying around in the warm sun all day, then relaxing to the sound of waves at night. Not having a care in the world. It sure had to be a lot better than the grief he was involved in.

Even being called "Boss" didn't make him feel any better now. What kind of boss gets taken down by a bunch of stupid jerks? Especially at his age. Dominic needed this like he needed a hole in the head.

Yes, it was definitely time to get out. The only thing standing between him and Phil in Florida was money–lots of it–and someone he could trust to send him his sweet little cut every month.

The hundred keys, along with what he already had stashed, would've given him enough to retire very comfortably, thank you. And as far as someone taking over his action, he had his eye on someone for that too–the kid, Jorge Rivera. Sure, the kid was a spic and the boys might not like it, but he was honest, tough and loyal, and Dominic knew the kid could keep things together. Besides, having a spic running the operation would help keep it plugged into the Hispanic groups that were pushing out old Anglo organizations like his and Phil's.

Yeah, letting Jorge take over was just smart business. Change with the times. Let the greasers stand up front; let them think they're running the show. As long as those fat envelopes kept flying south every month, why should he care if they were sent by a guy named Jorge or one named Tony? Either way the drinks would be just as cold, the sun just as warm, and the broads just as hot. Amen.

But right now the laugh would be on him if he didn't

get those damn duffel bags back. Dominic didn't doubt he'd get the bags back along with every last stinking football that was in them. He'd get the guys who swiped them too. Make himself sick watching what he did to those assholes.

Good thing the doc wasn't taking his blood pressure right about now. And he'd been doing so good too.

Chapter 4

DAN GLANCED AROUND his small cottage, his gaze lingering on the beach memorabilia scattered here and there: A jar with shells and smooth stones he'd found walking along the beach with his kids. Framed photos of happy summers they'd had here together.

All just memories now.

That's when Dan started to think of making the call. He knew he shouldn't; it was a bad move. These calls had never turned out well in the past. Still, the more beer he drank the less that realization mattered. Finally the beer-soaked side of his brain rooting him on to make the call won out.

Before he could change his mind, he picked up the phone, punched in the numbers, looked at the ship's clock on his cottage wall. 11:20 p.m. He adjusted himself confidently in his easy chair, listened to the phone ring.

She answered drowsily on the fourth ring. "Hello?"

"Hello, Sharon. It's me. How are you doing?"

She suddenly sounded wide awake. "How am I doing? What are you crazy? You're not supposed to be calling here. I'm hanging up, Dan."

"Don't hang up. I want to see the kids."

"Are you high? It's eleven thirty at night."

Dan cleared his throat. "I know what time it is, but I've been working a lot of hours and this is the first chance I've had to call. I'd like to see the kids. I haven't seen them in a while."

"You are high."

He felt his anger rising slowly; she still knew how to push his buttons. He tried to control his voice. "No, I'm not high. I've told you I'm not doing that anymore."

Her voice became angrier. "You've told me a lot of things. A lot were lies."

Dan took a couple of deep breaths. It didn't help. When he spoke there was a slight quiver in his voice. "You're right, Sharon. But all that is in the past. Everything's good now."

"Calling at eleven thirty at night and demanding to see the kids doesn't sound good."

Dan sat up straight. "I just want to see the kids. That's it. I won't even take them anywhere."

For a long time, Sharon didn't say anything. Dan's stomach tightened. Maybe this time . . .

"No."

"There'd be no problem. I promise you." Now there was more than a slight quiver in his voice.

"I've heard that before too."

Dan stared toward the window. A set of dim headlights crept past the cottage. Probably the neighbor's kids sneaking off for a late night party. The two boys were older than his kids and were always getting into trouble, something their mother blamed on their father abandoning them over ten years ago. "You shouldn't keep those kids away from me. It's not good for them."

"You should've thought of that a long time ago."

"Nobody's perfect, Sharon. Not even you." Dan squeezed his eyes tight. "Are you going to let me see the kids or not."

"You scared the hell out of them the last time I let you see them."

"That was a long time ago."

"Not long enough. I still remember it all. Want me to remind you?"

"Forget that. I just want to make arrangements to see the kids."

"I don't have to let you see the kids. Remember? The judge?"

His voice cracked. "You can overlook that for one short visit it you want to."

"But I don't want to. Go to bed, Dan. Sleep it off."

Dan took a deep breath, struggling to keep the anger out of his voice. "I told you I'm not . . ."

Silence. The line was as dead as the beach in winter.

Dan slammed the receiver back into its cradle, then grabbed the entire phone and hurled it blindly across the room. The phone sailed over the couch, hit the end of its cord, and flopped onto the cushions like a fish he'd just hauled from the sea.

He'd screwed up again. Made a bad situation worse. Sharon was never going to understand that today's Dan Marlowe was not the same person who in the past would regularly pass out in a beach motel after a three bender with no sleep.

All because of cocaine. It had ruled his life for way too long. And he'd paid a big price for those mistakes. But he'd thought he'd left all that behind. That he was in control. But he wasn't in control. The bills just kept coming and coming.

Dan looked at the dark bedroom door, envisioning the double-barreled shotgun lying under the bed. He'd picked Betsy up during a drug-induced bout of paranoia and couldn't quite seem to part with her now. He could feel her lying there, her two black eyes staring out at him.

Daring.

Like a man in a slow-motion movie, Dan stood and moved toward the bedroom. There was no life if he couldn't see his children. They were the reason he'd cleaned up his act. Resisted the cravings. The cravings he still suffered with every day. The cravings that bubbled up from his brain at the most inopportune moments, persistent and painful as a bloody sore.

Two steps from the bedroom, Dan spun around and headed into the kitchen. There were other ways to forget all this. Less permanent ways. He tore open the refrigerator door, grabbed another beer, and popped it open. Sharon was right–he was hopeless. A worthless piece of shit not worthy to spend time with his own children.

The bottle's lip banged against his teeth. The familiar scent filled his head. He tilted the bottle up, up, up. Felt the cold liquid touch his bottom lip.

He killed it. Then opened another. He had to.

Chapter 5

BUZZ CRAVEN, at the wheel of the little white Sentra, was driving north on Route 95 near Newburyport, Massachusetts, not far from the New Hampshire border. Beside him, riding shotgun, sat Skinny Halliday. They were headed to Hampton Beach to retrieve the hundred kilos of coke they'd lifted off the fishing boat before that same boat had mysteriously been found hung up on the jetty with two dead bodies inside.

"I still don't get it, Buzz," Skinny said. "Why we going back now? I thought you said we should leave the stuff there until things cooled down. So why we goin' back now, huh?"

For the umpteenth time since they'd gotten involved in this thing, Buzz had to fight the urge to put his big hands around Skinny's pencil-thin neck and squeeze real hard-like. Maybe never stop. Or better yet–beat the thin man's face in till it looked like used silly putty. Yeah, that'd feel real good. But he couldn't do it. Not yet. Whether he liked to admit it or not, he needed Skinny. For now.

"Listen, you stupid shit. For the last time–we left the stuff at that cottage the night we grabbed it because there's only two ways out of that beach. If anything went wrong, no way was I going to get popped with it. My buddy said I could use the dump for a couple of weeks, so no problem there. As long as the weather didn't get too hot. Then we'd have to move real quick before the stuff got damaged. That's why I'm watching the weather. And yeah, I said we'd hang tight 'till things died down, but things have changed. I got somebody interested in the whole load. They want a showpiece and I'm going to give it to them. Dealing with one reliable person is a heck of a lot better than piecing it out to the fucking lowlifes you know. Now do you get it?"

Buzz realized he must have been talking real loud or something because Skinny was looking back at him with a terrified look on his puss, his fingers working a mile a minute on his pockmarked face.

"Well, do you get it?" Buzz said again, and damn, he *was* talking loud–very loud.

"I get it, Buzz," Skinny answered as he fidgeted around in his seat. "I get it."

"And speaking of lowlifes, don't forget to keep your trap shut with them like I told you. This isn't like the other things we been involved in before; this is serious shit. One hundred fucking keys. Remember?"

"I remember, Buzz," Skinny said, his ordinarily shrill voice going higher. "A hundred keys. Sweet Jesus, how could I forget that?"

As Buzz took the Route 286 exit off 95, he wondered if anyone, even dumbbell Skinny, could forget how serious one hundred keys were? Even he-a guy who'd seen his share of weight during all his years with the D.E.A.-couldn't forget. In fact, this particular little heist had been all he'd been able to think about for the past couple of months, ever since he'd first gotten wind of the load over that beautiful golden goose of an illegal wiretap he and Skinny had placed on Dominic Carpucci's Lynnfield home.

Buzz'd been hoping to get a line on one of Carpucci's distributors-take the guy down when he was holding-money preferably, although powder would've been cheerfully accepted. Buzz was figuring maybe ten or twenty grand, or if they got real lucky, hell, even fifty wouldn't have been impossible. He never even considered ripping off Dominic Carpucci himself. The man was too cautious, too ruthless. Anyone who tried would probably get their balls cut off-if they were lucky. All Buzz was hoping for was a nice little score. Easy in, easy out. Nothing more.

Until he heard about the boat scam. Then everything changed.

At first, he didn't think the tap was going to pay off. Carpucci kept yakking about this and that, but nothing that smelled like money. Then Carpucci mentioned "footballs" and Buzz's ears perked up. The creep had been talking in code, but that hadn't kept Buzz in the dark. Hell, he'd been deciphering dealer's chatter so long he was better at it than a C.I.A. cryptographer. Seemed Carpucci and his right-hand man, some spic–Jorge something or other–had a load of blow they were expecting. And what a load. One hundred keys! Shit, that was over 200 pounds. Buzz hadn't had to reach for a calculator to know that was talking millions. When he heard about that dream shipment, the idea of hitting one of Carpucci's distributors went right out the window.

Sure, it would be dangerous to try to rip a man like Carpucci–real dangerous as a matter of fact–but this wasn't a little flurry of cocaine. It was a fucking blizzard! So it was damn well worth the risk. Besides, it wasn't like him and Skinny hadn't done things like this before. Hell, they'd pulled lots of scams. Maybe not as big, but smooth and pretty profitable–ten, twenty, even thirty grand once. Some in cash, some in merchandise. Only one problem– there was never enough cash or merchandise in one score to quit. And that's what Buzz wanted most of all– enough dough to quit.

He didn't mean just the rip-offs either. Buzz was ready for a major career move–from D.E.A. to retirement. He'd had it up to his nose with that organization. All these years the idiots had kept him from moving up the ladder like he knew he deserved, keeping him hanging around with the promise of that stinking pension at the end of the slog. A pension he'd never see if they ever caught him in one of his little side enterprises with Skinny. All the time he'd given, the risks he'd taken, the scum he'd had to associate with, and at the end nothing but a paltry pension? Not likely.

And now he had a hundred kilos just waiting for him to presto chango it into dollars. He had to pat himself on the back–the heist had gone real smooth. Listening in on the tap had not only opened the door on the hundred keys, during that same conversation Carpucci had been kind enough to reveal what time the boat was coming into Hampton Harbor. Buzz would have to thank Carpucci for that someday. How easy the man had made it for him and Skinny. All they'd had to do was wait on that little motorboat. And then board that treasure ship like they'd been a couple of modern day pirates. It'd been that easy.

To add to the run of luck, the two fools on board weren't even armed. If you didn't count the fishhook one of them was waving. No matter. Buzz killed them both. There was no way he was going to leave those two alive. He and Skinny wore masks but that was more to keep Skinny in the dark about what he was going to do. This was the score; there could be no witnesses. Masks or no masks. So he did what he had to do.

And now he had the hundred keys. Not some greaseball guinea down in la-te-da Lynnfield. And boy, did that make him feel good as a hard-on as he drove along. Even had to shift his ass a bit on the seat.

"Buzz."

Damn. That shrill voice of Skinny's was enough to turn a sane man into a raving maniac. "What?" Buzz tried to keep the annoyance he felt out of his voice. One day soon he'd leave that grating voice behind. His nerves would definitely appreciate the reprieve.

"Can I ask ya something?" Skinny said, snapping his gum every second he wasn't talking.

Was it him, or was Skinny's voice really that bad? The moron's screeching jangled his central nervous system like a kid with his first electric guitar. Buzz almost wished the skinny little shit had ratted him out somewhere along the line, just so he wouldn't have to be here now listening to it. But he never had; had to give Skinny that much. All the rip-offs they'd pulled through the years and Skinny'd actually managed to keep his pie hole shut. Amazing. Could have something to do with Buzz's six-foot-two, 210-pound frame. Years ago, Buzz had used his size to scare the little weasel shitless. All it took was a glance and Buzz could see that nothing had changed in all the time they'd been working together–Skinny was still terrified of him. Anyone could see that.

"What?" Buzz asked, controlling his voice, not wanting Skinny to jump out of his skin. "But don't make it stupid. I'm cranky enough."

Skinny cleared his throat, and when he spoke it was

with a slight quiver. "Whattaya gonna do with your share, Buzz?"

Despite his irritation, Buzz felt a grin spreading across his face at the thought of what he'd do with all that bread. "My share? Well, first of all I won't be hanging around with you anymore, that's for fucking sure."

Skinny's face collapsed like a dynamited building.

Buzz sighed. What the hell. "Travel, that'll be the first thing."

"Yeah?" Skinny said, his eyes shining as much as someone like his could. "Where?"

"The islands. Caribbean," Buzz answered, really getting into it now, enjoying the pictures he was conjuring up in his mind. "Anytime, anywhere I want. Maybe have a nice place down in Jamaica. On the sand. West coast. Too much trouble over the other side."

"You gonna keep working?" Skinny asked, really working his gum now, bobbing his little head like he couldn't wait to hear more.

"Do you have rocks in your head?" Jesus, could this guy be that dumb? "Soon as we turn the stash into cash I'm gone. Quick as a MEGABUCKS winner."

Skinny furrowed his one eyebrow. "What about that pension you're always talkin' about?"

"This is a two or three million dollar score we got here, birdbrain. My seventy-five percent of that is–well, even you don't need a calculator to know that's a lot of money." Buzz could tell that he must be sounding real hot again by the frightened look that came over Skinny's face. But that didn't cool him down any. "All these fucking years I been busting my ass, taking dope dealers down, risking my life. And for what?"

Skinny cowered against the passenger door.

"So some suit in Boston or Washington can get all the glory. And me? What do I get? I'll tell you what I get. Bounced around to every two-bit, rinky-dink task force they feel like forming. Like the damn hemorrhoid I'm stuck in now." Buzz continued in a sing-songy voice, "Northern Massachusetts, Southern New Hampshire Drug Task Force . . . It's all bullshit. Nothin' but a bunch of staties and locals who know absolutely nothing. Stupid morons are chasing high school kids for joints when there's big shit like this going on. Right under their noses too. And why do I get stuck in something like this?"

Skinny looked real antsy now, like maybe he knew what was coming.

"Cause of that goddamn lousy ten grand missing from that crack bust. I'm risking my fucking life and they make a big deal out of that? And it was a Dominican's ten to boot. For Chrissake, the guy's lawyer would've got a judge to return it to him anyway, and the spic would've Federal Expressed it home to relatives faster than you can take a shit. Probably would've gone for chickens and goats." Buzz stomped on the accelerator and the puny car jumped from sixty-five to seventy-five.

Skinny let out a little screech. "You wanna know what

I'm gonna do with my share, Buzz?"

Buzz could've given a rat's ass about Skinny's plans. But he needed to keep the little weasel in the game for a while longer. "What, Skinny? What are you going to do with your share?"

"Open a nightclub," Skinny said, raising himself up an inch or two in the seat.

"A nightclub?" Buzz had to fight to keep from laughing. He had a hard enough time picturing Skinny running a hotdog stand let alone a nightclub. Christ, he made one of those zit-faced, young geeks at McDonald's look like Donald Trump.

"Yeah, a nightclub. And maybe I'll have a restaurant to go along with it. With nice grub too, fried fish probably. Clams, maybe. There's a lot of money in clams. Not the chewy kind either that you gotta spit out. The sweet ones. Yeah, that's what I'm gonna do." Skinny's eyes glazed over and he let out an audible sigh.

All that fryolator grease'd probably rot the weasel's face off. At least the parts that weren't rotted already.

"Sounds good." But it didn't really because Buzz knew it was never going to happen.

They were crossing over the Hampton Bridge now–a green two-lane drawbridge spanning the water that led from the Atlantic Ocean to the harbor, separating Hampton Beach from Seabrook, New Hampshire. The sun above shone big and bright, reflecting off the dome of the nuclear power plant to his left and glittering on the rippling water. They cruised past the state park loaded with cars and a string of RV's along the water's edge.

Buzz banged a right onto Eaton Avenue. Halfway down the short street, he pulled the car into the driveway of a dilapidated one-story wood cottage and stopped.

Old lobster traps littered the crooked stairs that led to the front porch of the ramshackle building. A worn sign, which at one time probably announced the cottage's name, swung loosely from a single fastener. A rusted bike frame, absent tires, rested against the building. The entire structure was covered in cracked, multi-colored asphalt shingles. It was an eyesore.

Buzz didn't care about any of that. To him it might as well have been the Taj Mahal, all glittering gold. A beautiful sight. The answer to his prayers. This was it.

Skinny snapped his gum and Buzz turned to look at the thin man seated beside him. A thought crept into Buzz's mind–maybe this was as good a time as any. Let Skinny help load the car. Then go back inside with him, and lights out. Death by misadventure. Too much coke. Just another dead junkie found in a Hampton Beach hovel.

Buzz knew he'd have to do it sooner or later anyway. Skinny was a liability. He'd never be able to keep it together. The only reason he'd made it this far without getting shot in the head or thrown in the joint was that he had Buzz running interference for him. No other reason. The thin man couldn't hold onto a dime, let alone a bundle like this was going to be. He'd get his cut and it wouldn't two days before he'd be doing just a couple of lines, and then before you could say, "Pass me the pipe," he'd be a crazy, crack-smoking madman again.

And then the money'd be gone–real quick, crack-quick.

Buzz didn't have to wonder where that would put him. Skinny with no money and craving blow would start pulling all sorts of shitty little scores. Till the inevitable happened and he got popped and they jammed him up. They'd offer him the standard deal–who and what do you know? And wouldn't they be surprised with what the skinny little junkie came back with–a real interesting story about an ex-D.E.A. agent who ripped off 220 pounds of cocaine and was retired now in Jamaica. You could almost write a book about it. The cops would offer Skinny the moon.

Where would Buzz be then? After the thin man told them the whole story?

And that was the main reason the man now sitting beside Buzz would never have to worry about all the troublesome paperwork involved in running a business.

"Buzz," Skinny said. "We goin' in?"

"Yeah. Let's go."

They climbed out of the car and went up on the rickety front porch. Buzz unlocked the door and they went in. They walked through the main room with its two tattered easy chairs and ratty sofa and into the first bedroom on the right. The moment he stepped into the bedroom Buzz's stomach flip-flopped. There on the floor was the wooden cover he'd left secured over the opening in the ceiling that led to the tiny attic.

Buzz dashed to the only closet in the room, looked up, and sure enough there was the attic entrance–wide open. "Boost me up quick," he shouted.

Skinny squeezed in the closet and made a stirrup with his bony hands. Buzz stuck his foot in and raised himself up so his head was sticking through the opening in the ceiling. He peered around the tiny room. The only things in the attic now were spiders and webs.

Buzz jumped down and shoved Skinny out of his way. He headed back through the cottage.

"Are they all gone?" Skinny whined, running to keep up.

"No, you fucking nitwit. They left one as a present. Of course, they're all gone."

"Who do you think?" Skinny asked. "Kids?"

"Kids don't go searching around for a little trap door in the ceiling of a bedroom closet." Buzz jumped down the few porch stairs and hopped in the driver's seat of the car.

Skinny climbed in the other side. "Who then?"

"How the hell should I know?" Buzz peeled backward out of the driveway, reversed direction, and headed back down Eaton to Ocean Boulevard. He banged left and headed back over the bridge.

"Where we going?" Skinny asked.

"Back to Carpucci's in Lynnfield. Somehow the bastard

must've found out where it was stashed." Buzz glanced hard at Skinny, then shook his head. Skinny wasn't smart enough or desperate enough to deal with the big boys. Someone must've seen them and gone directly to Carpucci. That's the only way the stash could've disappeared far as he could tell. "One way or the other, I'm going to get that coke back."

Buzz slammed the wheel with the palm of his hand. His big dream had been this close and he'd be damned if he was going to see it all go up in smoke. He hit the gas hard and Skinny grabbed the dash with both hands, clinging tight as the car sped back across the Hampton Bridge.

Chapter 6

LIEUTENANT RAY CONOVER, of the New Hampshire State Police, knew this was a big case–a double homicide with possible drug smuggling ties. The brass had made sure he understood that. So it was only natural that he and his partner, Sergeant Vincent Bartolo, had been talking to a lot of people up and down the seacoast trying to shake something loose. Someone in the area had to know something. Bartolo and Conover were determined to find out who that someone was and what they knew, almost any way they could. That's what they were doing now–rattling another cage, putting pressure on another somebody. Hoping that one of those somebodies would tell them what he knew about a boat smacked up on the Hampton Beach jetty with two dead bodies in it.

Bartolo was doing the dirty work as usual. Conover was keeping an eye on him, letting Vinny do his thing, but making sure his partner didn't get carried away like he sometimes did. Right now Vinny was yelling and screaming at a short, heavy guy with gold chains around his neck. He was right up in the guy's face. And right now Tony Peralta, the guy with the gold chains, didn't seem like the tough coke dealer he was supposed to be either–he was cowering like a punk at the tongue lashing he was receiving.

"Look, you fucking scumbag," Bartolo said, punctuating each word with a jab to Peralta's sternum. "You think you're hot shit just because you live in a nice place. I got news for you, dirt bag. You don't help us, you can kiss all this goodbye." He waved his meaty hand at the surrounding room, barely missing Peralta's cringing face.

Conover hoped the threat would be enough to bring the guy around. Otherwise, even though he didn't like the thought of it, he'd probably have to look the other way while Vinny got a little rough. People had died, after all. If something didn't give quick, maybe more would. Hopefully, the guy would cave before Vinny decided to draw blood.

Conover glanced around. The punk wouldn't want to give this up. Who would? It was a beautiful home, brand new construction. Couldn't have been more than a few years old. Perched high on the rocks of Boar's Head, a peninsula that jutted out into the Atlantic at the north end of Hampton Beach. The place must have more than a dozen massive rooms. If they were anything like the room they were in now, then they must be really something.

The room he was standing in now was a sunken living room on the first floor, with loads of expensive furniture and a well-stocked polished-stone bar. The wall behind Peralta was floor-to-ceiling glass looking out over the ocean. A sliding door opened onto a patio, and beyond that there was an expanse of beautiful golf course-like grass with an extra long picnic table and lounge chairs scattered about. The grass ran right down to rocks that dropped at an angle fifty feet to the ocean.

Yeah, it was a hell of a place and Conover didn't think anyone, let alone a character like Tony Peralta, would want to lose it.

"I told you, I haven't heard anything about the murders," Peralta whined. "It's an enigma."

It was Conover's turn to cringe as Bartolo's hand suddenly cracked across Peralta's face. Peralta's head snapped to the side and he staggered back a step.

"An enigma?" Bartolo scowled. "Don't talk to me like that, you fucking asshole. We know all about you, you worthless piece a shit. The only reason you're living up here like King Tut is 'cause you ratted out some people to the D.E.A. And you're still feeding the feds names, aren't you, sleazeball? You think we don't know that? You think we're fucking stupid or something? I wonder what'd happen if word got around that you dropped a dime as big as a manhole cover on some of your business competitors? That you're still ratting on people? I bet you'd have to move out of this palace. Wouldn't you? And that's if you were lucky."

"Whoa, whoa, whoa," Peralta said, holding up his hands. "You got me all wrong." Sweat poured down his big forehead.

"I got you wrong?" Bartolo said, first pointing to his chest, then Peralta's. "No, you got it wrong." He went nose to nose with the dope dealer. "And if you don't cooperate, in one minute I'm going to throw you through that big fucking window behind you, beat your fat body 'til you're bloody as raw meat, then toss you down that cliff. And if you live, I'll put the word out in every bar on the seacoast that you're a federal informant before you can even dry your hair–or what's left of it.

Conover could see that Bartolo had worked himself into a frenzy, and that his partner wasn't going to wait for Peralta to answer him. And he was right. Bartolo grabbed Peralta by his loud Hawaiian shirt and introduced the dope dealer's cheek to Bartolo's massive fist. The blow hit hard and Conover thought he heard something crack. Peralta went flying backwards, landing heavily on his ass. Blood spurted from a gash, splattering down Peralta's face and shirt.

Conover didn't like the action one bit, but he didn't make a move to stop his partner. He could let it go a little longer if he had to; the image of the murder victims in his mind made sure of that. He watched as Bartolo pulled the man up from the floor by his shirt and cocked his big right fist.

"All right, all right," Peralta said, his voice shaking, his hands up trying to protect his face. "I'll do whatever you want." He gingerly touched his cheek. "My god, I think you broke a bone."

"So what?" Bartolo said. "You're lucky it wasn't your nose. Then you'd have to lay off sampling your wares for a while."

Conover knew it was his turn now. "Forget about your ugly face, Peralta, and tell us what you know about the murders down at the harbor."

"I don't know anything about the murders except what I read in the papers," Peralta said as he wiped the bottom end of his shirt across his face to sop up the blood.

They had some intelligence that a large load of cocaine might have been the motive behind the murders. Maybe it was time to pursue that avenue and see where it led. "You heard of anyone trying to move any weight of coke? Maybe somebody new?"

"Yeah, you should know about that, you fucking sleazebag." Bartolo moved in close again. "You like moving powder. Getting people all strung out. What do you care, right, shithead?"

"If it wasn't me, it'd be someone else. You know that as well as I do," Peralta said as he wiped his face one more time.

"You mother . . ." Bartolo raised his fist again.

Conover moved between them; he couldn't let this

deteriorate further. They had a job to do. A job that didn't involve beating a suspect senseless. "I asked you if you heard of anyone trying to move a lot of coke. A new player maybe?"

Peralta started to say something, hesitated, then started again. "Nothing. I haven't heard anything unusual."

"Well, you better clean out your ears and hear something we can use," Bartolo said. "And it better be fast."

"The bottom line is we want whoever's behind these murders. And we want them bad," Conover said. "We also don't want any big loads of dope flooding our state. We're going to break hard on every goddamn dope dealer within fifty miles of here until we get what we want. You find out something for us. And when you're asking around, you tell them what I said too. They're all going to feel more heat than they knew could exist until we get some answers. And I don't care whether they're moving ounces of weed or pounds of blow. They aren't going to be able to make a dime and that'll be if they're lucky. Now get us something and get it quick."

"And don't forget what I promised you if you don't come across," Bartolo snarled, a wicked smirk on his face.

"I'll get you what you want," Peralta said. Blood dripped from his chin, spotting the thick beige rug.

"And remember–make it fast," Conover said. He took one of his business cards from his wallet and flipped it onto the sofa. Then he and Bartolo turned and walked out the front door.

When they reached their car at the end of the gravel driveway, they both stopped and looked back. It was a sunny day with low humidity, and they could hear the sound of the surf pounding the rocks below the house.

"I know it's the way it is," Bartolo said, staring at the house. "But I still don't like it."

"What's that?" Conover asked, even though he already knew the answer.

"This dirtbag, Peralta. Here he is dealing a ton of coke and who knows what else and he's living ocean front. We'll never see that."

"He'll get his someday. What goes around, comes around," Conover said, and he believed it too.

Bartolo snorted. "Maybe, but I'm not holding my breath. The fed's are protecting him."

"You know them. They'll protect him only as long as he's valuable to them."

"A guy like him doesn't deserve to live," Bartolo said. "All dope dealers deserve to die, but this guy should die twice. Somebody should take him out."

"Somebody will, one way or another," Conover said. "Someday."

"Maybe, but I don't know who's worse–guys like this or the feds that let them operate." Bartolo scowled.

"Six of one, half-dozen of the other," Conover said, shaking his head. "Let's travel, partner."

"Yeah, yeah. Sure. But you want to know something else, Ray?"

"What's that, Vinny?"

"It felt real good clocking that guy," Bartolo said, holding up a fist and shaking it.

Conover had to chuckle. "Yeah, I bet it did. I bet it really did."

They both got in the car and headed down the road and off Boar's Head.

Chapter 7

MID-MORNING ON FRIDAY and the beach was already starting to fill up. Dan Marlowe was walking north on Ocean Boulevard on his way to work. Occasionally he had to step off the sidewalk and weave around people; it was that crowded. The sun shone hot and bright and he was feeling pretty good, considering.

Enough time had passed since the murders down at the jetty that they weren't the only topic of conversation among the regulars at the bar anymore. And that was all right with Dan, he was sick of hearing about it anyway.

When he arrived at the High Tide, Dan went through the motions getting the bar ready for the day. Shamrock wasn't about, but a couple of the waitresses were setting up the tables over in the restaurant side of the building. He could see the waitresses moving around on the other side of the shoulder-high partition. He made small talk each time they got close enough while doing their setups. And he felt like he was forcing himself to even do that, his heart sure wasn't in it. He'd do okay for a couple of minutes or so, but then his mind would drift back to the same thing it always did–his wife and kids.   The waitresses knew the score–he used to be their boss, after all–but they didn't bring it up. They weren't the kind to kick him when he was down, a fact he was definitely thankful for.

Dan was making the cash banks for the waitresses when he heard someone call his name. He'd already let in a couple of regulars, so when he looked up from the cups he was filling with bills and change, he expected to see one of them waving their beer glass for a refill. But it wasn't one of the customers at the bar.

Two men stood just inside the front door. Cops, by the look of them. In fact, Dan would've chugged a fifth of Seagram's if the pair turned out not to be cops. Both stood over six feet tall, a bit on the stocky side, sporting shades you could see your reflection in. They both had on short-sleeve sport shirts and ties. Only plainclothes cops and real estate agents wore ties at the beach in the summer. He closed the cash register. "Can I help you?"

"We'd like to talk to you for a minute," the older one with the gray hair said, flashing a badge too fast for Dan to make out. His tone of voice didn't sound like he was asking either. "Outside." He nodded toward the door.

Dan called to one of the waitresses behind the

partition. "If Dianne comes in, tell her I'll be right back," he said, referring to the owner. "I have to step out for a second."

The two cops walked outside. Dan started to follow. As he passed the customer side of the bar, Paulie, a long-haired retired mailman nursing a beer, grabbed Dan's arm.

"Be careful," Paulie whispered. "That's Plainview Bartolo, a state cop."

Dan pulled his arm free from Paulie's grip and gave a tight smile. "Thanks for the heads up."

Dan shoved through the front door and nodded at the two cops waiting outside. When they saw Dan they resumed walking. He followed them around the corner to the rear of the High Tide where there was no one to hear their conversation.

"I'm Lieutenant Conover and this is Sergeant Bartolo," the older cop said, jerking his thumb toward his dark-haired companion. Bartolo stood there not saying a word, a real tough guy look on his face. Dan knew even before the introduction that he had to be the one Paulie had referred to as "Plainview."

"New Hampshire State Police," Conover added.

Dan nodded. His stomach felt like it had an ulcer in the making.

"We'd like you to tell us everything you know about Michael Kelly," Conover said in a businesslike tone.

"Who?"

"Come on, come on," Bartolo suddenly said. "Don't fuck

around with us. Kelly. Shamrock Kelly."

For a moment Dan hadn't realized that they were talking
about Shamrock.   It was rare that anyone used the
Irishman's real name.

"I don't know much," Dan said warily. "Why?"

"Never mind fucking why," Bartolo growled. "What
do you know about him?"

Dan didn't like this a bit. He had no idea what was
going on, but it didn't sound good for Shamrock. So he
decided not to give them any information they probably
didn't already have. "He's the dishwasher and maintenance
man at the restaurant."

Bartolo suddenly shoved his face close to Dan's. So
close Dan could smell the coffee and cigarettes the man
had for breakfast still lingering on his breath.

"What are you, a smartass?" Bartolo said through clenched
teeth.   "There are two dead people and we think this
Shamrock buddy of yours is involved. We know he's a
goddamn dishwasher. Tell us something we don't know.
Like why the hell a dishwasher's telling certain people he's
got a lot of cocaine to sell?"

"Shamrock?" Slowly the puzzle began to slip into place.
Shamrock hadn't been trying to get Dan to talk about
the past this morning. The Irishman had been talking
about the future–a future that suddenly looked pretty
dicey if Dan was doing his math right.

"You got wax in your ears?" Bartolo said. "Tell us what
you   know   or   you're   going   down   for   withholding

information."

"Shamrock's never said a word to me about having any coke." Not exactly the truth, but close enough. Dan forced himself to look the detective in the eye.

"Bullshit," Bartolo said. "Word on the street is that you two are closer than gum on shoe leather."

The cop was fishing, Dan was almost certain of it. Didn't make all this questioning any easier on his nerves. "Look, I told you what I know. Yeah, I work with the guy. I guess you could say we're friends. Work friends. But when work is done, we both go our separate ways."

"I don't believe you," Bartolo said, sticking his thick index finger into Dan's chest. "You're involved in this thing, and you're going to tell us what you know. Otherwise, we're gonna bust your ass from here to Kingdom Come. How's obstruction of justice sound? And that's just for starters." The last few words were emphasized with hard pokes to Dan's chest.

"Keep your finger to yourself," Dan said. "Or you'll be wearing it in a cast."

"And you'll be wearing an 'assault and battery on a police officer' charge. I'd love to have that leverage on you, punk."

"Screw you."

"Why, you little asshole." Bartolo lunged towards Dan.

Dan tensed, but just before Bartolo got a chance to strike, Conover stepped between them. The older cop grabbed Bartolo by the shoulders and told him to cool down. Dan had seen this routine a few times on the Late Show but he was glad to see it again, especially now.

Finally Conover got his hot-headed partner under control. He told Bartolo to wait back at their car. Bartolo glared at Dan, leaving behind the impression that Dan definitely hadn't made a new friend here today.

No problem there. Dan had never been one to make friends easily.

After Bartolo stalked away, Conover turned back to Dan. "He can cause you a lot of trouble. I could probably convince him otherwise, but you've got to give me something."

Dan waited. No use saying anything more until he heard what the cop had in mind.

"We know this Shamrock character's trying to move a lot of cocaine," Conover continued. "Coke that was probably ripped off during those murders down at the harbor. Doesn't sound like he's smart enough to do all of that himself. Somebody else a little more savvy has to be in with him. You look like a good candidate: You lost your business due to your coke problem; Kelly works with you. The way my partner has it figured is that you're trying to get that business back by moving one big load of stuff. I haven't decided yet if my partner is right. I'm leaving it up to you to convince me otherwise."

Conover stared hard at Dan for a long moment. "You know we can make things real warm for you, buddy. Shut down whatever action you got going on for yourself.

Matter of fact, we plan to make it real uncomfortable for every dealer on the seacoast until we wrap this thing up."

Dan couldn't believe what he was hearing. Dealer? Did they really think he was dealing coke? "I haven't touched that stuff for a long time, for Chrissake," he said. "And there is no action." Somehow he didn't sound convincing even to himself.

"Sure," Conover said. He gave Dan the once-over, like he was measuring him for a prison jumpsuit. "Once a junkie, always a junkie."

Unfortunately for Dan the man looked like he believed it. And this was the more reasonable cop?

"I don't care what you believe," Dan said. "But I'm telling you, I'm clean. Haven't touched the stuff in a long time."

"One thing about junkies that always stays the same. They're always innocent. Doesn't matter if you catch a guy with a needle in his arm or snow all over his nose. You're gonna have to prove yourself to me, you hear? Give us something, something we don't already know—like where your buddy was when the bullets started flying or where he stashed the coke–and maybe, just maybe, I'll give you the benefit of the doubt." Conover turned like he was going to leave, then turned back. "Otherwise, we'll have no choice but to assume you're more than just a bartender. Know what I mean?"

Yeah, Dan knew what the man meant. Made him

sick to his stomach. This clown was going to use Dan's past to justify what? Harassing him? Or worse, have his pal "Plainview" plant something on him? Hell, Dan wasn't a kid. He'd been around a while and he was anything but naive. He knew what was possible when the cops wanted somebody bad. Nailing a double murderer in New Hampshire would definitely make their day.

Once again Dan was in trouble up to his neck. If Sharon could see him now, she'd nod her head in that I-told-you-so way that always made him feel like he was at fault no matter what the circumstances. He had to be careful. Wouldn't be good to antagonize this cop. Not now. So all Dan said was, "Yeah, I know what you mean."

"Good," Conover said. He took a business card from his shirt pocket and handed it to Dan. "When you got something, call. But you better make it quick, for your own sake."

Dan shoved the card into his jeans pocket and nodded. He watched as Conover turned and walked up the side street back to Ocean Boulevard and wherever his car and Bartolo were waiting. Dan stayed put until Conover was out of sight, then gave him another minute. By the time Dan worked his way to the main drag the two cops were nowhere in sight.

He should get back to the bar. Instead, Dan found himself gazing across Ocean Boulevard at the water. Clouds had rolled in and there was no sun shining off it now, so the water looked dull. People milled about on the beach and along the boulevard. Across the street, leaning against the gray metal railing that separated the parking lot from the sand, stood a local character everyone called the Bird Man. He was feeding the pigeons just like he did every day. But Bird Man didn't feed pigeons like an ordinary person. He treated the birds like they were his kids, letting the damn things sit on his arms and eat right out of his hands. Dan usually got a chuckle from watching the guy, but today the strange sight didn't even make him smile.

Dan was in big trouble. If he didn't come across with something for this state cop, Conover, the outcome wouldn't be pleasant. One of those Catch 22's. If Dan had known anything, he still wouldn't have told the cops. You just didn't rat. But he didn't have a clue what Shamrock might be up to anyway, which somehow made the whole situation feel worse. Hard to believe that Shamrock would be involved with anything having to do with cocaine. And he definitely wasn't the type to get himself wrapped up in a double murder. Hell, Dan had been around the Irishman long enough to know the man wasn't capable of hurting, let alone killing, another person.

So what the hell was going on? And more importantly– considering the threats made by Conover and his partner– what would be the repercussions for someone who wasn't even involved. Namely one extremely nervous Dan

Marlowe.

No matter what the answers to those questions turned out to be, Dan was still stuck right smack dab in the middle of the mess. And what a mess it was–king-size. Had him worried plenty. He didn't have to be a rocket scientist to know whatever happened wouldn't be good. For anyone involved. Including himself.

He had to do something and quick, but what? He might as well get back behind the bar–a man could think there as well as anywhere else, sometimes even better. It was that kind of work. Besides, the last thing Dan needed now was to lose his job. After all, he didn't have much else left.

Before he turned to go back in, he gave the Bird Man one more glance. The icon stood posed like a scarecrow on the sand with his arms extended out from his sides. And the pigeons? For God's sake, he had one perched on each arm and a third plunked down on his noggin, right on top of a big-billed baseball cap. Seagulls strutted around him on the sand. Dan wondered if he got shit on much and if the man knew pigeons were filthy birds? He shook his head, turned, and headed back to the Tide.

Chapter 8

DAN KNEW IT COULDN'T be good news. Shamrock had asked to meet that afternoon at The Crooked Shillelagh, an Irish bar/restaurant situated at the south end of the beach not far from Dan's cottage. The location wasn't a surprise. Shamrock could usually be found at the Shillelagh when he wasn't at the High Tide. What was a surprise was the nervousness Dan detected in Shamrock's voice and that he'd called at all–he never had before.

So that was why Dan found himself on the sidewalk in front of the building, mulling over the possibilities in his head. Suspended over the front door of the one-story wood structure was a large wooden shillelagh. And yes, it was crooked. Plastered along the length of the restaurant's windows were posters depicting kelly green shamrocks and glasses of dark Guinness beer, each with a perfect foamy head.

Dan took a deep breath, entered, and immediately saw Shamrock in his kitchen whites sitting alone at a corner table. Planted on the table in front of him was, naturally, a glass of Guinness beer just like the ones in the windows. Probably not the first of the day. Or the last.

Shamrock looked up as Dan reached the table. "Danny, may I buy you a Heineken?"

Dan shook his head. "No thanks, Shamrock. Too early. Ginger'll do."

Shamrock shrugged, brought the beer up to his lips, and took a healthy pull. He set the glass down with an audible sigh, a creamy white mustache lingering on his upper lip.

A young waitress approached the table. She definitely fit the motif with her braided red hair and her black apron with the green Crooked Shillelagh logo stitched across the front.

"What can I be getting you, sir?" Her brogue made Shamrock sound as if he'd been born stateside.

Dan grinned. "Just a ginger ale, please."

She looked at Dan quizzically, like she'd never heard that request. Finally she said, "Some food you'll be having then?"

"No thanks."

She glanced at Shamrock staring into his glass like it would disappear if he didn't keep his eye on it, then turned and walked away.

Shamrock, for a change, didn't seem in any hurry to

speak. Dan glanced around, noticing that there was only one other occupied table and maybe a half-dozen customers at the bar. Early. Quiet. Soon enough the place would be packed with a rowdy crowd listening to "Seven Drunken Nights" played over and over by the house band. He'd listened to it himself many times through the years.

Dan turned his gaze back to Shamrock. The man was still staring into his beer, only this time the expression on his face seemed to say that beer wasn't doing its job anymore. "What's the matter, Shamrock? Something wrong?"

Shamrock finally raised his beery eyes. "Danny, I, I, ahh . . ." His shoulders slumped and he let out another sigh.

"How about I start?" Dan leaned back in his chair. "Two state cops came in the Tide. They were asking questions about you."

Shamrock's eyes widened. "About me?"

Dan took a quick look around, lowered his voice. "You and cocaine."

Shamrock quickly brought the Guinness up to his lips. Dan could hear the glass bang against the man's teeth as Shamrock drained the contents in one long pull. He put the glass down. Stared morosely at the foamy sides. "I . . ."

Dan held up his hand, interrupting Shamrock before he could go any further.

The red-haired waitress deposited a ginger ale in front of Dan and an unasked-for Guinness in front of Shamrock. "Anything else, gents?"

Shamrock waved her off, and before she could even turn to go, had the beer tipped greedily to his lips.

When he'd placed the half-empty glass down, he said, "God have mercy on me, Danny. I think I'm in a hell of a lot of trouble."

Dan took a sip of his ginger, wished it could have been something stronger. "I figured you might be after talking to those two cops."

"That's all I need, Danny. Cops on me back. And that ain't the worst of it. I think there's some bad people wanting to talk to me. And I'm afraid they might be wanting to do a lot more than just trade jokes with me. I think I did it this time, Danny. I'm scared. I don't think kissing the Blarney Stone is going to help me now." He swiped up the beer, took another pull, then set it down.

There was one thing Dan had to know before he got any deeper into this. "Shamrock, I have to ask you–did you have anything to do with those murders?"

Shamrock shook his head like he was trying to twist it off. "Murders! No, no, Danny. I swear to baby Jesus." He quickly crossed his heart. "I had nothin' at all to do with that. We . . . ah . . . I just saw where they put the stuff."

"We?"

"A slip of the tongue." Shamrock grabbed both sides

of the table, his knuckles white. "It was me, Danny boy. Just me."

"All right, Shamrock, I believe you." Dan kept his voice calm. "You didn't kill anyone. But you did take the cocaine."

"Yes, Danny, yes. That's it. I'm in awful trouble." Shamrock raised his face to the ceiling. "Oh, Heavenly Father. I wish I'd never even seen the stuff. I don't know what I was thinking."

Dan reached across the table and grabbed Shamrock's arm. "Get hold of yourself, Shamrock. We'll think of something."

Shamrock stared at him, eyes desperate. "You'll help me then, Danny? I got no one else. No one."

Dan looked back at Shamrock. He slowly released his grip on the man's arm, pulled his hand back. He didn't want to get involved. In fact, he shouldn't get mixed up in anything involving drugs–especially this. It could blow back on him in a hundred ways. But this was Shamrock, after all. And he liked the man. Besides, Dan didn't have many friends left; he couldn't afford to lose any.

Besides, it hadn't been that long ago when he'd been as bad off as Shamrock and had needed help. People had been there for him (at least what'd been left of him). And that was the only reason he was still here today–sitting with Shamrock, both of them having no family–because someone took a big risk for him. So what could he do?

Say no and walk out the door onto Ocean Boulevard, with
the sun in his eyes and the sea air in his nostrils, whistling a
happy tune? Not likely. He had to shave every morning,
didn't he?

"All right, my friend. All right."

The Irishman gave a weak smile. "Ah, Danny. You'll
help me then? You promise? You promise you'll help
me with this?"

"Yes, Shamrock, I promise. We'll figure this out somehow."
Dan slowly stirred his drink with the straw. "So you have
it? The cocaine?"

"Yes, Danny. I have the god-awful stuff. But I don't
want it. Maybe I'll just throw it in the goddamn ocean."
Shamrock raised the beer, polished it off, slammed the
glass down on the table.

Dan sat back, alarmed. "You don't want to do that. No
one would ever believe you. They'd treat you just like
you still had the stuff stashed somewhere. And that
wouldn't be good."

Shamrock shook his head. "All right, Danny. I wasn't
really serious. It's just that I'm at my wit's end. Maybe if
I tell you everything, we'll think of something else to do?
Right?"

"We'll figure it out somehow." Dan looked at his
wristwatch. "When are you working?"

Shamrock glanced up at the big Boston Bruins clock
on the wall. "Sweet Jesus, I'm late. I'm never late. I got
to go. Can we talk again tomorrow, Danny?"

"Sure, Shamrock. We'll talk tomorrow."

Shamrock slid his chair back and stood up. "You're a saint, Danny."

"My wife doesn't think so. But we'll figure something out. And try not to worry."

Shamrock turned and hurried out the front door.

Dan lifted his soft drink, studied it, set it down. This whole setup wasn't good. He knew it. He felt it. He didn't have a clue how he was going to get Shamrock out of this mess and not have the whole thing blow up in his face. Too bad he couldn't follow the advice he'd given to Shamrock–about trying not to worry. Because right now he was plenty worried. Worried enough for both of them.

Chapter 9

JORGE RIVERA made the rounds, telling everyone he knew who was big in the business to let him know if they heard of anyone new trying to move weight. He'd already spoken to people in Boston, Lowell, Manchester, Concord, and Providence. Now he was going to reach out to associates in New York. Then he was going to stop up in Lawrence, his old stomping grounds, before heading up to Hampton Beach. He couldn't leave any stone unturned. Not with this load.

Jorge pulled his black Lexus up to a pay phone on Route 114 in Middleton, grabbed his address book from the glove compartment, and walked up to the booth. He opened the book and then hesitated for a minute, running through his mind the discreet words he'd use to disguise the purpose of his calls to anyone eavesdropping. He fished out a pocketful of change and made three calls to

New York.

Satisfied he'd spread his net wide enough, Jorge got back in the Lexus and headed north to Lawrence, his home town. Back where it had all started for him so many years ago. He thought about that now, like he did occasionally, as he drove in that direction.

Lawrence, Massachusetts. An old mill city with no jobs and no future. He couldn't wait to get out of there when he was a kid. When he was old enough to go in the army, he did. For four years. And when the four years were up, where the hell did he go? Right back to Lawrence. He'd been hoping at the time–maybe dreaming was more like it–that the city would've changed. And change it had. In fact Lawrence, Massachusetts had taken a major nose dive. Unemployment among the large Hispanic population was sky-high. Besides a few low-paying jobs at factories that had once been some of the most ancient mills in the State, there was nothing. Except drugs. A lot of heroin and cocaine were being sold on the city's streets. So that's what Jorge gravitated to: small-time dealing. There were no other opportunities for someone who had no marketable skills. At least that's what Jorge thought.

Until Dominic Carpucci came into the picture.

Jorge could still remember the first night he'd met the old man. He'd been working a side street off Essex Street in downtown Lawrence. Nothing big–grams and eight balls. He'd been making money, but he wasn't getting famous.

Made enough to pay the bills and live a little high–for Lawrence, anyway. He had good quality powder and a pretty regular clientele.

Unlike most of the other dealers in the area, Jorge didn't buy his coke from fellow Hispanic wholesalers in Boston, New York, or Rhode Island. He didn't buy from the larger local dealers in Lawrence or Lowell, either. His community was filthy with informers and rip-offs, so he figured the less everyone knew about his business, the less chance he'd have problems.

His excellent command of English combined with his stint in the service made him feel at ease around Anglos (and they with him). He used both to his advantage when faced with the opportunity to score his coke from a non-Hispanic–Rocco, an Italian guy from Revere who handled only quality. Jorge got his coke on the arm from Rocco and paid him back quickly. He believed in being a fast-pay. Besides, the sooner he handed the money to Rocco, the sooner it wasn't his responsibility anymore. He made things as easy and pleasant for Rocco as possible. Jorge's motto was keep your connection happy and your customers happier.

So one evening when Rocco pulled up in his Caddy and told Jorge someone wanted to meet him, Jorge hopped right in the car. Why not? After all, he had a clear conscience.

When they reached Revere, somewhere near the beach, Rocco parked the car, and the two of them walked down the street to Rocco's apartment building, a brick garden-style job. That was when Jorge began having second thoughts. They always conducted business in various parking lots throughout the Merrimac Valley–never the same place two times in a row. What the hell was going on?

Rocco didn't say a word as they rode the elevator to the third floor. He led Jorge into the apartment and closed the door behind them.

There was a man sitting in an overstuffed chair in the main room of Rocco's gaudily decorated place. The man stood as they entered the room. He looked Italian–class Italian, not street Italian like Rocco. He was short but well built and obviously took care of himself. His grooming and clothing were impeccable. Suit, tie, the works. He extended his hand to Jorge.   No surprise–a firm handshake.

"Jorge, my name's Dominic Carpucci," the man said, in a voice that told Jorge that he too had come from the streets, no matter what his appearance said. "I've heard a lot about ya."

"Nice to meet you," Jorge said. He glanced at Rocco, noting the way the other man deferred to the slick-looking Italian. This must be Rocco's connection.

The three men sat in chairs around the room. Jorge close to Dominic, Rocco farther back.

"Can Rocky get you anything, Jorge?" Dominic Carpucci asked.

Jorge cleared his throat. He wasn't sure how to

address this man so he decided to take the neutral
approach. "No, thank you." Just keep it polite, Jorge
thought. Let the man say what he's going to say in his
own time.

Apparently, Dominic Carpucci didn't believe in
wasting that time. "I know you're wonderin' why I had
Rocky bring you here, Jorge."

"I'm curious."

Rocco sat silently, off to the side, as if he were as
important in this as the furniture.

"Rocky tells me you've had some special training in
the military," Dominic said. "Tell me about it."

"A special ops unit," Jorge answered.

"Intelligence training? Weapons? Hand-to-hand? That
kind of stuff?"

"All of that and more," Jorge said confidently. There was
a fine line between confidence and arrogance. Hopefully, he
didn't come off on the too-arrogant side.

"Interesting," Dominic said. He nodded his head, then
looked intently at Jorge and gave a sly smile. "He tells
me other things too. Like you been with him awhile. That
you got a little business that you run nice. That you're a
stand-up guy who keeps his mouth shut. And that you
pay your bills on time. That right?"

"I believe in doing the right thing," Jorge said. Where
the hell was this all leading?

Dominic's face stayed smooth for a moment.
Noncommittal. Then he broke into a wide grin. "I like

that answer, Jorge. That's a pretty good answer, huh, Rocky?"

Rocco nodded his head stiffly, looking none too happy as far as Jorge could see.

"How'd you like to come and work for me?" Dominic asked. He leaned back in his chair, crossed his ankle over his knee.

"What would I be doing, Mr. Carpucci?" Jorge asked.

"A little of everything. Drive me around here and there. Maybe make some collections. Talk to some people for me. I'd start you off slow, see how it works out. The pay would be good and I'd keep you from getting bored." Dominic glanced at his Rolex watch. "Whattaya think, kid?"

Jorge wasn't sure what to think, except he knew he didn't like being called kid. But still, working for this guy who was obviously a big wheel, maybe even Mafia, had to be better than standing on a dirty street corner in Lawrence hustling eight balls. Yet there was one thing that puzzled him. "One thing I'm wondering, Mr. Carpucci? Why me?"

"You mean why would I use a Spanish kid like you when I'm Italian?" Dominic laughed and looked over at Rocco who forced a laugh. "Because you're qualified, kid. Aren't any Italian kids I know with your qualifications. Besides, I like having someone from outside who everybody don't know. It'll keep certain people on their toes. All right, kid?"

It was the best offer he'd had in a long time, or more

truthfully, the only offer. But there was one more item to straighten out. Jorge nodded, then said, "I have a little thing going on up north in Lawrence. I'm not getting rich, but it's not bad either. What about that?"

"If ya got someone you can trust to take it over, that's okay," Dominic said, waving his hand through the air. "Otherwise, you'll have to dump it. I don't want the heat. In that case, figure out what you been makin' and I'll beat it good. Either way, I'll make sure you do better. You keep me happy, I'll keep you happy. That's the way it works around here."

"All right, Mr. Carpucci, I accept," Jorge said.   He glanced at Rocco sitting like a mannequin in his chair.

Dominic must've read Jorge's mind. "Don't worry about Rocky. I'm going to take care of him too. Right, Rocky?"

"Right, Boss."

And that was the first time Jorge had ever heard someone called boss. It was also the first time he thought maybe he'd like to be called "Boss" someday too. Hell, at least it was something he could dream about, wasn't it?

Chapter 10

TONY PERALTA didn't waste any time making a move after the visit from the two state cops; he couldn't afford to. They'd been right about how much he loved his ocean front home and he wasn't about to jeopardize it just because some assholes had whacked two nobodies down at the harbor.

They'd threatened his business, too. He had a sweet operation going and it was very profitable. Nobody ever bothered him. Of course, the statie had been right— he did give the feds a name or two every so often to insure that things kept chugging along nice like. But hey, the drug business was a tough business and you had to do what you had to do. Working with the feds had paid off big for Tony. Any time local or state cops came snooping around, he'd just made a call to a certain federal agent and the pests had backed off.

But that same agent had called him first this time,

picking his brain about a large load of coke being shopped around. When Tony admitted being in the dark about this particular matter, that same agent told Tony he better start beating the bushes and find something out, or he could pack his bags for Club Fed. And it hadn't even been an hour after that call before he received another call. This one from one of his connections–a heavyweight Hispanic by the name of Jorge Rivera. And guess what he wanted for Christmas?

Hard to say what was worse: Bartolo, the state cop, threatening to take Tony's house and let everyone on the seacoast know he was an informer, not to mention throwing him off the cliff for good measure; the fed saying he'd send him away to college for who knew how long; or his Hispanic connection who . . . well, he didn't have to threaten anything, that's how real he was. Just the thought of that multiple choice question gave Tony the heebie-jeebies.

There was one thing in all this that didn't give him the shakes. Instead, it made him feel kind of excited. And that was when he thought about the likely size of this load everyone was after. It had to be one king-size mountain of snow to get all these heavy people's pants in an uproar. Kind of made him thankful he hadn't slipped and told anyone what he had heard recently from one of his own customers–that someone on the beach was trying to move a good amount of coke, cheap. When he'd heard who the so-called seller was, Tony'd just laughed and said, "Yeah, right."

But now, with what the staties had said and the two telephone calls, it didn't seem so funny anymore. Instead, it gave him ideas. Possible problems too. Even if he located the coke, no way could he keep everyone who wanted it happy. That left just one alternative–maybe, just maybe, he could grab the coke for himself and play dumb with the whole bunch of them. After all, he was a real slick guy, wasn't he? It was dangerous, no lie there, and he'd have to move quick if he hoped to pull it off. None of these characters who were trying to strong-arm him were the type who'd wait long.

So the first thing he did was call Wayne and tell him to get his ass over to Boar's Head, fast. Wayne came, of course, all 250 pounds of him. Wayne had slapped around a lot of people for Tony through the years, people who dragged their feet on paying or tried to move in on his outs. The six-foot-four-inch giant was damn good at his work and he enjoyed it.

Right now Wayne was enjoying his work again. This time at the High Tide Restaurant. It was six in the morning and the only people inside were Wayne, Tony, and Shamrock Kelly, Shamrock currently serving as the recipient of all Wayne's "enjoyment."

Wayne gave the little guy another slap upside the head. "You heard him. Answer the fucking question."

"I don't know what yer talking about," Shamrock said, his voice shaky and his brogue so thick Tony could barely understand him.

They were in the restaurant's kitchen, the Irishman backed up flat against a walk-in fridge.

"Word on the street is you have some snow that needs shoveling." Tony ran a finger across the walk-in's shiny surface, then slammed that same surface hard with his fist.

"I was only joking around," Shamrock answered, gazing around the kitchen as if looking for help. "Taking advantage of the situation with the ladies, if you know what I mean. I know nothing about the cocaine."

"Lying little harp," Tony said. "Give him another slap."

WHAP! WHAP! WHAP! Wayne hit the cowering Irishman hard with the palms of both of his huge hands, alternating one after the other, over and over again, a few of the slaps connecting hard.

Shamrock yelped like a wounded seal. When Wayne stopped the little man peeked up at him from between his fingers. "Stop! I'll tell you. I'll tell you. It was down there, that's where it was." Shamrock pointed.

"Where?" Tony said. "The other end of the beach?"

"That's it. Near the bridge."

"What side?" Tony asked.

"This side," Shamrock said.

"I know that, you stupid shit," Tony snapped. "I mean which side of Ocean Boulevard?"

"Near the water."

"Must be down near the old White Rock store," Tony

muttered.   He glared at Shamrock.   "What street? Atlantic? Boston? Huh, what street?"

"Eaton."

Eaton. Tony knew where that was. He remembered who lived near there too–Dan Marlowe, the bartender, ex-owner of the High Tide. Lost the place when he couldn't keep his nose clean. Everybody on the beach knew that.

Marlowe'd turned his life around or so he claimed. But the man was smart. Smart enough to put together something like this little scam. This dishwasher sure as hell couldn't. Another piece of the puzzle clicked into place. Tony just needed some verification; shouldn't be too hard. The little Irishman looked so scared now he'd probably give up his mother. Time to see what he'd do about someone who wasn't his mother.

"So Marlowe's mixed up in this, huh? He's the man who took the coke. Am I right?"

Shamrock's eyes grew wide as balloons. "Dan Marlowe? He's got nothing to do with it. I swear to God."

Wayne pulled down a metal kitchen pot the size of a volleyball from the pans hanging overhead. He held the pot by the handle, waved it menacingly in front of Shamrock's face.

"Should I see if these pots are any good, Boss?" Wayne asked, a maniacal leer on his face. "Maybe see if they're dent proof?"

"Where's Marlowe hiding the coke?" Tony demanded.

"I don't know anything about that," Shamrock said,

pleading now. He had big red welts on both sides of his face from Wayne's slaps, and his eyes were glued to the pot in the big man's hand. "I dunno. Sweet Mother of Mary, I'm telling you the truth."

Judging by the sound of his voice and the look of him, Tony was pretty sure the Irishman was telling the truth. After all, Marlowe wouldn't be stupid enough to let this guy know where the stuff was stashed. Still, it wouldn't hurt to be certain. "Go ahead, Wayne. See if that pot'll dent."

Shamrock howled as the first blow from the pot bounced hard off his arm, breaking the bone with an audible crack. "I swear . . ."

Wayne swung the pot fast and hard, over and over, like he was trying to eradicate a cockroach infestation. The attack was so quick and ruthless it even caught Tony by surprise. He jumped back out of the way, narrowly avoiding a wild swing.

Shamrock howled–the desperate sound of a dying animal–and crumpled to the floor, his bloodied arms raised to protect his head. "I'll tell . . ."

The air hissed as Wayne swung the pot directly at the Irishman's head. Shamrock ducked, then looked up at Tony with pleading eyes.

"Wayne, you ignoramus, stop. Stop. He's ready to talk."

Wayne took one last swing. The pot connected with Shamrock's head in a sickening thud that made Tony's stomach do flip-flops.

"Jesus Christ, Wayne. Stop it." Tony slammed his fist hard into Wayne's back.

Wayne stopped and stood panting, the big pot dented and dangling loose in his right hand. Shamrock lay face up on the floor, not moving, blood everywhere.

Tony pushed around Wayne and looked down at the bloody mess. "This is just fucking great," he said softly.

"Did I hit him too hard, Boss?"

"Are you serious?" Tony had to look back over his shoulder at the big man to see if he was serious. He was.

Wayne shrugged, "Well, at least we found out one good thing."

"What's that?" Tony asked, already dreading the answer.

Wayne held up the blood-stained kitchen pot. "These pans ain't worth shit," he said with a stupid grin on his puss. "They dent."

Tony just shook his head and groaned.

Chapter 11

SOME DAYS YOU JUST KNOW Life is going to give you trouble–you stub your toe when you get out of bed, the coffee maker breaks just as you're brewing your first cup of coffee, you get to work and the door's locked when it should be open.

Saturday morning, cloudy with a chance of rain. Matched his mood. What the hell was Shamrock thinking, leaving the door locked? When Dan finally got the door open, he found the lights off, and by the time he'd found the light switch, he'd managed to bang into a mop and bucket, bruising his shin and making his bad mood worse.

Dan scowled as he shoved the bucket and mop back against the wall. Nothing had been right since those two state cops stopped to chat with him. He'd been tossing around what they'd said and mixing it up with a few other things that'd been rattling around in his brain recently, but he hadn't been able to put any of it together yet.

Maybe Shamrock had gone out for a box of sinkers. A couple of donuts would sweeten both their moods.

Dan made his way out front to the bar, turned on the overhead TV's, and flipped on the radio that piped soft music throughout the restaurant area. He took a cloth and swiped at imaginary spots on the bar, not quite ready to get to work–he still couldn't get the two state cops out of his mind.

Conover and Bartolo. They'd wanted information, information Dan wasn't willing to give. They wouldn't be too happy that he hadn't called, especially that Bartolo. Not too many things more dangerous than a pissed-off cop, especially one with the moniker, "Plainview." A cop who wasn't above saying that seized evidence had been in "plain view" when it hadn't been certainly wasn't above planting evidence when he felt like it.

It all boiled down to the fact that Dan had decided not to do anything except maybe pray that the whole crazy thing would just fade away like a bad dream, although he knew there was fat chance of that happening. Still, knowing what he now knew was like sitting in the path of a tornado just waiting for the storm to hit–knowing it was coming and hoping for the best, but expecting the worst.

Dan walked over to the front door and unlocked it,

just like every other morning. Even though the day felt heavy and portentous there was no reason to believe there were boogiemen hiding behind every doorway. He didn't mind if he had a customer or two while he was getting everything ready. The kitchen wouldn't open for a while so they couldn't order any chow, just a beer or a drink. Easy.

As he pushed the door open a bit to make sure it was unlocked, he glanced across the street at the ocean. It was calm, only a few white caps. Heavy clouds hung in the sky and the humidity was already building. Not unusual for this time of the year. Hampton got maybe a couple of weeks of high humidity each summer–if you added up all the humid days. He tugged at the shirt sticking to his chest, walked back to the bar, flicked on the air conditioner switches.

Next he pulled the fruit trays from the refrigerator underneath the bar, put a set of each at both ends, then took a stack of clean ashtrays and set them at intervals along the shiny surface. His movements were automatic. His thoughts, not so much.

What the hell was Shamrock thinking when he took that cocaine? Considering his old addiction, Dan figured he should be able to sympathize with the Irishman, but all he could do was think how stupid a move like that was.

Dan grabbed a five-gallon bucket from under the sink and headed through the kitchen to the ice machine. When he reached the machine, he set the bucket on a wooden counter and flipped up the cover. The machine had been making ice all night long and was practically overflowing. Dan used the big, metal scoop they kept beside the machine and started to shovel ice into the bucket.

No matter how stupid Shamrock had been taking the stuff, he was even stupider to think he could get away with it. Someone was bound to figure out where the coke had gone. No matter how hard Dan tried, he couldn't figure out a way to help the Irishman out of the hellhole he was in.

Dan's scoop hit something hard. Something definitely "not ice." He pushed the ice off to one side. Sometimes, the waitresses left a metal water pitcher inside and it'd get buried as the machine made new ice. He shoveled a few more scoops out of the way, moving ice into the bucket before he realized that what he was uncovering was definitely not a water pitcher.

Dan's stomach flip-flopped. The scoop fell from his hands and clanged on the floor. He used his hands, feverishly raking ice out of the machine and dumping it on the floor. It didn't take long before he'd cleared away enough ice to see why Shamrock hadn't unlocked the door.

"Jesus fuckin' Christ." Dan stumbled backward, heart thumping. He swallowed hard, grabbing his stomach to keep from losing his breakfast. He stared, stunned, at Shamrock's semi-frozen face. The Irishman's skin glinted with white frost and dark blood, looking more like a frozen pumpkin that some kid had done a poor carving job on than a human face.

After a long moment, the adrenalin kicked in and Dan tore at the ice with both hands like an animal, raking the cubes out and onto the kitchen floor in huge piles. He had to get the Irishman out of there. Find out if he was still alive.

While there was an off-hand chance Shamrock was the victim of a random robbery, Dan knew in his heart there was only one reason Shamrock would end up on ice–the harbor incident. And that meant Dan was in big trouble; Shamrock too, if he was still breathing.

Dan slipped on the pile of growing ice, regained his balance, shoveled some more.

Somehow he had to get them both out of what was turning out to be a deadly situation. But who could he trust? Certainly not the local cops. It was out of their league. And then Dan realized he had the answer right in his back jeans pocket, in his wallet–Conover's business card.

Suddenly Shamrock's shoulders were free. Dan reached under the Irishman and wrapped both arms around Shamrock's chest, then straightened his legs and pulled hard. The body unfolded and broke free, sliding out of the bin in a shower of falling ice and almost carrying Dan to the floor with it.

Dan stretched Shamrock flat on the floor and ran to the phone, struggling to hold his balance as he slipped and slid through mounds of ice. He grabbed the receiver from the wall phone and dialed 911 as fast as his shaking fingers would go.

Chapter 12

LIEUTENANT RAY Conover had a problem–too many donuts and not enough running. He was jogging north on Hampton Beach at an easy pace and already his lungs ached. The low tide left the sand hard, making a good running surface. It was 7:30 in the morning. The sky was a clear blue, the sun bright, and the ocean shimmering. This should've been an easy run, not a freaking endurance race.

There were only about a dozen people scattered along the entire length of the beach, some walking, a handful running. A few seagulls circled overhead, squawking. An orange parasail floated high enough above the water that the tourist strapped between the sail and the towing boat was an amorphous blob. Up ahead, leading by maybe a hundred yards, was Dan Marlowe and he was jogging too.

Conover swore at himself for not keeping in better shape.

He needed to find something besides his own pain to think about. Immediately, a picture flashed into his mind: the mug of the Irishman, looking like a frozen turnip, staring up from the floor of the High Tide Restaurant. The poor soul's head had been bashed in with a kitchen pot. The little guy must've had been born with "The Luck of the Irish" because somehow the Irishman survived. He was in the Intensive Care Unit.

A couple of the local cops who'd been hanging around the crime scene insisted that the incident was a restaurant burglary-in-progress that Shamrock had inadvertently interrupted. One look at the Irishman's bruised face and Conover knew this was no burglary. Looked like the word he and Bartolo had picked up on the street–that the Irishman was trying to unload some serious blow and that blow had gotten him into some serious shit–was a more accurate scenario. You didn't have to be Einstein to figure there might be a tie-in with the murders down at the harbor.

There was always the chance the Irishman had spilled the beans and told whoever was beating on him where the coke was. If that was the case, that same somebody more than likely had the entire stash in his or her hot little hands. At least that would put an end to the rough stuff on Happy Hampton Beach. But Conover couldn't make assumptions. Except for one–if Kelly hadn't talked, then someone was still out there looking for the cocaine. And they would do anything to get it.

But who in the hell would beat a man almost to death with a kitchen pot and stuff him in an ice machine? Took a sadist who really enjoyed his work to pull off a mess like that. Conover had put a lot of guys away during his career, but none of them could hold a candle to this guy.

He'd discarded Dan Marlowe as a suspect right off the bat. After all, Marlowe had called right after he'd hung up with Emergency Services. The guy'd sounded really shaken. Said he'd found out a few things. That they had to talk. Definitely not a killer-like move unless Marlowe was trying to throw him off the track. But Conover had a good feel for people–had to in his business–and Marlowe didn't seem the type to go around pulverizing people's brains.

The jury was still out as far as the cocaine heist went. Marlowe was denying any involvement, but more and more it seemed that anyone and everyone could be mixed up in that kind of shit. And with what they had found out about Marlowe's past . . . well, he just wasn't sure.

Better than even odds that Marlowe was in danger either way. Marlowe sensed it too. His connections to the High Tide and Kelly, not to mention the fact that his history with coke was known up and down the beach, made him a prime target. If the coke was still out there waiting to be found, it wouldn't take long for whoever tried to turn the Irishman into a popsicle to connect all the dots. Those dots would lead them straight to Marlowe, and they wouldn't hesitate to introduce Marlowe's head to a kitchen pot, see what he had to say.

Conover wasn't happy with where his thoughts were heading. Happy or not, there was no doubt Marlowe was his best lead.

When Marlowe called, Conover had stayed away from pressuring the man about the coke. Instead, he hammered away at the danger Marlowe was in, pointing out whoever had battered the Irishman had probably been after him too, or would be soon. After some initial resistance, he'd finally convinced Marlowe to let him shadow him for a while. Marlowe had demanded only one assurance–he didn't want Bartolo anywhere near him. Conover had a chuckle over that and then had given his word.

Conover kept his eyes focused on Marlowe's jogging outfit–black t-shirt, black jogging shorts, white sox and white sneakers, Walkman in hand, earphones on his head. About the same getup that Conover was wearing, except instead of a Walkman Conover carried a small brown bag with a 9mm Glock pistol inside.

They'd started the run down on the sand at the south end of the beach and now Conover was across from the Casino, a two-story gray building two blocks long that contained everything from arcades to a miniature golf course.

Up ahead Marlowe clambered over a jumble of rocks separating the main beach from another short stretch of sand. The sandy spit was only about 50 yards long.

Marlowe would have to turn and retrace his steps as soon as he reached the end.

Marlowe dropped out of sight and Conover picked up his pace. As he raced toward the rocks a feeling suddenly came over him, the same feeling he'd had off and on over the years. Something bad was going on behind those rocks. Something he couldn't see. It was ridiculous getting all worked up about a feeling, but Conover found himself pouring it on, his arms and legs pumping faster.

When he finally reached the rocks where Marlowe had disappeared and scrambled to the top he didn't feel quite so ridiculous anymore.

Instead, he felt worse.

The little spit of land was deserted except for Marlowe and two masked figures–a short pudgy guy and a muscle-bound giant–mixing it up at the far end. The giant yanked Marlowe toward the seawall. Didn't look like Marlowe was going easy. He landed what looked like a decent blow upside the giant's face, but the big man wasn't fazed. The smaller character danced out in front, motioning the bigger guy on.

Conover yanked his gun from the paper bag as he took two quick steps down the rocks and onto the sand. He paused a moment, uncertain who he was dealing with. No one had drawn a weapon yet. At least, not that he could see.

Conover raced toward the small group. "Stop. Police."

The words came out more like a squeak instead of a

shout. Marlowe stayed put while the other two bolted for the seawall. They reached the wall just as Conover stopped next to Marlowe. He bent his head, put his hands on his knees, and tried to slow his breathing.

"Are . . . you . . . all . . . right?"

"Yeah, sure," Dan answered, sounding shaken. "I'm okay, I guess."

And except for a couple of red marks on his face he did look okay to Conover. "Who were they?"

"I'm not sure."

"What'd they want?"

Suddenly, a voice shouted out, "Hey, asshole."

Conover glanced up at the seawall near Ocean Boulevard. The big guy stood there, pistol held across his body like he was preparing for inspection, then he turned and leveled the barrel at them. The second it went off, the explosion that made his whole body jump told Conover the weapon was a magnum.

He and Dan both hit the sand. The big man fired the cannon once more, the bullet whistling as it passed close by. Conover lifted his face from the sand and watched the shooter turn and disappear beyond the seawall.

"Stay here." Conover jumped up and ran to the seawall where he boosted himself up onto the concrete and then over the gray railing onto the sidewalk. A silver Mercury Sable came peeling out of the parking lot that separated the north and southbound sides of Ocean Boulevard, and there was that jerk again riding shotgun with his cannon waving out the window, yelling obscenities, and then another god-awful explosion as he fired again. Conover found himself hugging the sidewalk. By the time he got up he knew it was hopeless, but he was so pissed he still raised his Glock in a two-handed grip and fired off half a magazine in the direction of the speeding car.

Dan was on his feet when Conover got back. "You sure you don't know who that was?"

Marlowe looked away. "I don't think so."

"Sooner or later we're gonna figure out who they are," Conover said, gun in his hand hanging at his side. "One thing we don't have to figure out, though, is what they're after. The coke. They think you got it."

Conover looked at Dan, waiting for him to respond. Dan looked back.

After a long minute of silence, the two men–Dan holding his Walkman and Conover his gun–turned and started walking back south along the beach.

Chapter 13

"HEY, THERE GOES the turn," Wayne said as they drove past the street that led up Boar's Head to Tony Peralta's mansion. They were in the rented Sable, Tony driving, Wayne riding shotgun, his head brushing the roof.

"I know," Tony said, his right hand on top of the steering wheel. He glanced over at Wayne beside him. The big lummox was staring out the window, a huge shit-eating grin on his face. How the hell could he be so calm–trading shots over the seawall with some jerk one minute, sitting there like nothing happened the next?

Probably didn't have a high enough I.Q. to worry about it, Tony realized. But he, unfortunately, did.

Tony turned his attention back to the road, every so often shooting a look up at the rearview half expecting to see a string of Hampton cruisers chasing them. "We aren't going back to the house right now. We'll go for a little ride first. Just in case someone's following us."

"No one's following us, Boss," Wayne said. He let out
a little laugh. "That asshole's probably still hugging the
ground. Besides, I feel like a beer."

"Fuck you and your beer. I think I know that guy with
the gun back there. He's a state cop, for Chrissake. And
he wasn't hugging the ground when he got those shots
off at us, was he?"

"Wild shots," Wayne said, shrugging his wide shoulders.
"He wasn't going to hit nobody like that." Wayne picked up
the .357 magnum he had in his lap and gave it a loving look.
"Especially after he almost took one from this baby. He
was probably shaking like a leaf."

Tony looked at the gun and furrowed his brow. "Will
you put that thing away. You missed him, but with the
luck I've been having lately you'll probably shoot me."

"No problem," Wayne said, reaching down and sliding
the gun under the seat.

Tony drove the car along Route 1A, past North Beach
and into North Hampton. He'd just keep driving north
for a while. Maybe go all the way to Portsmouth or a
little father even, into Maine. Anything but going back
to Boar's Head right away. After all, he wasn't stupid
like Wayne. Tony wasn't about to lead Marlowe's white
knight–cop or otherwise–right back to his home, that was
for sure.

Maybe he wouldn't drive back to Boar's Head period,
at least not in this car. He'd been careful and had a stooge

rent it, but if the guy back there was lucky enough to get the plate number, the stooge might give Tony up. Especially if that character on the beach turned out to be the statie Tony thought he might be.

The guy'd looked a little like Conover, but Tony couldn't be sure. He'd been too far away and things had happened too fast. Could have been that some schmuck jogging down the beach decided to play hero. A schmuck who just happened to have a gun.

No, Tony realized. It had to be Conover back there with the gun. And if it was, things had just gotten a thousand times worse.

"You know something?" Tony said, glancing back and forth between Wayne and the road. "You're a fucking asshole."

Wayne frowned. "Geez. Whattaya mean?" he asked, sounding more like a hurt little boy than a 250-pound man.

"What do I mean?" Tony answered. "What do you think I mean? I ask you to give me a little help with a few problems I got–those two staties squeezing me, threatening my business and my beautiful home; the fed; and the connection giving me grief. You're supposed to help me with all that. Instead, you got me mixed up with that little Mick fiasco down at the High Tide and now you're shooting it out with cops. And when you're with me to boot."

"Hey," Wayne said apologetically, "the guy we put in the ice machine . . . he's alive, so that's no big deal. And that doofus back there, I don't think he was any freakin' cop."

"The guy you put in the ice machine. You. I didn't touch him."

"Yeah, but we thought he was dead. You said stuffing him in there would obituate the evidence."

"It's obliterate, dunce. Don't bet that guy on the beach wasn't a cop, either. Who the hell do you think he was, a lifeguard, for Chrissake? Lifeguards don't pack automatics, they pack sunscreen." Tony glanced in the rearview mirror again. "From now on if you feel the urge to kill anyone, do it on your own time. When I'm not around. Understand?"

"Yeah, yeah, whatever you say. Can we stop for a beer now?"

"Forget your beer," Tony answered. They were somewhere in Rye now and Tony caught himself going over the speed limit. He slowed it down. This was no time to draw attention from the law. "We still have to get this Marlowe jerk and find out two things. One, where's the coke? That's for me–I want it. Number two, who killed those two sailor boys down at the harbor? That's for the staties–keep them off my back. No way I'm losing my business and palace because of those two assholes. Who the hell were they to me six months ago? Nobody, that's who. Now I have to devote all my precious time to chasing people around the beach for them? I don't think so."

Tony drove in silence for a couple of miles. Finally he said, "The mistake we made was trying to take Marlowe on his jog. Out in the open like that. I thought it was smart, but it wasn't. It was stupid. The smart way is to grab him at his cottage when he's alone. I heard his wife and kids left him or something, so nabbing him shouldn't be hard. We'll get him when he's sleeping. What could go wrong then?"

Tony glanced at Wayne. "You can control yourself this time, can't you?"

"Sure I can," Wayne said.

Right. But Tony had to have some muscle along. If not Wayne, then who? There was nobody else. Besides leg breakers were all the same–all muscle, no brains. The job description didn't include being the shiniest shell on the beach.

"Hold the steering wheel," Tony said. Wayne reached over with his left hand and held the car to the road. Tony reached under the big man's arm, popped the glove compartment, and removed a small glass vial of coke. He quickly unscrewed the cap and dipped a tiny spoon attached to it by a thin chain into the vial. The spoon came out with a mound of white powder. Tony put the spoon to his right nostril and quickly snorted the coke. He repeated the process with the other nostril, put the cap back on, and tossed the vial back into the glove compartment.

"Hey, what about me?" Wayne asked.

"Coke's for management," Tony replied. "Not workers." Last thing he needed was Wayne on coke.

Tony took back the wheel. He'd been feeling muddled before. Now his thoughts were crystal clear. He'd use Wayne again. The two of them would go to this Dan Marlowe's cottage. Scare the prick a little. Find out where the coke was and who did the harbor job. When Tony had the coke safely tucked away, he'd give the names of the shooters to those two goddamn cops, Bartolo and Conover. Then he'd do his best to play dumb with the fed and his connection. Tell them he tried hard but couldn't turn up anything.

He hoped Marlowe wouldn't turn out to be the one who whacked the guys at the harbor. That would present a problem–like maybe Marlowe trying to stay off death row by telling the cops who had the coke after Tony was done with him. Maybe he'd let Wayne have his fun with Marlowe, after all. Just like he did with the Irishman. Except this time, Tony'd let Wayne finish the job.

He'd find someone to take the fall for the Marlowe murder rap. Some poor sap who didn't know his head from his ass. That way Tony'd still have his nice little business and his nice little house, both of which were anything but little. To top it all off, he'd have the coke too.

Nice and easy. Just the way he liked it.

They were coming into downtown Portsmouth with a

small pub on the right and a donut joint on the left. Tony pulled into the parking lot beside the pub. "You still want that beer, Wayne?"

Wayne smiled like a kid. "Sure I do. I love beer."

"All right then," Tony said. Damn, he did feel better about this now. Everything was going to work out just fine. He could feel it in his gut. "Come on. Let's go get that brew."

Wayne reached under the seat. Tony grabbed his arm. "Leave the gun here," he said, feeling good but not crazy. "My limit's one gunfight a day. All right?"

"Okay, Boss, okay," Wayne said, an ear-to-ear grin stretched wide across his face. "Whatever you say."

Tony let Wayne get out of the car. Then he reached over, took the vial from the glove box, and put it in his shirt pocket. What the hell–things were looking good and he'd be a fool not to want to keep them that way. Besides, they had a lot of heavy work ahead of them. He might as well get fortified. Tony climbed out of the car and followed Wayne into the pub.

Chapter 14

JORGE HAD CALLED AND told Dominic he had a line on the captain's brother. Dominic had told Jorge to sit on the guy, he was on his way and wanted to handle it himself. And so Dominic was headed to Hampton Beach in his big, black Lincoln. Sal, Dominic's driver and bodyguard, was behind the wheel, looking exactly how a bodyguard named Sal was expected to look.

Jorge's call wasn't the only reason Dominic wanted to travel to that damn beach. He wanted to check out the area where the rip-off went down. He'd been around for a long time and had a good sixth sense in this business. If he could get a look at the place, get a feel for it, he might be able to figure out who pulled the job, or at the very least, what direction he should be looking to find them.

What he didn't have to figure out was what he was

going to do to whoever pulled the heist once he caught up with them. No, he didn't have to figure that out at all. And now, after telling Sal to speed it up, he stretched and tried to relax, daydreaming about what he would do to those poor pricks when he got his hands on them.

He wouldn't have the kid shoot them in the head, at least not right away. That'd be too easy. No, first he'd tie them to a goddamn tree. And he'd find a tree at the beach even if he had to plant one himself. Then he'd use a baseball bat–no bat?–then a fat limb from the tree would do just fine. God, it'd feel good whacking those cocksuckers. Wouldn't take long before they'd be begging him to let the kid put a bullet in their slimy skulls to put them out of their misery.

"No one's ever hit Dominic Carpucci and gotten away with it," he muttered.

Sal must have heard him because he said, "What'd you say?"

Dominic answered angrily, "I didn't say nothin'. Just keep driving. How close do you think we are?"

"Fifteen minutes maybe, Boss."

That word "boss" again. That's a fucking laugh, Dominic thought. Somehow through the years he'd stopped enjoying being called boss and started dreading it. Especially today. Today all the word "boss" did for Dominic was remind him that his stuff was running around loose somewhere with some goddamn punks. And because he was the boss, and it was his stuff, he couldn't just walk away. If he wasn't the boss–the big shot–he could just tell some other jamoke, "Go screw yourself. Get your own fuckin' stuff." But he couldn't do that when it was his stuff, his trip. He was stuck. So much for the fun of being a boss.

He was supposed to be getting ready to head down to Florida, not sitting here in this damn car chasing down some sleazeball who thought he was better, smarter, tougher than Dominic Carpucci. Time to let someone else be the boss while he hit the beach like Filthy Phil, laying in the sun with the broads and the booze and not a care in the world. Not to mention the few million bucks he had stuffed in safe deposit boxes.

Dominic scowled. All the dough he'd made through the years should add up to more than a few million. Probably ten or twenty million easy. Except for the fact that what he did wasn't a secret to law enforcement anymore. And that'd meant extra expenses–big extra expenses–which made what he'd be retiring on smaller than what it should've been. But it'd have to do; he'd had enough. And to Dominic right now it felt like what he had stashed away would do just fine, thank you.

Unless he didn't get the load back, that lovely score that could make all his retirement dreams come true. Not only would losing that load throw a monkey wrench into his retirement plans, he'd have to come up with the dough to pay the Colombians for the load in the first place, seeing most of it was on the arm. Because the

Colombians, they didn't want to hear any sob story about a supposedly ripped off load. No way. They'd want their money and Dominic would have to pay them whether he got the product back or not.

And that was real bad because it meant no retirement. Worse, it'd mean starting all over from square one, trying to get ahead again and put together a big enough stash to get the hell out of the business. It meant more scams, more hustling, more risks. Prison, maybe. Even death.

Sounded real bad to Dominic now. A lot worse than it had twenty-five years ago. He'd really be pushing the odds this time. And the odds were a lot less favorable now than they'd been back in the day. But even worse than the things he faced out there if he had to start all over again, was the way he felt inside–his heart just wasn't in it anymore. He didn't have the desire to do it all over again. He wasn't young enough or hungry enough anymore. And because he didn't have the drive, things would never work out. It'd only end up one way–bad.

On the other hand, if he could just get his product back, he'd be out of this shit and on his way to Florida. Just like Phil Garrola. No troubles, no worries. It'd be real nice–no, more than nice–it'd be a lifesaver. That's why he wasn't going to blow it, not after getting this close. He was going to get that product back and make his retirement a reality. He was sure of it.

He'd wondered off and on how he'd feel after retiring.

Would he miss the action? Calling the shots? Probably not. If things worked out the way he planned–at least the way he'd planned before these slimeball thieves got into the act–he'd have the best of both worlds. Not out front with the headaches and danger, but behind the scenes. Bigger than a boss, still calling the shots with his own man in there and tribute sailing down south to him every month, just like it did to Filthy Phil. Wouldn't that be the balls.

And who'd be sending him those envelopes? Dominic smiled as he sat in the back seat of the Lincoln and pictured Jorge Rivera. A spic boss. Ha, the boys'd really love that. Since he and his late wife Esther hadn't had any children, there was no son to take over the family business. So fuck them all.

The kid would do just fine, Dominic was betting on it. Jorge had the look in his eye. He was hungry. He wanted to be a boss–the man.   And Dominic was determined to make sure the kid got what he wanted. The kid was loyal and could be trusted, which was more than he could say for the young Italians Dominic had working for him. Those Guidos thought the world owed them a living. If the feds ever put any pressure on them to give up Dominic? They'd talk so much the cops would have to slap them to shut them up. No balls.

Jorge was different. The kid had a pair and he was stand up. Besides, he'd be so grateful to Dominic for giving him the chance to move up, that he'd never miss sending one of those beautiful fat envelopes south every month to keep Dominic living in the style he'd be accustomed to by then.

Dominic chuckled–a spic boss!   Christ, that'd be something. Course he knew the kid'd have to get some fresh blood. Some of the goombahs would never work for a spic. Stupid shits would rather starve first and probably would. But recruiting new men would be no problem for the kid.   There were a million wetbacks looking for a hustle and for somebody to tell them what to do. The kid'd have his pick of the best. Didn't bother Dominic at all, the thought of handing everything he'd built up over the years to Jorge and his people. Hadn't Luciano done the same thing seventy-odd years ago when he'd let Lansky and the Jews in on the action? Lucky had played it smart back then, and he, Dominic Carpucci, was going to play it smart now.

All he had to do was collect on this scam and maybe a couple of repeats, get his envelope every month, and Jorge's group could have the rest. Good luck to them.

The car screeched to a stop. Dominic sat up straight, frustrated by the sudden holdup. "What's the matter, Sal?"

"Friggin' bridge is up, Boss. They're lettin' some boats through."

Dominic squinted through the front window. Sure enough the Hampton Bridge was up and open. "Think it'll it be long?"

"Nah. I see the boats goin' under. Ain't they pretty."

Dominic shifted uncomfortably in his seat. Through his window he could see the Seabrook Nuclear Power Plant. With the luck he'd had lately, odds were that place could blow any second. He turned back just in time to see the bridge finish its descent and click back into traffic position. He gave Sal a couple of taps on the shoulder. "Come on, come on. Let's get outta here."

As the Lincoln started to move forward with the other cars, Dominic glanced once again at the domed nuclear plant and tried to get his mind back on something he hoped he might have some control over.

Like getting his damn product back.

Chapter 15

THE DRIVE FROM Dan's cottage to Exeter Hospital took only about fifteen minutes. It had been quite a while since he'd been to the hospital. The last time he hadn't been driving and he hadn't been a visitor. Not a good trip. He didn't expect this one to be much better.

He pulled his car into the parking garage and walked the short distance to the Alumnae Plaza entrance. He walked up the concrete steps to the impressive glass-and-brick-covered front, shoved through the glass turnstile door, and found himself at a receptionist's desk in the lobby.

The black man behind the desk gave Dan directions to the Intensive Care Unit. Dan followed them. He found himself in front of a set of locked double doors. A sign instructed visitors to press a button on the wall. He did. Within seconds the doors swung outward, allowing him to enter.

Dan approached a young nurse seated behind a command desk. She was dressed in blue scrubs and a white coat with blue flowers sprinkled across it. "May I help you?"

"I'm here to see my brother, Michael Kelly," Dan answered. He suddenly recalled the feeling he'd had when he was under twenty-one and trying to buy beer.

"Your name?"

"Dan Kelly."

The young nurse studied a clipboard on the desk in front of her. For a long moment Dan had a feeling she was going to question him further. Instead, she turned her swivel chair and pointed in the direction of a group of rooms to her left. "You want 205."

"Thanks." Dan walked quickly to the room marked 205. The door was ajar. He pushed it open and stepped inside. In front of him sat a bed concealed by a wraparound beige curtain.

Dan took a deep breath, almost gagging on the strong sickroom smell. "Shamrock? It's me, Dan."

Silence.

Dan pinched the curtain and slid it slowly around until the bed was fully exposed. He dropped the curtain in shock and took a step back. "Jesus Christ, Shamrock. What've they done to you?"

The Irishman was completely unrecognizable, looking more like the Invisible Man than a real man. His head was fully swathed in bandages. Only his closed eyes, nose, and mouth were exposed. A breathing tube draped from his mouth. Dan stared at the other end, realizing the ventilation machine there was responsible for the faint sighs he was hearing. IV lines ran from Shamrock's arms to bags hanging from metal poles. A heart monitor beeped ominously. The rest of his body was covered by sheets.

Dan swallowed hard. This was worse than he expected. Much worse. "Shamrock?" Dan said softly. "Shamrock?"

He reached out and touched the Irishman's arm. Cold. Icy cold.

He'd been told the Irishman was in bad shape, but for some reason he hadn't thought it would be this bad. He'd figured he'd walk in and find Shamrock sitting up in bed, regaling nurses with his endless repertoire of Irish jokes as they prepared to move him to a regular ward. But the Shamrock laying in front of him couldn't tell a joke if his life depended on it.

The heart monitor's beep became frantic, tiny eruptions of sound that set Dan's nerves jangling. He stared at the erratic peaks on the monitor screen and held his breath until the beeps finally resumed their regular rhythm. Then he turned his attention back to the bed.

"I know it's kind of late, Shamrock, but I'm still going to keep that promise I made. As best I can, anyway. If we'd just had one more day, you'd have told me where you put it. Now I don't have a clue where to look. And without it . . . Jesus, things are going to be hard. If we'd just had that one more day . . . Christ, maybe you'd still be telling jokes back at the High Tide."

He'd been thinking about buttonholing Shamrock's doctor and asking about Shamrock's prognosis. But staring down at the little Irishman all bandaged up like a mummy, with the tubes and the monitor and the throat thingamajig, made Dan reconsider. Probably better not knowing than dreading the future.

Then again, maybe Shamrock truly had the "Luck o' the Irish." Time would tell soon enough.

Meanwhile, he'd do his best to keep the promise he'd made to his Irish friend. After all, his word was about all he had left.

Chapter 16

WHEN BUZZ'D FOUND the cottage on Eaton Avenue empty, the coke gone, he'd almost broken down and cried. There was a small chance some local B&E kids had just stumbled on a jackpot, and if that were the case, he was screwed. The kids would start snorting and selling to anyone on the beach who'd buy, including the cops. Then the cops would grab the load and that would be the end of that.

But the more likely scenario, and the one that gave him some hope, was that somehow that bastard Carpucci had gotten wind of where the coke was and had stolen it back. Even if that thinking was wrong, it was all Buzz had to go on. Besides, if Carpucci didn't have the coke, he'd be looking hard for it. And if the drug lord had any luck . . . well, Buzz and Skinny were going to be there to take the coke back. No way was Buzz going to let anyone–Carpucci included–steal that coke and get away with it.

He and Skinny had gone back to Carpucci's estate in Lynnfield and kept the place under surveillance. And they weren't there long before Carpucci came out and hopped in the back of a big black Lincoln with some goon driving. Buzz had followed the Lincoln right onto Route 95 heading north. He'd kept a few cars between himself and the Lincoln all the way, not stopping until they got jammed up when the Hampton Bridge opened to let some boats pass beneath.

Finally the bridge had lowered and Buzz could see the Lincoln up ahead moving across the bridge. He stepped on the accelerator, following a couple of cars behind. One question kept running round and round in his head–did Carpucci already have the coke or not?

"I don't think he'd be coming up here if he already had the stuff," he said. "He probably has a line on it, though."

"I don't know," Skinny said in between snaps of his gum. "Maybe he just likes the beach."

Buzz had to look over at him for a second to make sure he wasn't joking. Skinny looked back, snapped his gum, and shrugged.

"He may like beaches, but not this one, shit-for-brains. Remember, this is where he lost his load."

Traffic crawled across the bridge. Buzz concentrated on keeping his eyes on the vehicle in front of them and tried to ignore Skinny's popping gum.

"Why do you have a little car like this, Buzz?" Skinny whined. "We coulda lost 'em on the highway in this thing."

Buzz clenched his jaw, grinding his teeth.

"You narcs used to always have big Fords. What happened to them days anyhow? If you gotta have something small, it oughta be a Vette or a Porsche you seized. Right? So why do you have this little crate?"

"Because this is what they fucking gave me," Buzz answered, thinking how he'd love to stick his thumb in Skinny's eye, see just how high that aggravating voice of his could really go. "We can't ride around in navy blue Fords with blackwalls all the time, you little nimrod. The bad guys'd figure it was us and then we wouldn't be undercover anymore, would we?"

Nice story, but the real reason Buzz got issued this tin can was because the higher ups were hoping he'd get sick of it all and hand in his resignation. Just more of the shit end of the stick the suits in the agency had been giving him for a long time now. And all because of a few missing crummy dope dollars, which they couldn't prove he'd ended up with anyway. What kind of a crazy country was it anyhow when scuzzball dope dealers like Carpucci got rich and Drug War soldiers like himself got screwed?

Skinny turned to look at Buzz, his pockmarked face looking like he'd bit into a lemon. "Yeah, but a Jap car? They ain't fast. They ain't comfortable neither." His spaghetti-thin body bounced around as if he were sitting on a hot plate.

"Relax. We got more important things to worry about than your sore little ass." Judging by the frightened look that came over Skinny's face, and the way he stopped bouncing and kind of oozed closer to his door, Buzz's voice affected Skinny just as much as the little idiot's voice affected him, only Buzz's voice generated fear instead of disgust. Good. Quiet the skinny little shit right down.

The Lincoln banged a left when it finally got across the bridge, disappearing down a sloped driveway behind a one-story white building. The sign on the building read, "Renaldo's Restaurant," and the stench of garlic filled the little car as Buzz followed. He coasted past the building a few feet, then pulled the car over to the shoulder. The gravel road marched on ahead, leading down to the harbor and the docks. The Lincoln was down there, pulled up in a parking lot beside another car. Carpucci had the back window down and appeared to be talking to the driver of the other car.

"Who . . . uh . . . who do you think that guy is?" Skinny asked.

"That's the spic's car," Buzz answered. Then he added, "I'll tell you one thing, they either got the coke or they know who does. They aren't all here to go deep sea fishing. That's for sure."

Skinny clammed up for another minute. "What'll we do when we find out where it is?" he finally asked, his voice cracking.

Kill them all. Not a thought he could voice to Skinny without the little guy having a heart attack. "We'll handle it the usual way," Buzz said. Which meant they'd go in masked and with guns drawn, grab the goods, and leave the dealers bound and gagged, not knowing who the hell stole their stuff.

That was the usual way. But since the stash was in Carpucci's hands again, the rip-off would have to go down the same way it did when they took the boat in the harbor, though Skinny didn't need to know that. Not yet. With a man like Dominic Carpucci there was no other choice. If he was there when they took it, he'd have to die. If they left him alive, the bastard would somehow get a line on who they were, and then he'd chase Buzz forever. The man would never let it go. Buzz wouldn't be safe in Africa let alone in Jamaica. Not with a man like Carpucci after him.

No, they'd have to go all the way–the practical way. Carpucci, and whoever else was with him when they scooped the coke, would have to go. No loose ends on this one. Especially if Buzz ever wanted to relax with all that money, and more than anything, that's what he wanted to do. But he couldn't tell Skinny any of this. Christ, Skinny had almost passed out when he'd seen Buzz do those two dickheads on the boat.

Which reminded Buzz of another problem he had: Skinny. And what to do with him when this was all over. Buzz tried to shove that thought right out of his mind because, for some crazy reason he didn't understand, every time he thought about sending the little guy to a better place, it made him feel kind of bad.

Skinny started bouncing in his seat again. "I hope we find out where it is quick," he said in that shrill voice that went through Buzz like fingernails on a blackboard. "My ass hurts again." Skinny let that last word stretch way out, his voice getting even shriller.

"Shut up," Buzz said. "Look."

The spic got out of the Lexus and Carpucci's driver hopped out too. Both men walked across the parking lot to a small run-down cottage that looked like it belonged in Appalachia. They went up on the porch, opened a screen door, and stepped inside out of sight.

This could be it. Buzz could tell by the acid churning in his stomach. Talk about a gut feeling. It seemed like hours, but was only a few minutes before the two men reappeared, pushing a third man in front of them. They forced him down the cottage steps and across the parking lot. Then they shoved him in the backseat of the Lincoln with Carpucci. The Lincoln's driver got back in behind the wheel and the spic jumped in the Lexus. Both cars pulled out of the lot with the Lexus leading.

"Get down," Buzz ordered. "They're coming right by us." He grabbed Skinny's shoulder, pushed him down hard, and ducked down himself just as the Lexus and Lincoln zipped right past.

Buzz sat up and backed his car all the way to the main

road, catching a strong whiff of garlic again. He could see the two black cars over near the state park, heading for the bridge. He brought his car around and followed after them.

Skinny slowly sat up in his seat, moving his face, neck, and shoulders like he was doing Isometrics. "I think you pulled a muscle in my neck, Buzz," he said in a whining tone.

"I'll pull more than a fucking muscle in your neck if you don't shut up," Buzz said. He squeezed and pushed the steering wheel with his left hand almost hard enough to crack it, and with his right he rubbed his face from forehead to chin. No, he reminded himself, he couldn't do it now. No matter how crazy Skinny was making him, Buzz needed him. He couldn't even look at the man for fear he might lose it. Instead, Buzz let a maniacal grin cross his face and a little rhyme run through his head over and over: *Skinny Minny with the meatball eyes, punch him in the belly and you get french fries.* And that helped–a little.

Chapter 17

"YOU DIDN'T REALLY THINK you were gonna just waltz away with all that stuff, did ya?" Dominic Carpucci asked. In front of him, seated in a straight-back chair in the middle of Dominic's basement, was Tommy McGee, brother of Bill McGee, the murdered boat captain. They'd picked him up in Hampton Beach and let him do a bit of thinking on the way to Lynnfield. Dominic had found that a little thinking time often did a better job of loosening a man's tongue than starting in on him with both fists.

McGee's arms were handcuffed behind the chair so the only way he could run was if he took the chair with him. Jorge and Sal stood on either side of Dominic.

Dominic was proud of his basement and took a moment to look around, giving the guy in the chair a little more "thinking" time.

As far as basements went Dominic's was pretty nice.

Of course, the guy in the chair could have cared less about the decor, but the room was finished and divided into two areas. The entertainment section had a big-screen TV, a well-stocked bar with captain's stools scattered along its length, and a wall lined with shelves crammed with books of all types, fiction and non-fiction alike. Facing the huge TV, with their backs to the bookshelves, were two expensive brown leather chairs and a matching sofa.

The other half of the basement was equipped for a woodworking hobbyist. Dominic had played around with woodworking for a while after Esther, his wife, had died. He'd been desperate then for anything to keep him busy, to help him forget. The hobby had worked, but not for long. Finally he'd lost interest in all the sanding and sawing and hammering, and had thrown himself right back into the one thing that kept his mind off everything else–the good old cocaine business.

Cocaine was a lot more profitable than making little end tables and the work definitely kept him busy. He hadn't used the woodworking area for so long that all the hammers, saws, and screwdrivers hanging from the wall above the workbench were covered with a thin layer of dust. The cleaning lady was never allowed to tend to this level of the house. This was Dominic's private refuge, a place where he could get away to read his books or watch TV and escape from the craziness of his business if only for an evening. Besides, having a little dust around was a small price to pay for the assurance that everything–book, clicker, corkscrew–would be right where he'd last left it.

It was in this woodworking area that Captain Bill McGee's brother was seated. He was fortyish–thin hair, plain features, dressed in restaurant whites. And scared. Real scared. His blood-shot eyes looked from man to man.

"So, you don't wanna talk," Dominic said. He whipped the back of his right hand hard across McGee's mouth. McGee's head snapped back as if released from a spring and blood spurted from an ugly ring gash just above his chin.

"Maybe ya like that instead?" Dominic savored the sting in his hand. Sal, big and dumb looking, let out a laugh. Dominic gave him a look that usually shut up anyone he used it on, even big guys like Sal. It worked again–Sal shut right up.

Dominic turned his attention back to McGee, staring at the blood running down onto the man's white top. What was the best way to play this guy? How the fuck did he think?

He'd asked himself similar questions in the past, but never with so much at stake as today. Back in the day, it'd been a lot easier. Most of the time he'd usually known the man he was grilling–either it'd been a business associate of his who hadn't been associating in a way Dominic'd liked, one of his own boys who'd been caught holding out a little more than was reasonable, or some competition that'd been getting a bit too competitive.

Whatever the reason, he'd been familiar with the scumbags, so he'd known their weak points beforehand. That was the key to getting information–you had to figure out what your opponent's weak point was. Everyone had their weaknesses–muscle, bribery, threats on their family. All men held things in different value and would react differently to each tactic. He just had to figure out who was who.

Some guys all you had to do was say "boo" and they'd give up their mother. Other guys, a few promises (later broken, of course) would get their mouths moving. With some, a threat against their family was the way to go. Still others had to be beaten and broken–to one degree or another. At least until they had enough marks on their bodies to convince themselves that they'd stood up as well as anyone could be expected to. Although Dominic had heard of men who'd taken secrets to their graves, he'd never had one seated in front of him. All the ones he'd worked on in the past had told him what he'd wanted to know or agreed to what he'd demanded. Some had just required a little more time and effort.

But this time it was different. The man seated in front of him was an unknown. He'd have to go through his options quick. Dominic couldn't afford to have his product floating around much longer. Coke tended to disappear real fast when it was out there loose like his was.

Might as well start with the fatherly approach.

"Look, McGee. It was your brother brought the load in. You gotta know something. Besides, restaurant people hear everything. I know anyone farts the wrong way on Hampton Beach you know it, so I bet you got a pretty good idea who pulled that rip-off, don't you? Don't you want to get back at whoever killed your brother? You tell me who it was. I'll send someone to pick 'em up. If you told me straight, then no hard feelings. You'll be free to go. We'll even give you a ride back to the beach. How does that sound?"

Tommy McGee looked like he didn't have a clue what Dominic was saying. Stupid bastard. He was either playing games or he really didn't know. Maybe he didn't understand that he was playing in the big leagues, but he was about to learn fast. Real fast. Dominic didn't have the time to play footsie with this guy. He had to find out who had his product and now.

"Where's he work, Jorge?"

"The Crooked Shillelagh. Irish place around the corner from his dump."

"So he lives and works right at the harbor. Convenient. And his brother brought in my load. Too coincidental. If he don't know something, I'll eat sand."

Dominic looked over at big Sal. "Bring him over here."

Sal picked up McGee, chair and all, and followed Dominic across the large room to the workbench. Dominic gave a quick nod and Sal set McGee down. Jorge moved into position behind and a bit to the left of McGee. Dominic reached over and flicked on the switch of a drill press mounted on the workbench. The drill bit whirred and McGee's eyes popped open like a shutter on a camera.

Now that was more like it.

Dominic didn't have to say anything to anyone-everyone knew their roles. McGee snapped back in his chair as if he were trying to jettison himself across the room.

Jorge bent over and unlocked McGee's handcuffs. He grabbed McGee's left arm and held it tight while Sal yanked the man's right arm straight out. McGee struggled, but he still hadn't said a word. Sal stretched the man's hand, palm down, on the drill press pad.

One look at the punk's face told Dominic this wasn't going to take long. He let out a chuckle and grabbed the wheel that brought the drill bit down. He turned the wheel slowly, dropping the bit closer and closer to the back of McGee's hand.

McGee's eyes bulged and his body heaved as he struggled to break his hand loose. Sal held tight, keeping the palm pressed to the pad. When the bit was only a couple of inches away from the pounding pulse on the back of his hand McGee finally cracked.

"All right. All right. I'll tell you what you want to know." His voice shook so much Dominic could hardly understand him. But the game wasn't over. Not yet. Dominic played the game his own way, and it wasn't the way Tommy McGee probably hoped.

The bit dropped lower. "Sweet mother of God, please stop," McGee shouted. He was frantic now. "I'll tell you everything I know. Sure, I knew my brother was up to somethin' but I didn't know what. Me and my buddy, we just happened to be down in the state park drinking that night. We saw someone hiding it. We didn't know what it was. Not till the next day when we heard about my brother and then figured it out. We went in that night and got it. Figured my brother was owed something. But we didn't know there'd be that much. We don't know what the hell to do with it anyhow. You can have it all." His gaze darted from man to man, eyes pleading.

Dominic was really liking this. Time to teach this asshole a lesson he'd never forget–nobody steals from Dominic Carpucci. The spinning bit was almost touching McGee's hand.

McGee thrashed wildly but he couldn't move his hand an inch. "Please, I'll tell you anything. Please don't."

The sound of the spinning drill brought back memories that suddenly had Dominic feeling nostalgic. "Jeez, you know something, Sal? This kinda reminds me of shop class." He laughed like a maniac and drove the drill bit home.

Dominic felt the skin on McGee's hand give beneath the boring bit. Smoke rose from the tearing flesh as the bit burrowed a large jagged hole through the hand. McGee's screams hurt Dominic's ears and the smell stunk up his nostrils.

It felt good to pay someone back for what they stole, even if the guy wasn't one of the original thieves. He was from Hampton Beach. Close enough.

It only took seconds for the drill bit to get through McGee's hand, but reversing the wheel and getting the bit out took a little longer. The bit refused to reverse itself properly and stuck fast. It took a few hard, ragged tugs to tear the bit loose from the hand. McGee passed out on the second try. Probably a good thing–Dominic wasn't inclined to be gentle.

The metal was coated with blood when he finally worked the bit free. A small strip of flesh dangled from the tip.

"Gee, that was something, Boss," Sal said with admiration.

Good. Another story added to his reputation. Stories like this were good for business. They helped keep other punks–punks who might think Dominic was getting too soft or too old–in line.

"Sal, toss some water on him," Dominic ordered. "Find out where my product is. Jorge, you go get it. We'll keep him here until we hear from you."

"It's late."

"I give a shit? Get up there in the morning then."

It was going to be a long night for all of them.

Chapter 18

DANGEROUS THINGS WERE happening on the beach and somehow he, Dan Marlowe, lowly bartender and ex-coke addict, was right in the middle of it all. During the last couple of days, he'd been accosted by cops, had a friend beaten to a pulp, and had almost been kidnapped by goons.

It was around eleven at night and Dan Marlowe was sitting in his favorite chair in his cottage down in the Island section of the beach. He'd given up on the crime novel he'd just set down. Now he was just sipping Heineken, trying not to think about what might have happened if Conover hadn't shown up when he did. He owed the cop a favor. Big time.

Yeah, his life was definitely a mess. No wonder his wife wouldn't let the kids come visit him. She'd heard about Shamrock, knew something bad was going on, didn't trust Dan not to be in the middle of it all. This time Dan had to admit she was probably right. It wasn't a good idea to have his children around. Not until he got this mess straightened out, whatever the hell it was.

That gave him an incentive, a big incentive, to get this trouble over with quick, one way or another. If he didn't get to see his kids, at least every so often, even the sea air and Heineken wouldn't be enough to keep him from eventually ending up like the Bird Man–down on the beach with pigeons roosting on his squash.

Which was why he was nursing this beer and trying to figure it all out. It had taken him a bit, but Dan had finally placed the voice of the man who'd tried to snatch him on the beach. Tony Peralta. A bragging blowhard who'd held court at the High Tide regularly through the years.

Somehow this whole mess was tied together: murders and a cocaine rip-off; Peralta, a big seacoast coke dealer, trying to snatch him; Shamrock being turned into a snowman because he'd asked some stupid questions about cocaine around the beach; and two state cops named Bartolo and Conover after the cocaine; and who knows what or who else.

Dan killed the bottle of Heineken he was working on. No use sitting here alone, drinking and thinking about what might happen. Christ, if he dwelled on it too much, he'd be down at a little hovel he knew on Ashworth Avenue and before you could say, "Two grams, please," his wife would be proven right again. Yeah, he didn't want to end up there. After all, you never knew which time would be the last time.

He turned off the lights, locked the front door, and went into the bedroom. Outside the surf pounded loud against the shore, probably high tide, and he was glad of that. Maybe the sound would help lull him to sleep. It had worked before. Dan stripped off his pants, crawled into bed, listened to the surf through the open window.

Just as he was about to drop off, Dan suddenly heard a noise he didn't like–the screen out in the main room being raised. There was more than one window in that room, but unless someone had a ladder, they could only come through the front porch window.

Dan rolled over to the edge of the bed and reached under it. With shaking hands he slowly pulled out Betsy, his Overland double-barreled shotgun. Betsy was a replica of the stubby old-fashioned shotguns they used to use in the Old West, with the hammers on the outside. The type of shotgun that could do a lot of damage at close range. He could hear whispering from the direction of the other room, and to his horror, the sound of scraping as someone climbed through the window.

His heart thumped hard against his ribs. This was it. The real deal.

He quietly slid open the drawer on the little end table beside his bed. Inside he had a box of 00 buckshot and a box of birdshot shells. He started to reach for the 00, then changed his mind and grabbed the birdshot. Sure he was scared, but no use hurting an innocent, or semi-innocent, person. Could be just a pair of kids coming in to steal the TV, for Chrissake. It was the beach, after all. He fumbled two birdshot shells into the shotgun and quietly closed the breach.

Someone else was coming through the window now, trying to be quiet, but still making enough noise he could tell when they were both inside.

"Go ahead. There." The whisper sent a shiver up Dan's spine.

Enough was enough. "Get back out through that window the way you came in. I've got a shotgun," Dan said in what he hoped was a commanding voice. He was still prone on the bed, right next to the open bedroom door. If he peeked around the corner, he'd probably be eyeball to eyeball with whoever was out there.

"Sure ya do, Marlowe," a deep voice said from the other room.

Definitely not kids.

No time to swap out the birdshot for the 00; he'd have to make do with the birdshot.

"Maybe you got a shotgun and maybe you don't, but we got this," the voice added.

Dan jumped as a shot echoed through the cottage. They were shooting at him! The noise had barely subsided when he heard another noise even more ominous–footsteps moving slowly toward his bedroom.

They were close, so close he thought he could actually

hear them breathing. Or was that him?

Dan slid off the bed and scooted over to the door. He poked the barrel of the shotgun through the doorway, cocked just one hammer, and pulled the trigger. The twelve gauge roared, kicking Dan's arm back hard against the door. His ears rang, and for a second, he thought he'd completely lost his hearing.

Then he heard shouts from the other room. The front door banged open and footsteps thudded out onto the porch. Dan ran back to the nightstand, grabbed a fistful of birdshot shells and jammed them in his t-shirt pocket. This damn thing had to end one way or another and the sooner the better. He raced from the bedroom, scowled at his blown-out TV, and leapt out the open front door.

The moon shone high overhead, bathing the neighborhood with its bleached light. Ahead Dan could see two men hightailing it between cottages. He sprang down the steps onto the walkway and took aim. Before his finger closed around the trigger, he lowered the shotgun. Stray pellets could go through somebody's window, and one thing Dan didn't want was collateral damage.

But he had to do something. They were getting away.

"Stop or I'll shoot," Dan yelled. How the hell did he end up standing around in his underwear sounding like a bad cop show?

Didn't really matter. The two guys dodging between cottages must've been hard of hearing. Either that or they didn't believe Dan would actually hit anything. He pointed the shotgun skyward, cocked the other hammer, and let off a blast that reverberated through the entire neighborhood.

Satisfied, Dan lowered the shotgun, expecting to see the two men turn back towards him, hands raised.

Instead the fools ran faster.

Dan bolted after them. They were across the next street now, squeezing between parked cars in a darkened driveway, moving fast. Dan broke the barrel open as he ran, fumbled two more shells home, and snapped the breach shut. It felt good holding Betsy in his hands. Solid. Bold.

Dan raced between the cottages, not caring about the doors and windows slamming open.   Give people something to talk about in the morning–a wild-eyed man wearing a t-shirt and underpants waving a shotgun and chasing two other men.

Adrenalin tightened in Dan's stomach as he burst onto the open street. He could see the two men clearly in the moonlight–one tall, one short–and they were headed straight towards the state park. They'd hopped a short railroad tie fence on the far side of the street that led to nothing but a 100-yard run, out in the open with no protection except foot-high dune grass.

He almost floated over the little fence. The men were right in front of him with no cover. They'd made it so easy, Dan almost felt bad for them. Almost. He jogged a few more steps, raised the shotgun to his shoulder. He lined up the two figures silhouetted in the moonlight, the tall guy out in front. He almost yelled another warning, but what the hell. They probably wouldn't have stopped anyway. Besides, he was using birdshot, and they wouldn't be hurt seriously anyhow.

He aimed low, firing first one and then the other barrel within seconds of each other. The shorter guy jerked forward real fast twice, like a big hand had smacked his bottom a couple of times. Kind of funny, really. Almost like one of those cartoons. The guy was even yelping like a coyote.

Dan ran forward again, breaking the breach, dumping the old shells, and trying to slam in new ones. He bobbled the shells and that was lucky for the two ahead of him. By the time he got the shotgun loaded, they'd hopped into a red Jag parked beside the bathhouse. The engine turned and the car fishtailed down the gravel drive towards Ocean Boulevard.

Dan raised the shotgun to his shoulder again. He didn't have any hope of stopping them, not at this distance, especially with birdshot. But standing there in the moonlight with the dunes beside him and the salt air in his nostrils, Dan tingled with an exhilaration he hadn't felt in a long, long time. Damn it made him feel good. Almost forgot he was in his underpants.

Everything in his life had felt so out of his control for so long . . . He tightened his finger on the trigger, let both barrels go in quick succession. And when he heard the pellets ping off the Jag's body, let loose a howl that would've done a wolf pack proud.

Chapter 19

TONY PERALTA LAY NAKED on a sofa in the middle of his sunken living room. He was back in his house on Boar's Head, on his elbows with his ass stuck up in the air. Rhonda–a twenty-something hard-bodied blonde in a red thong bathing suit–leaned over him, tweezers in hand.

"Toneeey," she said shrilly. "Keep still or I can't get them all out." She had a sewing needle in one hand and the tweezers in the other. A small bowl on the table beside her already held a half-dozen tiny pellets she'd removed from Tony's fleshy rump. Occasionally she stopped to dip the needle or tweezers into a bottle of rubbing alcohol. She'd then touch the wet end of the instrument to a small pile of cocaine that was also on the table. When she raised the needle or tweezers there'd be a bit of the glistening white powder stuck on the end.

"I never thought I'd live to see you like this, Boss,"

Wayne said. The big dolt was sitting in an easy chair across the room, long legs hanging over one of the chair's arms, smoking a cigarette and drinking a beer. His gaze shifted back and forth from Tony's ass to Rhonda's ass. When he looked at Rhonda, his expression became serious, lustful. When he looked back at Tony's injured hiney, a big smile spread across his face. "Real embarrassing, ain't it." He chuckled, then swallowed hard when Tony glared at him.

"There's nothing funny about this," Tony said.   "I could've been killed. If you'd done your job right when we were in his cottage, I wouldn't be lying here now getting humiliated like I am."

Wayne dropped his legs and sat up straight, an indignant look on his face. "The man had a shotgun."

"Excuses. Fucking excuses. Every time I'm with you something screwy happens. You got me shot at on the beach, almost got me mixed up in a murder, and finally managed to actually get me shot. What'll you do next to help me? Throw me off a cliff?" Tony grit his teeth and grabbed the fabric of the sofa with both hands as Rhonda probed for another pellet. "Motherfucker. How many more?"

"You big baby," she said in a singsong voice. "I'm almost done."

"Not even Schwarzenegger'd go up against a shotgun," Wayne said, folding his big arms across his puffed-out chest. "Everybody knows that."

How the hell had he ended up in a situation like this–
with a ditsy broad yanking birdshot out of his tender ass
and an overgrown juvenile delinquent sitting over there
arguing with him?

"Apparently I don't know anything anymore," Tony
said. Then he added sarcastically, "Maybe my brains are
on the fritz or something. That's the only thing that could
explain what I'm doing in a fix like this. Yeah, that's
probably it. Maybe I got some exotic brain fever. Burned
them all up. Baby, feel my forehead."

"Don't worry, hon. Your brains'll grow back," Rhonda
said. She dipped the needle in the pile of coke, and as
she pulled the needle out, she held it high, studying the
white powder with a gleam in her eyes.

Shit, she was as serious as Wayne. Tony rolled his eyes.
"Yeah, maybe. But that fucking Dan Marlowe won't be so
lucky. Nobody does this to me and gets away with it.
When I get my hands on him I'll shove that shotgun of
his up his ass and pull the trigger."

Wayne let out a wicked chuckle. "That'd sure take
care of him."

"You bet your ass it will," Tony said. He pictured
Marlowe standing in the sand shooting at them as they
drove away, Tony leaning hard on his side trying not to
bleed on the Jag's upholstery. "And if he got one goddamn
scratch on my Jag from that shotgun, I'll pull the trigger
twice. Bastard."

"He ain't got no respect," Wayne said.

"Give me some of that blow, Ronnie," Tony said. "No sense wasting it all on my handsome butt." Rhonda dipped a small silver spoon into the coke and reached around to hold it under Tony's right nostril. He supported himself on one elbow and brought his left index finger up to block his left nostril. With a loud snort, he inhaled the blow up his pipe. Rhonda got another spoonful and they repeated the process for the other nostril.

And suddenly Tony's ass didn't bother him so much anymore. He was getting such a good sensation in his cock that it overshadowed the pain on his opposite side. "Yeah, I'll get him real fucking good," he said, sounding– and feeling–oh, so confident.

"Sure ya will," Wayne said. He nodded his big head, never taking his gaze off Rhonda's scrumptious body. "We'll both get him."

"There. I'm done, honey," Rhonda said, plastering the last of two large bandages on Tony's buttocks. "You should feel fine now."

Oh, he felt fine, that was for sure. But it didn't have anything to do with Rhonda's nursing. Gingerly, Tony turned on his side on the large sofa, propping himself up with his left elbow. "Two more, Ron," he said. And Rhonda's tan arm with the gold bracelets brought the coke-filled spoon up to his nose twice more. And man, did his cock start to vibrate.

Tony looked over at Wayne, winked and said, "We'll see you later, Wayne. I'll be calling you, so don't go far from your phone."

"Yeah. Sure, Boss. See ya later." After a short hesitation, Wayne got up, crossed the room, and walked out the door.

Tony studied Rhonda as she sat on the edge of the couch beside him, her bare leg touching his. Beautiful, tanned face, made up so hotly, surrounded by that gorgeous blonde hair. Gold chains around her neck. Skimpy red thong bikini. Wheew! Rhonda and the coke were making his cock ache, and wicked thoughts were running amuck in his mind. "Oh, baby, do I fucking want you."

"But Tony, your buns hurt," she said in a sympathetic voice.

"Not that bad they don't." Tony rolled over on his back, shoving a fat end pillow under his ass as he moved. "You do all the work, baby. Blow my mind."

"All right," Rhonda said. She stood, stepped backwards halfway across the room, and shook her mane of blonde hair. Tony watched as she unfastened the top of her bathing suit and let it fall. Two gorgeous tan breasts spilled out. Then she unsnapped her tiny thong and tossed it aside. Tony could see that she'd been sunbathing nude again, and that all she was wearing now were gold chains around her neck, wrists, and ankle. Tony's cock really started to hum as Rhonda leaned over and inhaled a spoon of coke up each of her cute little nostrils. Her nipples instantly turned hard as rocks and she let out a small moan. She looked at Tony through half-closed eyes. "Baby, I am going to blow your mind. Right now."

She walked slowly over to Tony. He tapped his fingers impatiently, anticipation building until he thought he would pop. He knew what was coming; he'd made it with her this way many times before. With one hand he pulled the small table with the coke on it closer to him, and with the other he reached up, grabbed Rhonda's arm and pulled her towards him. She fell right on top of him, all hot smells, tanned skin, gold chains, and hard body. And for the next couple of hours she did blow Tony's mind.

Chapter 20

JORGE HAD PLENTY of time to think on the drive back to
Hampton Beach. The drill press was a nice touch, he had to
give the old man credit for that, but Jorge would have
handled it differently. He'd thought about giving the old
man a suggestion or two, but the old man would have cut
him off. The way Jorge had it figured, bringing McGee
along would've made for a nice intimidating introduction,
what with the hole in his hand and all. But the old man
wouldn't have gone for it because he didn't think of it.

That's why Jorge was on his way back to Hampton
Beach–to get his hands on this Shamrock Kelly McGee
had fingered, find out where Kelly had stashed the stuff,
and bring back the coke. McGee'd sworn Kelly hadn't
told him where it was, just that he had a good place.

McGee had said that he and this Shamrock character,
a neighbor and drinking buddy, were down at the state

park on the evening of the harbor killings swigging beer.
They'd spotted a car driving up Eaton Avenue with its
lights out. The car went down the driveway of a cottage
that butted up to the state park. They'd sat there quietly,
sipping their beer, watching as two men skulked back
and forth lugging duffel bags between the car's trunk and
the cottage. McGee had said the only light they could
see in the cottage was an occasional beam from a
flashlight. Close to an hour passed, then the men drove
away with the car lights off again.

McGee and Kelly had their suspicions about what went
down, but it wasn't until the next day, after they heard
about the killings, that Tommy McGee threw the deal
his brother was involved in into the mix. He and Kelly
put two and two together and came up with coke-loaded
duffel bags. That night they got those bags out of that
Eaton Avenue cottage faster than the mystery men had
gotten them in.

Yeah, it did sound a little off the wall to Jorge. Yet,
he'd heard of people occasionally hitting a jackpot in some
weird way in this business. Hadn't it been just last year
some dealer up in Lawrence had a connection who died
after mixing an eight ball into beer and drinking it? The
dealer'd owed the connection almost $250,000. No one
ever came to collect. So maybe it was possible that these
two sad sacks just got lucky. It could happen. But it still
didn't reassure him any.

So what would he do if he came up empty-handed?

Maybe Kelly would give him a hard time or maybe he already got rid of the coke and wouldn't want to say to who. The old man would say to beat the shit out of Kelly if he was a problem. If that didn't work, do the same to his family one at a time, until the guy decided not to be a problem anymore. But Christ, that wasn't Jorge's style–slapping around somebody's family just on the strength of what might turn out to be a fairy tale. How could anyone respect someone who'd slap around a woman and kids?

That was one of the big differences between him and the old man–respect. The other difference was class. He had them, or would soon. The old man didn't, not anymore.

Respect and class, Jorge knew instinctively, were two things you had to have to be a boss. The old man'd had them at one time; otherwise, he'd never have gotten to the top. But somewhere along the line he'd lost them. Jorge had been pretty sure of that for a while now. The old man no longer had what it took to be a boss. The way the old fool had handled this crazy boat scam right from the beginning proved it. The old guy was incompetent. And that made Jorge real nervous. Nervous because he had plans and the old man losing it now and blowing everything would screw up those plans good.

Jorge had picked up on the old man's intentions to retire to Florida. The old man hadn't come right out and told Jorge his plans; he wasn't stupid after all. But he'd let little things slip, things he thought no one'd pick up on.   During Boston snow storms the old man would wonder out loud about what the temperature was in Miami.   More than once Jorge had caught him listening a little more intently than usual to the people coming back from vacation saying how nice and warm it was down there.   And what about those sales brochures from Florida boat dealers scattered about his place?   Not to mention the phone call Jorge'd answered once when the old man wasn't there.   Seemed some broker down in Lauderdale had heard Mr. Carpucci was looking for property.

Yes, it was pretty clear to Jorge that the old man was going to retire, just like that big tub Filthy Phil before him.   And that would've been okay with Jorge, except for one thing–where would that leave him?

And the answer to that was easy–nowhere.   The Italians in the old man's crew would never accept Jorge as boss, and the old man must've known that too.   A Puerto Rican?   Christ, they only put up with where he was in the organization now because the old man was making them all so much money with his coke thing that they didn't want to get on his shit list by bitching.   No, it wouldn't be him the old man would choose to fill his shoes, that was for sure.   Once the old man was gone, he'd be out in the cold.   The old man would designate one of the goombah punks as his successor, and Jorge couldn't think of one of them who had much love for him.   No, he'd be out, or at the bottom at best.

There was only one way to handle the problem–get rid of the old man and take over the crew. Anyone that didn't like his sudden advancement would have to go, quick like. He was the only one that knew the whole operation–the old man's connections and all his outs. He was the only one that could keep the money machine going and that might be enough to keep most of the Italians in line. And if not, then hell, he had enough Hispanic brothers up in Lowell and Lawrence who would give their mothers to move up in the coke trade. Those guys would think wiping out a few guineas was a cheap price to pay.

The key to his making a successful transition, besides eliminating the old man, was this large load of coke. The one they couldn't quite seem to get their hands on. With that he could go right to the customers, product in hand, and show them he could produce as a supplier. Cocaine, and the prospect of big money that could be made from it, had a way of cooling feelings of bigotry or revenge.

The old man had screwed up everything when he'd abandoned their old tried-and-true way of driving the product up from Florida. He'd gotten greedy and come up with this boat scheme to smuggle it into the country himself and look where that had gotten him. Chasing fools around New England, trying to get the coke back. Not Jorge's idea of a good deal. The old man was making a mess of the retrieval, too, and that's what frustrated Jorge the most.

He'd watched the old man fuck up before and it hadn't bothered him too much, but this time was different. Without the coke his plans to take over the old man's organization would never work. No one'd go along with him, not the Italians or even his people in Lawrence. So that was why he had to make sure the old man didn't blow it completely.

The other reason he wasn't going to let the old man screw everything up had to do with a woman. Helen was her name. She lived in affluent Andover, right beside Lawrence. And did Jorge dig her or what? Even now the thought of her had barely entered his mind and he could already feel a tent growing in his pants, right there driving along Route 95 somewhere near Newburyport, heading back to Hampton Beach. Suddenly he had an uncontrollable urge to hear her voice. Now.

Jorge pulled the car off at the next exit and headed for the first pay phone he saw. He parked and jumped out. He dropped some coins in the slot and automatically dialed the number. He couldn't wait to hear Helen's voice. On the third ring, a woman with a Yankee inflection answered the phone. Jorge's stomach sank, just like it did almost every time he dialed this number.

"May I please speak to Helen," he said.

Helen's mother answered with ice in her voice. A real snot. "Helen is not here right now. Whom may I say has called?" Like she didn't know.

"Tell her Jorge called."

"Certainly." The phone on the other end went down a bit harder than was normal.

He hung up the phone and sagged against the phone booth. Helen's mother and father had never had much use for him. But he loved Helen and she loved him, or at least she had. Lately, he'd gotten the impression that her parents were finally convincing Helen that he was no good for her. To them he was nothing but a Puerto Rican, a spic. Period. People like Helen's parents thought most Hispanics were nothing but street-level drug dealers and those were the ones who were doing good. Maybe that's how Helen was beginning to think of him too. The way she'd changed toward him lately–avoiding him most of the time and cool as a cucumber when she couldn't make up an excuse not to see him.

Maybe they were right. Maybe he really wasn't much better off than somebody up on a Lawrence street corner moving crack. That was another big reason this plan to take over the old man's business had to work–to prove to himself as well as to Helen's parents that he was worthy of their daughter. Their attitudes about him, both Helen's and her parents', would change. They'd do a complete 180 when he was not just rich, but richer than any of them could ever imagine.

It only took Jorge another fifteen minutes to reach the Hampton Bridge. Traffic delays cost him another fifteen to get across the bridge and another fifteen to get up Ocean

Boulevard to the High Tide Restaurant. Parking was tough, so he gave five bucks to some enterprising kid on a side street who was packing cars into an empty lot. Then he walked the short distance to the High Tide.

It was as crowded in the place as it was out on the street. Jorge worked his way through the crowd waiting for tables and grabbed the only vacant stool at the bar. On one side of him was a young chick talking to a just-as-young guy beside her; on his other side, an old-timer in worn clothes and a painter's cap who desperately needed a bath.

Jorge tried to catch the eye of one of the two bartenders who were busy as one-armed paper hangers. When he finally succeeded, he ordered a Corona with lime and a frosted glass. He glanced at the old man beside him. A cigarette dangled between the man's nicotine-yellowed fingers.

"Always this crowded in here?" Jorge asked nonchalantly.

The old-timer turned his grizzled puss to look at him.

"Every goddamn summer, every goddamn day," he answered bitterly. His lips stretched in a tight scowl over rotten teeth. "Winter time you don't have to put up with any of this shit. No crowds and I'm treated like a king. Summer they push you around like cattle. Half the time I come here in the summer I can't even get a goddamn seat. And the noise, aaah."

Jorge lifted his glass of Corona to his lips and almost

spilled it as he got jostled from behind by someone trying to squeeze between him and the crowd of standing patrons.

"I see what you mean." If it had been somewhere else, a club in Boston maybe, he would have made an issue of it. Maybe give the jostler more than a little jostle right back. But not now, not in this place. He was here for something more important and had to keep focused.

Jorge signaled the bartender to bring a drink for the old-timer. When what appeared to be a cola was placed in front of him, the old man reached over with a pencil-thin arm, ripped the straw out of the glass, and threw it down on the bar. "How many times I gotta tell ya–no damn straw." He turned toward Jorge. "Haven't been able to drink for twelve years now, and I've hated every goddamn minute of it." He raised the glass to his thin lips and drank the soda as if it were medicine.

Enough chitchat. Time to get down to business. He talked to the old-timer's reflection staring back at him through the back bar mirror. "You wouldn't know a guy named Shamrock who works here, would you?"

He caught the old-timer in the middle of taking a drink. He spewed cola into his glass, splashing the bar with his backwash. He looked at Jorge. "I hope he ain't a good friend of yours?"

Jorge didn't like the look in the old-timer's eyes, so he answered cautiously. "No, not a good friend. I met him once, long time ago. That's all."

"Well, that's goddamn good," the old-timer said around

the bartender wiping up the spill. "They found him beat to shit in the ice machine here yesterday morning. He was frozen like a mackerel. You ever see a frozen mackerel? That's what he looked like. Except someone beat his head in, so naturally, he looked worse, I guess. Least that's what I heard. I didn't see him. He's in Intensive Care. Don't know if he'll make it. It's hard to thaw out a man."

Crap. His one good lead looked like it was going down the toilet. He took another sip of beer as the bartender slid a fresh cola in front of the old geezer. Jorge waved at the bartender, intending to have the drink put on his check, but the bartender signaled back that there was no charge. When the bartender moved on to help the next customer, Jorge tried one more time. "They know who did it?"

The old-timer crooked his index finger. He wanted Jorge to come closer. Jorge bent over until he was almost head to head with the old geezer. "See that bartender," he said, breathing into Jorge's face.

Jorge swallowed hard to keep from gagging. He glanced down the bar at the bartender working the other end. He was a tall, thin guy with salt and pepper hair and a mustache. Jorge nodded.

"They think he's mixed up in it somehow," the old man whispered. He beckoned Jorge closer. "You hear about those fellers on the boat they found down at the harbor, both shot in the squash?"

Jorge nodded and refused to breathe.

"The word is that guy," the old man nodded in the direction of the bartender again, "and Shamrock Kelly had something to do with that. Supposedly a lot of dope involved too."

Jorge straightened up and breathed deep. Maybe he still had a lead after all. "Do the cops know this guy had something to do with it?"

The old-timer cocked his head in disbelief. "Of course they know. He's the one found Kelly stuffed in the ice machine. They probably don't think he did it and I don't either. Them being good friends and all."

"Good friends?"

"Damn right. He used to own this place and Shamrock worked for him. Course, that was before he got hisself all screwed up on drugs and lost the place."

"What's his name?"

"Shamrock . . ."

"No, not him," Jorge said, anxious now to wrap up this conversation. "The bartender."

"Dan. Dan Marlowe."

"You know where he lives?"

The old-timer pointed with his thumb over his shoulder. "Down there somewhere. One of them streets by River Street. I ain't sure which."

Jorge got up from his stool, threw some bills on the bar, and told the old man to have another cola on him. Within a couple of minutes he was headed back home.

Christ, he'd known all along that this thing wasn't

going to be easy. Now he had to go back and tell the old man that Kelly was incommunicado. The old man'd probably really go over the edge this time, maybe do something really crazy, something that'd queer the whole thing for good. Then they'd never get the product back and that'd be it for Jorge and his plans. Without that coke he was up Shit Creek, or worse–up the Merrimack River and back in Lawrence. With no money, no being boss, and worst of all, no Helen.

He'd really have to sit tight on the old man now. Make sure he didn't blow up. If it looked like the old man was starting to slip, Jorge would have to act a little earlier, that was all. No way he was going to let anyone, including the old man, stop him from reaching his big dream. Not when he was this close. No way.

Chapter 21

LIEUTENANT RAY CONOVER leaned back against the metal railing that ran the length of the boardwalk across the street from the High Tide. He was holding the *Boston Herald* so the paper obscured most of his face. It was mid-afternoon and he'd been in the same place for hours, so he'd read everything in the *Herald*, including the ads, twice. He'd long ago stopped reading and switched to counting every life preserver, fake seagull, and lobster trap that decorated the front of the building.

Dan Marlowe was inside working while Conover stood watch outside on the off chance that the two men who'd tried to kidnap Dan on the beach came back to try again. It was probably a long shot, especially in broad daylight at a crowded restaurant, but it was the only lead Conover had on the harbor murders. Besides, he wanted another crack at those two punks. Especially the big one who'd taken pot shots at him. This time someone else would be kissing the pavement.

So far he hadn't seen anything out of the ordinary. A lot of customers coming and going and that was about it. He kept peeking over his paper and shifting from foot to foot, hoping the jerks he was interested in would show up again.

Suddenly a guy with a duck-billed cap–a guy he'd seen around the beach a couple of times before–stopped directly in front of Conover, obscuring his view of the High Tide. The man reached into the pocket of his lightweight coat and began scattering around some type of crumbs. Within seconds he'd attracted a few seagulls and a flock of pigeons.

"Hey, buddy. How about moving your little bird party to a better location," Conover said to the back of the man's head.

The birdman moved a few feet and took his friends with him, clearing Conover's line of sight. Conover tried to concentrate on the restaurant but found his gaze slowly sliding back to the fellow with the birds. They were crawling all over the guy now. On his arms, his shoulders, there was even one perched right on top of his head.

Conover forced himself to look back at the High Tide, expecting to see what he'd been seeing all afternoon–nothing. At least nothing worthwhile. This time, though, a thin, weaselly looking man, who seemed as out of place at the beach as an Eskimo, was at the side of the restaurant peering through the plate glass window. The man's hands shaded his eyes like a hat bill while he continued staring in the window for a couple of minutes. Suddenly, he scooted across the street to the opposite corner where he leaned against a building, keeping his face turned in the direction of the High Tide's front door.

Conover didn't recognize the weasel but he had a feeling about him. A feeling that made his stomach a bit queasy. He kept the newspaper high enough to hide his lower face and shifted his gaze from the restaurant to the thin guy on the corner and back again.

Nothing happened for a while. The thin man didn't move, and there was nothing happening with the restaurant except the coming and goings of patrons.

Then, about fifteen minutes after he'd first shown up, the skinny guy suddenly walked kitty-corner across the side street toward the back of the High Tide. Conover watched as the thin guy shanghaied an old man in a painter's cap and old clothes who'd just come out of the restaurant's back door. The thin guy grabbed the old man by the arm and shoved him against the wall of the restaurant. Although there was lots of foot traffic up near the front of the restaurant on Ocean, there wasn't another soul down near the two men at the rear side of the building.

The thin guy was jabbering right up in the old man's face. It didn't look like friendly talk either. Then the punk smacked the old man hard across the face with his open palm. Conover dropped the paper and started to move, then thought better of it. Unlikely that this dust-up had anything to do with why he was standing watch. If he went over and broke up the action, that'd probably be when something happened out front of the place.

Conover was distracted for the hundredth time by the guy with the pigeons who was now posing like some kind of statue with pigeons all over him. Conover turned back just in time to see the thin guy pull out a handgun and whack the old man across the side of the head with it.

Conover removed his Glock from his shoulder holster and moved it to the large pocket of his windbreaker. He kept his fingers wrapped around it.

"Hey, what the hell's going on?" he shouted and started walking in the direction of the two men. The thin guy saw him coming and took off toward Ocean Boulevard, leaving the old man sagging against the building.

Conover glanced at the old man. If he was still standing, he couldn't be too bad. He'd check out the old man as soon as he collared this slimeball. Conover cut diagonally across the parking lot separating the boardwalk from the street, moving at a normal speed. No use spooking the thin guy into running. The man continued south, occasionally glancing back over his shoulder.

It didn't take Conover long to come abreast of the man. The two of them on opposite sidewalks now, both heading in the same direction, only the two lanes of Ocean Boulevard separating them. Bumper-to-bumper traffic filled Conover's nose with exhaust fumes.

He was going to have to make a move sooner or later–the only question was when. Too bad there wasn't a local cop around; he didn't relish the idea of taking this armed guy alone. The street and sidewalk were so crowded that he wanted to avoid gunfire if possible. He kept his sweaty hand wrapped around the gun in his pocket.

When the thin man reached the corner of M Street, he glanced at Conover. There was an almost imperceptible change in the man's gait, not really faster, just different. Conover's hand tightened on the Glock. This was it; the man would start to rabbit any second.

Conover ducked as the thin man whipped out a gun and popped a shot in his direction. The man spun back around and broke into a full-out run, long hair flying in the wind. He sprinted right by a sub shop plastered with a hundred signs telling the prices of its sandwiches.

Adrenalin kicked Conover's heart into overdrive as he dashed between parked cars and out across Ocean Boulevard, dodging traffic as he went. He had his gun out now, barrel pointed down. No way could he get a clear shot, not with this many people around. The man was more than a half a block ahead of him now, all elbows and ass.

"Get out of the way," Conover shouted as he dodged around a couple on the sidewalk. Other people saw him coming, gun in hand, and jumped aside in fright. His feet pounded the cement and his lungs started to ache as he sprinted past N Street and a giant pirate holding a six-foot sword at a miniature golf course. Up ahead the thin guy was running like hell. The man banged a right onto O Street. Conover poured on the steam, dodging through the oblivious crowd.

When Conover rounded the corner onto O he could see the man hauling ass in the middle of the street about halfway down. No pedestrians on this side street–Conover had a clear shot. He stopped and raised the pistol with both hands. He started to shout a command but couldn't catch his breath. He took aim, steadied his shaking hands, and fired off a shot. The thin man dodged sideways as a jagged hole suddenly appeared in the rear window of a parked car next to him.

Conover was about to take a second shot when he saw a line of cars crawling past the end of the street on Ashworth Avenue. If he missed the guy again, he'd probably hit one of those occupied cars.

"Son of a bitch." Conover broke into a run again. He closed the gap a bit when the thin guy had trouble getting across the traffic on Ashworth. Brakes squealed left and right. The man barely made it past a car full of kids, but he finally reached the other side and continued heading south.

Conover didn't slow when he reached Ashworth. He barreled straight across the street, somehow managing to avoid becoming a pedestrian fatality.

They were both running south on Ashworth now.

Conover's lungs burned and his legs ached. If the thin man put any more distance between them, he'd never be able to make it up. He took heart knowing that they'd be at the harbor soon. The thin guy would be at a dead end–unless he planned to hotfoot it across the bridge toward Seabrook. If the creep went out on the bridge, Conover'd get at least one good shot.

At the last minute, the thin man banged a right down a gravel road toward the harbor where the party boats docked. Conover knew the area pretty well. As long as they both kept heading toward the water, there was no way out.

The thin man leapt onto one of the long wooden fishing boat piers and raced toward the far end. Conover hesitated when he reached the pier. He couldn't get a clear shot off–people were swarming off a party boat that had just gotten back to the pier. He broke into a sprint again, his feet pounding hard on the wooden planks. The thin man blew past two people, shoving them over a rail into the water fifteen feet below.

Someone screamed as Conover raced by waving his gun. The thin man suddenly dropped out of sight at the far end of the pier.

There was no way he could escape, Conover told himself. Somewhere nearby an outboard motor roared to life. Conover pulled up short at the end of the pier. About fifteen feet below, the thin man revved the engine in a small motorboat and pulled away from a tiny dock.

Conover ran down the gangplank to the dock, raised his weapon, and squeezed off a quick succession of shots. The dock rocked in the motorboat's wake and Conover had no doubt he'd missed.

There was a large party boat moored just off the dock and the motorboat angled around it. Conover dashed to the other side of the dock to try and catch the boat when it rounded the far end of the larger vessel, but the thin man was no fool. Instead of running the length of the party boat, he'd headed straight out. By the time Conover realized what had happened and got a bead on the motorboat, he knew it was too far away to hit even with a lucky shot. No use wasting bullets.

The motorboat headed toward the Hampton Bridge and the open sea beyond. There was no way he could beat the boat to the bridge even if he had wings. All he could do now was catch his breath and watch the motorboat until it disappeared.

Just before the boat went under the bridge, Conover swore he could see the skinny little weasel look back at the dock, his hand moving up and down in a rhythmic motion. He didn't actually have to see it to know that the prick was giving him the finger. Probably laughing at him too. Hard to tell which was worse.

Chapter 22

WHEN JORGE CAME BACK with the word that Shamrock Kelly was in the hospital indefinitely, Dominic went wild. At his direction, Jorge and Sal carried Tommy McGee, chair and all, over to the workbench again where Dominic forced McGee's head onto the drill press pad. The man was screaming and crying like a little girl.

All Jorge could think about was keeping McGee alive. He could know something about the bartender, Marlowe, that the old man at the beach had told him about. But this raving lunatic, his so-called boss, was about to blow the whole goddamn thing. He had to get Dominic back on track. Now.

Dominic was just about to drive the drill bit into McGee's ear when Jorge spoke up. "I got a line on somebody else. A bartender that worked with this Kelly. I got the word he might be involved. Maybe even the brains. Let's find out what he knows about him." Jorge nodded toward McGee. Poor guy looked ridiculous now with his head jammed under the drill press. Talk about frightened eyes!

Dominic was breathing short and fast through his nose, his face distorted with rage. He stared at Jorge like he was trying to digest what he'd just been told. Then he gave Jorge a wicked look. "Oh, yeah? Sure. We can do that, kid."

Dominic turned back to McGee, tore his head out from under the drill, and started beating him hard about the face with his fists. Jorge watched till it got so bad his stomach felt queasy. He was just about to reach out and put his hand on Dominic when the beating stopped as suddenly as it had begun. That's when Tommy McGee, spitting blood and teeth with each word, began to talk and talk and talk. So much so that finally Dominic started beating him again just to shut him up. By that time they knew more about Dan Marlowe than they wanted to know. But not much more about the product.

Jorge almost had a heart attack as he watched Dominic pick up the phone, call New Hampshire information for the High Tide Restaurant, then punch in the number. Marlowe must have answered the phone because a split second after the old man asked for Dan Marlowe, he started screaming obscenities over the line, ranting and raving about Kelly, Marlowe, and the stuff.

The old guinea was going to blow it for sure. Throw the whole damn thing away. Jorge felt like taking care of business right then and there–take out his piece and put it up to the back of the old man's head–and that'd be all she wrote. But that'd be as stupid a move as the one the old man was making now. He had to play it cooler. Everything was at stake.

"Boss," Jorge said gently. And when Dominic ignored him, he put his hand firmly on the older man's shoulder. Dominic looked shocked for a second. He stopped his screaming and acted as if he wasn't too sure how he should react to one of his subordinates laying a hand on him. It must have snapped him out of his rage though, because slowly a semblance of sanity returned to his face.

"Your product. That's what we want."

Dominic nodded slowly. "Yeah, yeah. You're right." He turned back to the phone. "I want my merchandise back, asshole. Fuckin' yesterday."

Jorge watched as Dominic listened to the answer coming over the phone. The old man's face grew dark again and his body trembled slightly. "Don't tell me ya don't know what the fuck I'm talkin' about," he shouted.

He turned back to Jorge. "Marlowe claims he don't know what Kelly or this sack-a-shit's brother were involved in." He pointed at McGee, then turned back to the phone. "Why you filthy, no good cocksucker. I'll fuckin' . . ." Before he could finish, Jorge put his hand back on Dominic's shoulder. Amazed, Dominic looked at the hand for a moment, then started to calm down.

"All right," Dominic said into the phone. "I've said

too much already. Here's the bottom line. If you want your family to keep on breathing, you call this number soon and set things right. I ain't gonna wait long." Dominic slowly recited the number of Jorge's beeper and slammed the phone down.

Jorge winced. "I wish you hadn't given him my number after threatening the man like that. You never know how someone's going to react to threats."

Dominic scowled. "Just gimme your beeper and don't worry about it. I hadda give him some number and I couldn't give him mine, could I?"

Just like Dominic to worry about himself and not his people. "We better get McGee out of here, Boss, and back up the beach." Jesus, did he hate using that word now. Boss, that is.

Dominic fluttered his hand. "Yeah, yeah. You're right. We got all we need outta this guy. Good riddance. Make sure the asshole's cleaned up before you bring him out to the car. I don't want nobody seein' him leaving here looking like that." Dominic nodded at Tommy McGee still strapped to the chair, head bowed, blood dripping from his chin to the floor.

Jorge reached over and lifted McGee's head. The eyes were closed and the skin felt cold to his touch. A stench rose from the body, making the room smell like a plugged-up crapper. "I don't think he's going back up the beach."

Dominic's eyes widened a bit, but only for a moment, as he stared disdainfully at McGee's body. "Well," he said, letting out a snort. "He was a punk and probably a rip-off anyway. Get rid a the fuckin' asshole, kid."

Jorge didn't know what he hated more–him having to call the old man "boss," or the old man calling him "kid." Both made him boil. But he didn't say anything; the time wasn't right. Instead, he and Sal did what they were told.

They got rid of dead Tommy McGee.

Chapter 23

THE HAMPTON BEACH fireworks were an institution. The town held them every Wednesday night during the summer, on the 4th of July, and on a few other special dates too. The display was usually pretty good, shot off from the sand just a little north of the Sea Shell where the bands played. The display always drew a large crowd with, unfortunately, a lot of traffic. And this Wednesday night was no exception.

Buzz and Skinny were right in the middle of it all, standing on the boardwalk (which long ago was converted to concrete) close to the Sea Shell, looking straight down at the beach. A pickup was parked in the sand and the men in charge of the fireworks were moving about. Out on the water, in the direction the aerial display would be aimed, lights sparkled from boats anchored off shore waiting for the show to begin.

Buzz, with Skinny on his right, stood shoulder-to-shoulder with the tight crowd. They were right behind the first line of people pressed against the railing that separated the boardwalk from the sand. Behind him Buzz could hear a cacophony of traffic noises, teenage shouts, and the bells and whistles of the arcades. He glanced up at the sky. A beautiful night for fireworks. The kind of night that made a man feel anything was possible.

He glanced at Skinny and scowled. The fruitcake was wearing a checkered sport coat held high to cover his chin, a pair of cheap sunglasses, and a ridiculous-looking porkpie hat. Skinny thought he was well disguised, but Buzz thought he resembled a bad scriptwriter's idea of a small-time bookmaker. If he wasn't so mad at the nitwit, he'd probably be embarrassed to be seen with him. But he was mad at him, real mad.

Buzz leaned down to speak into Skinny's ear. "I still can't believe you got in a shootout with a cop, you silly sack-a-shit."

"Buzz, I told you," Skinny said in that whining voice of his. "I didn't have no choice. He chased me clear across the beach. If I didn't have that motorboat stashed, you'd be bailing me out of jail now."

Buzz wasn't worried about the people around them hearing him and Skinny talk, the crowd noise was so loud they could barely hear each other. And Skinny's voice still twanged his nerves.

"Bullshit," Buzz said. "I wouldn't care if you rotted

behind bars. I tell you to do one little thing–follow the spic–and you end up getting in a gunfight with a cop. You know the trouble you could've caused me?"

He must've been talking pretty loud because a few people in the crowd started staring at him. He gave them a threatening glare and they looked quickly away. All of them.

"Sorry, Buzz," Skinny said, voice shaking. "But at least I found out about Marlowe." He nodded toward a man standing against the rail about five or six people to their right. "That's good. Huh, Buzz, huh?"

"Yeah, great. I just hope that old fart gave you the right scoop on who the spic was pumping him about." Buzz stared at the guy named Dan Marlowe, but instead of a man, he saw all those duffel bags of cocaine stuffed to the max with all that white powder. His heart kicked it up a notch. If everything went the way he hoped, he'd have all that cocaine back in his hot little hands before this night was over.

The plan was simple–the minute Marlowe started to leave after the fireworks show, he and Skinny would follow him. Somewhere between here and Marlowe's cottage at the other end of the beach, they'd take him. They'd escort him right off the boardwalk and down onto the sand where, with a little luck, there wouldn't be any people around. Then he'd force Marlowe to tell him where the coke was. It wouldn't take long either, Buzz was confident about that. He could size people up pretty good–had to in his line of work–and he was pretty sure that this Marlowe character was no tough guy. The guy'd shit his pants with a gun jammed in his mouth. Probably start sucking it like a baby's bottle. Buzz snickered.

"Sumpin funny, Buzz?" Skinny asked.

"Yeah. You." And boy did he look funny. A real piece of work. Buzz slowly stopped laughing. Nothing funny about having a simpleton for a partner.

Buzz glanced at his wristwatch: 9:30 p.m. He'd barely gotten his arm back down before a loud swoosh filled the air and the first rocket hurtled skyward. It exploded high above the water, illuminating the boats anchored below. The rocket was an old standard–a green and red pinwheel. The crowd around Buzz oohed. Except for the oohing and the traffic and a few scared kids beginning to cry, the night was strangely quiet all of a sudden.

More rockets, with short time lapses between each, flew skyward and exploded in various colors and shapes. Fifty thousand heads on Hampton Beach were tilted up, watching the sky. It was a terrific display and every so often Buzz had to remind himself why he was there. He glanced at Dan Marlowe staring up at the show like everyone else.

Then Buzz took a peek at Skinny. The thin man's eyes, visible through the shades, were as big as saucers, his mouth was hanging open, and he was oohing and ahhing with every burst of color. No big brain there, Buzz said to himself. But he had to admit, tonight's show was a real class act.

Before he knew it, the sound of multiple rockets leaving their tubes simultaneously slammed his ears. Finale time. Dozens of rockets shot up in the air in succession, creating a solid wave of sight and sound. Blam, blam, blam! The rockets shot faster and faster. Three . . . four . . . five . . . six at a time exploding overhead, their noise blasting his ears as the sound reverberated off the Casino and other buildings. The sky lit up like an aurora borealis, filled with a rainbow of colors. So many pyrotechnics going off all at once . . .

Buzz looked over in time to see Marlowe leaving.

"Come on, come on," he said, grabbing Skinny and propelling him into the crowd. "He's getting away."

Buzz used Skinny as a battering ram to force their way through the throng. It worked too, for a few yards at least. Until he pushed Skinny up against some no-neck twenty-somethings who had a good load on. One of the kids, built like a bull, shoved Skinny right back into Buzz.

"Watch where you're going, stupid tool," the kid said.

"Goddamn college boy," Skinny said and popped the no-neck right on his beak before Buzz could do anything to stop him. The kid looked stunned for a second and then launched into Skinny. Two of the kid's buddies, guys who looked like football players, started to close in too. Even though Skinny was swinging like an out-of-control windmill, Buzz knew instantly they'd probably need a paint scrapper to get what was left of him off the cement.

Buzz strained his neck trying to see over the melee in front of him, hoping to catch a glimpse of Marlowe up ahead. But the man was out of sight, lost in the crowd. Buzz almost went after him, but then he realized he'd have trouble getting around these rowdies. Besides, if he left Skinny alone and unprotected, he wouldn't be any help until he got out of the hospital.

Buzz sighed and balled his big fists. Then he waded into the group in front of him, cracked a couple of heads, and got Skinny out of his jam.

Chapter 24

IF YOU WANT your family to keep on breathing . . .

The voice kept echoing in Dan's head, bouncing back and forth, back and forth. No mistaking the tone in that voice. The guy it belonged to, the man claiming to be the missing cocaine's owner, had definitely made it clear he wasn't bullshitting. On top of everything else, Dan could now add drug smugglers to his worry list.

Only one problem–Dan didn't have the cocaine. Not that anyone believed him. Not this guy on the phone or the two state cops either. And he couldn't really blame any of them, because every time he denied having anything to do with the coke, it sounded like he was lying, even to himself.

Suddenly Dan felt like drinking a beer instead of serving it–maybe even a few. A cold glass or two might help him figure out what the hell to do. He glanced at the Budweiser clock over the bar. Almost time to punch out. He wrapped up his shift and turned the bar over to his relief.

Conover was out front somewhere, waiting for Dan to leave. He'd agreed to let Conover follow him which was probably a good thing considering how things had turned out on the beach. But tonight he had to get away. Somewhere he could be alone and have a few drinks. He didn't want a shadow along for that, least of all a state cop. So he left by the back door and headed down the side street to Ashworth Avenue.

He never drank at the High Tide, shitting in your own backyard and all. If he had to drink, it was either at home or at the White Cap. He felt comfortable there. The Cap was more like the Tide than any other joint on the beach. Unlike most of the other bars and restaurants on the beach, both the Tide and the Cap were open year round and both drew a steady crowd of tough winter people during the off-season. They also had a gang of regulars all year long in addition to the summer tourists. Both offered good food at reasonable prices, something you definitely didn't find at most of the other beach eateries. They treated you right so you liked going back. Which meant they were both usually packed in the summer, especially at night.

Dan squeezed his way through the front door, exchanged a quick greeting with the owner, and banged around the corner into the bar area. The bar itself was on the left and ran half the length of the room. Beyond the bar the room opened up with tables, chairs, a pool table, and room for the band against the back wall. He twisted his way through the standing-room-only crowd and plunked his ass down as a departing customer slid off a stool.

There were two bartenders hustling behind the bar, both so busy Dan got a headache just watching them. The TV above the bar was turned to some sitcom he didn't recognize and couldn't hear above the crowd. He'd been lucky to find a seat–customers were lined up shoulder-to-shoulder tighter than worms in a bait can. There wasn't an empty stool to be seen. Standing customers waved their hands behind those lucky enough to get a seat, shouting drink orders, grabbing drinks, and passing money. It was crazy, a madhouse. Just the way Dan liked it. At least for tonight. With all these partying people around he could sip his beer and relax and not feel like all the eyes were on him.

That alone was a treat, because lately he'd felt like everyone in the world was watching him. Conover was hoping that one way or another Dan'd lead him to the missing coke and whoever was responsible for the harbor murders. He had to admit it was reassuring to know Conover was there if Dan needed him again, no matter what the man's motivation was.

Then there were those two jamokes he'd chased out of his cottage with the shot gun. Probably the same two, Peralta and his sidekick, who'd tried to grab him down on the beach. Dan had a sick feeling in his gut that he hadn't seen the last of those two.

"Hey, Dan," the bartender shouted above the din as he set down a Heineken and a chilled pilsner glass in front of Dan. "How ya been?"

"Good, Tim. Slow I see."

"Oh yeah," Tim answered with a smile. "Always."

Tim was a young guy, younger than Dan by maybe ten years, maybe more. He was a good bartender too. You had to be to work a beach bar nights in the summer. If you weren't, you'd get buried. Tim started to say something else, but didn't get to finish it–shouts for his services were coming from the entire length of the bar. He gave a flip of his hands and was off in a blur.

Dan pulled his glass close. He rarely worked nights anymore and was glad of it. The money was better than days, but you earned every penny of it. Besides, moving for hours like a raped ape, by the time you finished, cleaned up the bar, and got home you were lucky if it was 2 a.m. Then you'd be so jacked up you'd have to have a few beers just to get to sleep.

No, being a night bartender was a young person's game. Dan had paid his dues and now he liked the slower pace of the day crowd. They were a little older and so was he.

He poured the beer skillfully into his glass, forming a small head of foam. Then he drank it, quickly. A cliche, but the first one really did go down the fastest. Tim slid another Heineken in front of him on one of his passes without being asked. Dan filled the glass again, took a small sip, and let out a deep breath. The knot in his gut started to loosen. With a little luck he'd be able to forget about all the craziness of the past few days, even if it was only for a few hours. He took a long swig. Then he took another.

He'd just about finished his fourth beer, with another already placed in front of him, when he heard her voice.

"Excuse me."

Dan half turned his head and there she was, right in his face, squeezed in between him and the guy on the stool to his left. All he could see at this close distance was her head and what a head! She was smokin'. Beautiful blonde hair, gorgeous face, thin gold neck chains, and tanned everywhere. And yeah, she was speaking to him.

Dan cleared his throat. "Yeah?" Apparently he hadn't gotten any smoother with age.

"I can't get the bartender's attention," she said, smiling. "Would you order me a Kahlua Sombrero? I've got the money." She handed Dan a few bills and he took them. It wasn't that he was cheap, just kind of shaken. Obviously there was something besides Conover showing up tonight that could surprise him.

Tim was so busy Dan had trouble getting his attention, but finally he did. Tim made the milkshake, set it down on the bar, and took off to fill another order. The woman didn't turn to go after Dan handed her the drink, just stood there jammed up close to him. She bent her head and pursed her lips around the straw, staring up at Dan with a look that made his face flush with heat.

She took her lips off the straw and twirled it in her drink. "Do you come here often?" she said loudly enough to be heard above the racket.

Now this he couldn't believe. He glanced around, half expecting some gorilla of a boyfriend to pounce on him. But none of the males staring her way looked like anything but males staring her way. "Not as much as I used to," he answered.

"It's a nice place," she said, still twirling the straw in her drink. "So crowded though."

"It's always like this in the summer." And then he got a whiff of her perfume. It smelled like cinnamon.

"I hate crowds." She slowly looked around the bar. Probably looking for a better prospect. She was the kind of woman who could choose from any male in the building, attached or unattached.

And speaking of attached–he was married, sure, but he was also separated, and he hadn't been laid in a long time, and the two of them were only talking, and she was such a knockout he was resigned to the fact that that's all that would happen anyhow.

He could take advantage of her temporary distraction though. Dan discreetly checked her out, up and down. And man, her neck down was as fine as her neck up. She was wearing a sheer white blouse with a neckline that plunged down, exposing the top of two tanned breasts that were perfect–not too small, not too large. Even though the blouse showed a lot, one thing it didn't reveal was a tan line. And the jeans she had on must have been applied by a paint brush. She was a ten, no debate there. In fact, this babe was so hot, he could feel his own jeans getting tight.

She looked to be in her early twenties, mid-twenties tops. Kind of young for him. Sure he ran every day, but there was no getting around the fact that he had a lot of years on this woman and he was feeling every one of those years right now.

And he was out of practice, to say the least. Nervous as a pimply teenager. Though it could be the nerves stemmed from the fact that he was a married man with two kids, a man who had never once cheated on his wife.

The woman leaned over and whispered in Dan's ear. "You like to go somewhere a little less crowded?" And you couldn't put on paper how she made that sound.

He didn't know if it was guilt or if he was burnt out because of what he'd been going through lately, or both. Maybe he'd just plain lost his mind. Dan held up his hand so she could see the gold band on his finger. "I'm married."

"That doesn't matter, honey." She ran a finger along the top of his shoulder. "We can still have a lot of fun. No one has to know."

Heat flushed his skin from head to toe, making him

feel like a goddamned Chinese lantern. Probably looked like one too. Dan took a deep breath and tried to slow his heartbeat from a dead run back to a jog. He could do it. Could go with her and probably have the time of his life. Problem was he had to live with himself the next day. And the day after that. "No thanks."

She looked at him, her gorgeous face all scrunched up like she couldn't believe what she'd just heard. "Come on, baby. We'll have a ball," she said in a low husky voice.

Now he really was feeling like a jerk. Who the hell else would turn down something like this? Only a crazy man or a gay guy. He reached for his beer and almost knocked it over instead. "No thanks."

Christ, he sounded like a broken record. But he couldn't seem to get any other words out of his mouth.

The woman's eyes narrowed. She whipped around, her blonde mane flaring wide, and stormed out of the White Cap. He watched her go, along with half the other men in the place.

Dan raised the glass to his mouth and killed the beer in one large swig. What the hell was that all about?

It took all of two minutes after she'd left for him to start thinking that maybe he'd made a mistake. What the hell had he been afraid of? He was separated after all and that was almost the same as being divorced, wasn't it? He'd been offered a once-in-a-lifetime opportunity and had blown it.

Maybe something like her was just what he needed to

make him feel the way he used to feel. Dan dropped a bunch of bills on the bar, slid off the stool, and maneuvered toward the exit, knowing deep down that it was only the beer motivating him now and that it really was too late–she'd be long gone. Because there was no way a woman who looked the way she looked would be loose and alone for long, especially on Ocean Boulevard.

Dan stepped out of the White Cap and walked down the steps to the sidewalk. The night was clear–all stars and salt air. He looked up the street toward Ocean Boulevard and then down the other way toward Ashworth Avenue. Nothing. There were plenty of people at both ends of the street walking by, but none that resembled Miss Hollywood. Yeah, that's who she was–Miss Hollywood.

Something or someone scuffed the sidewalk behind him. Before Dan could turn around, something hard jammed into his right cheek.

"You ever see a .22 slug bounce around inside someone's skull?" The deep voice sounded vaguely familiar.

"Not recently," Dan said.

A car screeched to a halt at the curb in front of them and the rear door flew open like maybe it was operated by a deranged cab driver.

"Then get in the car quick and maybe you never will."

Chapter 25

TONY PERALTA FELT GOOD for a change; things were starting to look up. They'd been after this Dan Marlowe character for a while now, blowing a couple of shots at him, and getting shot himself in the process. And now here was Marlowe, in the back of the rented Buick LaSabre, sitting there with Rhonda beside him, staring at the gun Tony was pointing at him from the front seat. Wayne was driving.

They only had a short distance to go once they finally broke free of all the traffic at the Casino on Ocean Boulevard. After that it was only a long minute before they were pulling into Tony's driveway on Boar's Head. A few minutes after that and they had Marlowe sitting in the middle of the main room in an antique chair, his hands bound with belts to the armrests.

Wayne and Rhonda lounged in the background as if this was something that happened every day while Tony kept his pistol pointed straight at Marlowe.   And Marlowe, with his beery eyes, was sitting there looking right back at Tony. The man wasn't really drunk though. He seemed to have sobered up fast the second Tony pressed the barrel of the gun against his head. The poor bastard had probably been hoping something a little more pleasant would be against his squash tonight–like Rhonda's tits maybe–except this nut sitting in front of him had blown Rhonda off.   Maybe the guy was queer or something. Passing up laying something like Rhonda?

She was pissed about it too. Tony let out a little chuckle when he thought of what her face must have looked like when Marlowe said no. Maybe it'd knock the broad down a peg or two.

But his mood didn't last long, because he suddenly remembered something else. "So, asshole, you think it was a big joke taking a pop at me with that shotgun?"

Marlowe didn't answer, but Wayne snorted.   Tony gave him a look.   Wayne cleared his throat and turned quiet. Rhonda just sat on one end of a long couch flipping through a magazine.

Tony turned back to Marlowe. "What? Forgot how to talk? You think it's a scream I had to get all those pellets plucked out of my rump? Huh? Think that's funny?"

"I was defending my property," Marlowe said, slurring his words slightly.

"Defending your property? What the fuck's that mean?

I wasn't on your property when you let me have it. I was in the state park. That's not your property. That's state property. And I'm a state resident. Taxpayer too. You shot me in the back, for Chrissake. I should let you defend yourself against this." Tony took a step closer and swung the .22 up like he was going to backhand him with the weapon. Marlowe's head jerked.

"Nah, with my luck I'd fucking kill you." Tony pointed the gun back at Marlowe's chest. "And I can't do that, at least not yet. You have to tell me some things first. And you will tell me what I want to know, especially if you want me to change my mind and let you crawl out of here."

Marlowe didn't say a word.

"I'll ask you straight out, Marlowe. Where's the fucking coke?" He gave the gun in his hand a little jiggle, just to remind the man it was still there.

Marlowe shook his head. "I don't have any idea."

"Well, you better get an idea and quick," Tony said. "I gotta itchy trigger finger." Rhonda giggled, Wayne choked.

"Look," Marlowe said, as if he were trying to sound reasonable. "I don't know why everyone thinks I know something about this coke, but I'm telling you the truth. I don't know anything about it."

"Well, the little Mick flipped on you like a pancake," Tony lied. "Said you were in on the rip-off with him. And I believe him. He didn't have the brains to do it himself. Although, after seeing you pass up Rhonda, I'm wondering if I might've misjudged your IQ."

Wayne snorted again and Rhonda tore a page in her magazine. Tony cleared his throat. "So where the fuck is the coke, Marlowe?"

Marlowe just shook his head.

"Let me have some fun with him," Wayne said, standing up from his chair. "I'll make him talk."

Tony waved him back down. "Won't do any good right now." He stroked his chin with his free hand. "We just need to make him a little more scared of us." He stuck his face right up in Marlowe's mug. "I heard something once. Something about you having a little problem with cocaine. That true, Marlowe? You used to have a problem with that stuff? Bad shit, cocaine."

Tony leaned back and waved at Rhonda. "Hey, sweet cheeks. We got any of that awful cocaine stuff around?"

Rhonda got up from the sofa and strolled over to a bookcase by the wall. She slid open a drawer and pulled out a flat hunk of polished stone. Piled on the stone was about a half-ounce of very fine-looking cocaine. She held the stone up toward Tony like an offering. At the sight of the blow sparkling in the light Tony suddenly felt like he had to crap.

Christ, the stuff was working already and not on Dan Marlowe either. He looked over at the bound man and tried to forget about his churning bowels. His little plan was working though. Marlowe didn't look like he wanted to take on the world anymore. He looked like he was the one about ready to shit his pants. The guy looked even more nervous about the blow than Tony's gun. Amazing what that stuff could do. Rhonda kept holding the coke out, occasionally cocking her hips from side to side.

"You know," Tony waved his index finger in the air. "Sometimes I forget to be a good host. But I guess it's never too late. Would you like some of this?" He nodded toward Rhonda and the cocaine.

Marlowe's voice cracked. "No . . . uhh . . . no." His face flushed fire-engine red and his Adam's apple bobbed as he swallowed.

"Sure you would." Tony grinned. This was going to be fun. He'd get his answers and revenge for being shot as well. "Rhonda, baby. Give our guest some of that fine blow. Go ahead, honey, give him a taste."

Rhonda set the stone down on a nearby coffee table. She pulled out a small coke spoon, bent over, and dipped the spoon into the coke. When she stood up, the spoon was overflowing with powder. She walked seductively over to Marlowe with a big smile on her face. She was really enjoying this. Payback time for Marlowe's earlier brush-off? Like they say–there's nothing worse than a woman scorned.

Rhonda moved the spoon toward Marlowe's head and as she did he sucked in his breath as if he might blow the cocaine away.

Tony stepped closer and put the barrel of the gun

against Marlowe's head. "Don't be rude, my friend," Tony said. "Just make the best of it. Things could be a lot worse than having a gorgeous hot woman piping coke up your beak. A lot worse."

Tony laughed. Rhonda's eyes narrowed and her lips parted as she moved the spoon under Marlowe's right nostril. Tony tapped the man's head lightly twice with the pistol, and Marlowe inhaled the coke up his nostril like he'd done it yesterday. His head snapped up and his eyes blinked rapidly a few times. Rhonda refilled the spoon and repeated the process with Marlowe's other nostril.

Tony pulled the gun away and watched Marlowe's reaction. The guy had definitely had a problem with the stuff at one time, that much was obvious. Being strapped to a chair would make anyone nervous, but not just anyone would change this much after just two lines. Marlowe fidgeted in his chair like he was sitting on a hot plate. His eyes bulged slightly and one looked like it was staring off to the side. His head swiveled back and forth, and every so often he'd glance around as if he'd heard someone sneaking up behind him. Tony brought the gun up quickly, stopping an inch from Marlowe's face. The man almost jumped out of his skin. Yeah, this guy'd had a bad problem. Tony laughed again. This could be almost as fun as making money.

"You seem a little nervous, Marlowe," Tony said. "Didn't you like my blow? Makes you feel real nice, doesn't it?" When he didn't get any response, Tony decided to have a little more fun.

"Look out, he's got a knife!" he shouted, looking over Marlowe's shoulder. The man's entire body jerked, almost tipping over the chair. Tony, Rhonda, and Wayne all burst into laughter. Tony stopped for a moment. "Sorry. I thought I saw someone." He laughed again.

"What's that?" Wayne suddenly yelled. No one jumped.

"Hey, how come it didn't work for me?" Wayne asked, sounding disappointed.

Tony rolled his eyes. "Because you're a moron, that's why. He'd have to be a lot higher before that'd scare him twice in a row."

Rhonda jumped in. "Can I try it?"

Tony rubbed his face from forehead to chin. "Maybe later. It's time to get serious again."

This time Tony went nose to nose with Marlowe. "Are you going to tell me where the coke is or do I have to get mean?"

"I . . . I . . . d . . . don't kn . . . know." Marlowe's voice shook.

"All right, asshole. You asked for it." Tony picked the cocaine up from the table and walked over to the bookcase. He set his gun down and held the stone over a half-filled glass of water sitting on the shelf. He picked up a business card and began using it to shovel an easy gram of cocaine into the glass. He put the stone down, picked up a pen, and stirred the cocaine-laced water. Mission accomplished, he grabbed his gun and the glass of cocaine water, and walked back to where Marlowe was sitting. He put the gun's barrel against Marlowe's temple and the glass against his lips. "Drink or die," he said.

Marlowe drank. Every drop.

When he was finished, Tony called Rhonda over. "Want to have some fun with him?"

Rhonda's eyes brightened. "I will if I can have a couple of lines."

"Okay, okay," Tony answered irritably. Rhonda bounced over to the bookcase and laid out two huge lines with the business card. She pulled a squished-up bill out of the pocket of her skin-tight jeans, rolled it right up, and expertly snorted both lines. Then she rose up tall, her body slightly shivering. She flipped back her hair and turned around.

Shit, she was hot as hell already. Her lips were parted, her mouth loose, and her eyes full of cocaine. She walked over to Marlowe, every step almost a sex act in itself. Tony could feel himself getting hard. Jesus, she was unbelievable even when she was straight, but on blow she was like an animal. He almost felt like taking her himself right here, right now. He forced himself to focus on the load of coke and what he had to do if he wanted to keep this beautiful house of his.

He'd let her blow this Marlowe's mind and see what the guy would do. Why Tony considered something like this torture, he wasn't sure. Just a gut feeling. And it was working.   Already Marlowe was thrashing around in the chair like a monkey in a cage. He was sweating and his face looked like he could use a blood pressure pill. And the cocaine water hadn't even kicked in yet. Then again, maybe it had.

"Come on, baby," Rhonda purred, as she stripped off her silk blouse, exposing beautiful tanned breasts. "I want to go crazy all over you. Mmmmmm." She was rubbing her breasts now with the flat of her hands, moaning, her head thrown back.

Tony cleared his throat. Jesus Christ. "What do you say, Marlowe? Tell me what I want to know and she's all yours. And I won't make you drink any more of my special cocktail either. Unless, of course, you want to."

Marlowe shook his head violently from side to side. Looked like the coke water was working; he was really bouncing around now. Tony could practically see the man's shirt expanding and contracting from his pounding heart.

"Ohhh," Rhonda breathed. She undulated her hips only a couple of feet from Marlowe's contorted face. "We'll do more coke and you can do anything you want to me." She unbuttoned her jeans. They were so tight she had trouble peeling them past her hips. But she finally did, and when her blonde hair was exposed she began stroking her thighs and whimpering.

That did it for Tony. This wasn't going anywhere anyhow. He grabbed Rhonda by the arm and dragged her toward the bedroom. As he went by the bookcase he picked up the stone with the coke on it. He glanced at Wayne, sitting ramrod straight in his chair. "See what you can do with him, Wayne. But be careful. Don't fucking kill him."

"No problem, Boss," Wayne said, jumping up with a grin. "It'll be my pleasure. I have a little tension to work out anyway."

Tony led Rhonda into the bedroom, pushing her in front of him as he went. He should be out there supervising the big lummox. After all, Wayne might get carried away again. But right now he was the one carried away and he knew it and he didn't care. He had to have some coke and this hot, beautiful bitch right now.

Tony turned and closed the bedroom door, grinning at the sight of Marlowe–bound and thrashing like a madman–in the chair with Wayne, huge fists balled at his sides, towering over him.

Chapter 26

MID-MORNING AND OVER twelve hours had gone by since Conover had lost Dan Marlowe. When Dan hadn't come out the front door of the High Tide within ten minutes of when he should have, Conover had gone right in and found out that Dan had gone out the back door. Why Dan would give him the slip he didn't know, but he didn't like it. He'd called Bartolo and the two of them had been beating the bushes ever since.

Conover shifted his feet on the Ocean Boulevard sidewalk and glanced over at Bartolo. Marlowe's disappearance threw up a red flag as far as Bartolo was concerned. His partner was more certain than ever that Marlowe was involved in the coke heist.

They were standing in front of Funland, listening to the sounds of arcade games and teenage voices spilling through the open front door. They had a kid backed against the outside wall of the building. He was about twenty, twenty-one, thin, greasy hair with a baseball cap planted backwards on his head. Looked like he'd been raised hard. Still, the kid looked plenty nervous. The conversation wasn't going anywhere and it was time to wrap it up, but Bartolo was busy playing tough guy again.

"You make sure you get your skinny little face right up to a phone if you hear anything, Freddy," Bartolo said, a menacing look on his face. "And don't fucking forget it."

"Yes, sir," Freddy said, his head bobbing up and down on his thin neck. "I'll call ya. Right away too. I won't forget. Not me, sir."

Conover rolled his eyes. The kid had probably already forgotten what day it was. He was definitely no genius. Their investigation of the harbor murders and last night's disappearance of Dan Marlowe was going nowhere. So he and Bartolo were reduced to scraping the bottom of the barrel for people like this Freddy.

"Come on, let's go," he said to Bartolo. He glanced at Freddy. "Have a good day."

"Yes, sir."

"And don't forget what I told you," Bartolo said.

Conover grabbed his partner's arm and gave him a jerk. "We're wasting our time here."

Conover led the way south on Ocean Boulevard. They cruised past jewelry shops, t-shirt stores, and fast food joints with the smell of fried dough thick in the air.

"What's the story on all these urine-colored people? How come they're the ones running these joints now?" Bartolo asked as they moved by another t-shirt shop with a dark-skinned man standing out front. The man gave Bartolo a dirty look.

"What d'ya know?" Bartolo said, not trying to hide the contempt in his voice. "He can speak English. I'll bet he isn't a citizen though. What do you think they're up to?"

"What do you mean up to?" Conover was irritated with the question. He had more important things on his mind than harassing the locals, citizens or not.

"You know what I mean, Ray," Bartolo said, sounding hot now. "You don't think it's strange that all of a sudden almost every goddamn t-shirt store on the beach is owned by an Iranian or Pakistani or whatever the hell they are?"

"No, I don't, Vinny. It's a free country."

"Yeah. And that's what we're giving it away for–free. Even the t-shirt stores, for Chrissake. See what I mean?" Bartolo nodded in the direction of another t-shirt joint and the men working it. "I feel like I'm in the bazaar in Baghdad walking around here."

Conover shrugged. "Hey, anybody can open a business. That's what it's all about."

"I still think there's something fishy."

Conover didn't want to go down this road with his partner, but still he had to ask. "Like what."

"Like where do they get the money for all of these

stores? Rents are big bucks around here for the season. You wanna know where I think they get it?"

"Okay, tell me," Conover said with a sigh. "Where do they get the money?"

Bartolo gave a smug grin and nodded. "The part of the world they come from . . . it must be either heroin or hashish. I'm telling you, they're hiding big action here."

Conover shook his head in exasperation. He already had enough to deal with without listening to his partner's crackpot ideas. "I doubt it. Besides, we already have enough action to keep us busy."

"Yeah," Bartolo said disgustedly. "But we aren't getting anywhere. And we've talked to every jerk on the beach."

"Then we'll start back at the beginning and talk to every single one of them again if we have to."

"If you'd listened to me, we wouldn't be traipsing around now looking for Marlowe, we'd have him in custody."

"I know, I know," Conover said. Bartolo'd been pushing to put illegal taps on the phones at both Dan Marlowe's cottage and at the High Tide Restaurant. Conover hadn't liked the idea one bit. Still didn't. Good old-fashioned footwork–chasing down leads and asking questions–had always worked for him before. It would work now.

They passed McDonald's and turned down D Street, heading toward the parking lot behind the Casino where they had left their car. It was a sunny, humid morning. Already too warm for even a lightweight sport coat. A great day to be home, air conditioner on high and a cold six-pack in the fridge. But he hadn't had a day off since this investigation started. The sooner they wrapped this one up, the better–for everyone involved.

As soon as they rounded the back corner of the Casino a Hampton police unit pulled into the lot and screeched to a halt in front of them. Two uniformed cops jumped out with guns drawn.

"Get your hands up," one of them shouted.

Bartolo shot Conover a quizzical look. "What the fuck?" he said.

"What the hell's going on?" Conover asked as another cruiser pulled into the lot, disgorging a pair of armed cops.

"I said get your hands up!" the first cop shouted again.

"I'm . . ." Conover began, and before he could finish, the cop moved toward them, his weapon pointed directly at Conover's chest. "Up against the building. Both of you. Now."

The other cops took the first one's lead, keeping their weapons trained on Conover and Bartolo and advancing like trained seals. Very dangerous trained seals.

"Are you crazy?" Bartolo started, but Conover put a hand on his partner's arm.

"I'm Lieutenant Conover with the state police and this is Sergeant Bartolo. We were in your station just the other day, talking with your chief."

"Yeah and I'm Elvis Presley," said another cop, a pimply-faced kid, as he spun Conover around and slammed him hard against the Casino wall.

"Hey, that's my fucking . . ." The first cop grabbed Bartolo, spun him around, and shoved him against the building.

"Look what I got," said Pimple Face, holding up the pistol he'd taken from Conover's shoulder holster.

"Check my wallet," Conover said. "My ID . . ."

"You bet your ass I'll check your wallet," Pimple Face said as he yanked the wallet from Conover's back pocket. He flipped it open. "Oh, oh." He held up the shield and squinted at it.

"Looks real," said the cop holding Bartolo against the wall.

"You bet your ass it's real," Bartolo shouted over his shoulder. "We're state police, you jackass."

Conover grimaced. Calling these jokers names wasn't going to win them any friends.

One of the new arrivals pitched in. "Look, pal, we got a call you just did a transaction with a known dope dealer up on the boulevard."

"Are you for real?" Bartolo growled. "Do we look like dopers? That was Fast Freddie. He couldn't deal his way out of a paper bag, for Chrissake. Besides, we're on an investigation, you nitwits. Didn't you get the word?"

"Easy, Vinny, easy," Conover said. Getting in a shouting match with these locals wasn't going to help. He knew some Hampton cops, but these guys looked like they were all summer help. "Look. We checked in with your chief when we got into town. We're working the Harbor Murders case."

"Well, we got a phone tip and we have to check it out," said another youngster, lowering his weapon. "If you're working the murders, why were you kibitzing with dealers up on the Boulevard?"

Conover took a deep breath. Before this case was over they might need help from one of these young policemen. No use burning any bridges. Besides, the kids were just doing their jobs.

"Following up a lead," Conover said, stretching the truth more than a little. That was the problem with this whole investigation–all their leads were leading nowhere except into trouble. "Your little 'tip' was probably somebody just trying to throw a monkey wrench into our investigation."

"This one's got a statie ID too," said the cop holding Bartolo. He lifted Bartolo's wallet so Pimple Face could see. "Matches his driver's license."

Pimple Face cleared his throat. "Let's take a walk across the street to the station." He nodded in the direction of the one-story cinder block building. "We'll let the chief straighten all this out."

"Hand over my gun," Bartolo demanded as he turned and smoothed his rumpled shirt.

Pimple Face thought for a moment. "We'll talk to the chief first. He says it's okay, we give them back. Come on, let's go. We'll walk."

Two of the Hampton cops stayed with the cruisers. The other two paraded across the parking lot toward the station with Conover and Bartolo in tow.

"Boy, am I going to bust these assholes' balls," Bartolo said. "Pushing us around like that."

"Forget it."

"I can't forget it. We could've been killed. Who the hell would've told them we were doing a dope deal on Ocean Boulevard anyway?"

"Maybe a urine-colored person who speaks English?"

"Why that fucking cocksucker. I'll strangle him when I get my hands on him."

"Come off it, will you," Conover said. "I got something else I want you to do."

"What's that?"

Conover didn't feel good about it, but he knew it had to be done. They were wasting too much time and getting nowhere fast. "Do the tap on Marlowe's cottage. But forget the restaurant. Too many people probably using it."

Bartolo punched air. "Yes! Now you're talking. When?"

"As soon as I explain our way out of this insanity. And could you please clam up and let me do the talking."

"Absolutely, Ray. I'll be nice and cool."

"Yeah, sure," was all Conover said as he walked through the front door of the Hampton Beach police station and up to the big wooden door marked "Chief of Police."

Chapter 27

WHEN HE FINALLY came to, Dan found himself in the dumpster behind the High Tide Restaurant with a bunch of seagulls high stepping in the dumpster around him. The sun was high enough to hurt his eyes and every bone in his body ached. It wasn't just the cuts and bruises left behind by the beating that caused the pain. He couldn't ignore the other pain, the pain in his head, from all that shit they'd made him take. It was a different pain–a pain he was too damn familiar with–just as intense as the pain from the beating, but this pain could last a lot longer.

He struggled to pull himself up on his elbows, scattering gulls in all directions. Dan touched his face gingerly. It was swollen badly, but he still located two eyes, a nose, and his tongue. Then he found the right number of teeth. It could've been a lot worse.

Judging by the sounds he was hearing, Ocean Boulevard

was pretty crowded. Dan shook his head very slowly, trying to clear the cobwebs away, but the cobwebs didn't want to go. It'd probably take a week or more before he started feeling normal again. And that was just to get over the cocaine he'd been force fed. He had no idea how long the physical damage would last.

Lying in all that garbage, with the stink strong enough to slice through his swollen nasal passages, it didn't take long before his brain started to clear enough to start torturing him. Even though all the details about Peralta and the coke and the chick without a tan line were still a bit fuzzy, he remembered enough to know he was lucky he hadn't died of an overdose up there on Boar's Head. Or from the beating. Seemed that guy Wayne had a lot of anger issues.

Dan let out a deep breath. It came out raspy, like he'd just come out of a coal mine. He pulled himself up a bit and looked over the edge of the dumpster. No one was around. Good time to move–if he could get his body in motion. Unless, of course, he wanted to be buried under garbage instead of just sitting on it.

He boosted himself up on his knees, rolled out of the dumpster, and landed on his feet. His legs felt a bit wobbly, but at least he hadn't passed out. His clothes were a mess– red shirt stained with blood, jeans all wrinkled and smelly.

Dan turned at the sound of voices. Three teenage girls were coming down the side street adjacent to the Tide. They were only a few yards away when they noticed him.

They hesitated for a moment, staring at him, then hurried off down the street. He must look even worse than he felt.

He wasn't likely to make it home in this condition. Somehow he had to get cleaned up and get some food into his roiling stomach. Then he could figure out what to do.

Dan stumbled up to the High Tide and pounded on the back door. In less than a minute the door opened, and Dianne stuck her head out. The current owner of the High Tide had a round face framed in long, frizzy black hair streaked with gray. She took one look at Dan's face and swung the heavy door all the way open. "Dan, my god. What happened?"

"I had an accident," he said. Lame excuse, but it was the best he could do right now.

Dianne closed the door after them, guided him over to her small office, and helped him into an old gray easy chair. Then she just stood there, hands on hips, looking at him like he was a kid with a raging fever. Brown stains spotted her white apron. Chili Day. That meant it must be Monday. Monday was always Chili Day.

"Don't move," she said, wiggling her index finger. "Just stay here."

"Don't worry," he mumbled. "I'm not going anywhere." The way both his legs and his belly were feeling he couldn't have gone anywhere even if he'd wanted to.

Dianne hurried out of the office and returned shortly

with some wet cloths and the small first aid kit from the kitchen. She wiped his face with a firm, yet gentle, hand. Every time she touched his face he flinched–it hurt like hell.

"Some of these look bad, Dan," she said. "You ought to go to a hospital and have them checked out."

He couldn't remember ever seeing her this concerned about anything and that worried him. Especially since she'd seen him in pretty bad shape before; not from a beating, of course, but otherwise. "I will. Maybe. Later."

"Dan, what the hell's going on?" she asked as she dabbed ointment on his wounds. "Someone almost kills Shamrock and now this. You're lucky you're alive. It's all about the harbor murders, isn't it? Shamrock . . . you . . . cops everywhere. What the hell's happening to our beach, Dan?"

He didn't think she was really expecting an answer so he kept his mouth shut. Finally, Dianne sat back and frowned. "Do you know who did this to you? Was it the people who beat up Shamrock? Or was it those two cops who've been looking for you?"

Dan shook his head. "I don't want to talk about it, Dianne. Not now." All he wanted to do was crawl into a hole somewhere and wake up in about a week or so.

He yawned even though it hurt, and let his eyelids flutter a little. Dianne didn't push him. Instead, she reached over like she was going to run her hand through his hair, then quickly turned and slid a case of empties across the floor. She grabbed his feet and set them on top of the case.

"All right," she said. "I'll keep everyone away. You stay here and get some sleep."

Sleep. Right. Like he could sleep after what he'd just been through. All he really wanted was a little quiet time. Time to think. Time to plan.

Chapter 28

THERE WAS NOTHING WORSE than knowing what was going down, and yet not knowing who the hell was behind it.

Ray Conover scowled through the binoculars pressed against his eyes. If Dan Marlowe was still alive, sooner or later he'd have to come home. So Conover had sent Bartolo off to check out a nonexistent lead, while Conover and his binoculars headed down to a cottage in the Island section of the beach with a clear view of Dan Marlowe's front porch and door. Conover's jacket and holstered gun were thrown on a dirty, threadbare sofa. A cold McDonald's burger was on a nearby metal tray table.

Conover's stomach grumbled, reminding him he hadn't eaten his food. The last time he'd eaten had been early in the morning, before he and Bartolo had been rousted by the Hampton cops. But he could go without a meal, maybe even two, if it meant connecting back up with Marlowe.

He could understand Marlowe slipping out the back door for an hour or two–maybe he wanted some privacy or wanted to have a few cold ones. But to be gone this long without checking in–that just wouldn't happen. Marlowe was too determined to get the guys who beat up his buddy and save his own skin in the process.

Conover'd been using this little cottage location for the same purpose off and on for the past few days. The foot traffic outside was heavy, even for a summer day. Foot traffic came with its own distractions–like the blonde in the skimpy bikini headed down to the beach.

He leaned back a bit in his metal foldout chair, took another bite out of the burger, and spit it out. Nothing worse than coagulated grease for lunch. Too bad the cottage wasn't as cold as the burger. Even with the windows open, this place was turning into a real hot box.

He dumped the rest of the hamburger onto the tray table, turned back toward the window, and glanced at Dan Marlowe's cottage. What the . . . ? He blinked a couple of times and grabbed the binoculars. A man dressed in pants, a t-shirt, and a Crocodile Dundee hat was standing on Marlowe's porch. A skinny guy. Like the one he'd chased and traded shots with down at the harbor the other day, the little prick who'd given him the finger as he went under the Hampton Bridge in that damn motorboat.

Conover watched as the Crocodile Dundee look-alike opened the screen door and tried the inside handle. After a moment he stepped back, let the screen door close, and looked slowly both ways.

The longer he watched, the more certain Conover became. When the guy walked over to one of the porch windows, lifted the screen, and climbed in, Conover knew he'd hit pay dirt. This was definitely the guy. How nice of the little weasel to walk right into Conover's hands.

He leapt up, almost knocking over his chair. He grabbed his Glock off the sofa, pulled it free of the holster, and hurried out the door. He was off the porch in one leap, jamming the pistol into the back waistband of his pants. No use scaring the natives any more than he had to.

Conover dashed across the street and pressed up tight to the side of Marlowe's cottage. There were two doors in these cottages, front and rear. No way could he watch both. He had to go inside and take him. Now. Before he got away.

He moved slowly along the side of the cottage–back pressed against the rough wood, gun in his right hand, barrel pointed at the sky. He reached the porch, took the steps one at a time, then crossed the porch quickly. When he reached the window he'd seen Crocodile climb through, Conover bent down and peered into the cottage's front room.

Empty.

Sweat tickled down Conover's sides. He took a couple of deep breaths and let them out slowly. He could crash through the front door, but that move would not only cost him the element of surprise, he could wind up with a broken bone or two. That left him with one option–the window.

Conover slipped the Glock back into his waistband, slid his right leg over the sill, and eased through the window onto a ratty couch. He drew his weapon and made another check of the front room. Off to the right was an open door that led to what appeared to be a bedroom. At the end of the small hallway directly in front of him he could see the corner of a refrigerator. The kitchen. And from the thumping and scuffing going on, it sounded like someone was getting an afternoon snack.

He rolled off the couch and rushed over to the wall, weapon at the ready. He swallowed hard to get some moisture back into his mouth and scooted along the wall toward the kitchen.

A quick peek around the corner showed the man with the Crocodile Dundee hat standing on a chair by the sink.

"Freeze! Police!" Conover yelled as he stepped into the kitchen, weapon pointed at the intruder.

The man jerked, bumping his head on a light fixture. "Ow!"

"Don't move or you're fucking dead," Conover said, keeping the Glock trained dead center on the man's back. "Keep your hands on your head and climb down off that chair. Slowly."

"I'll fall."

"Tough. Just do it. And you make one wrong move, you're dead. I've got a gun with a full clip pointed straight at the middle of your back. Give me a reason to see how fast I can empty it. Please."

The man bent his knees and took one step off the chair, teetered backward, then regained his balance, and finally came to a stumbling stop on the floor, hands still on his head.

"Good. Now turn around slowly."

Conover's stomach clenched like someone had head-butted him right in the gut. This wasn't the guy he'd chased down Ocean Boulevard. The guy he held at gunpoint was about sixty years old with a ruddy drinker's face. The only similarity was that he was as skinny as a rail.

"Who the hell are you?" Conover kept his weapon pointed at the man's midsection.

"They call me Fuckin' Schneider," the man said indignantly.

"Well, Fucking Schneider, what the hell are you doing here?"

"I'm fixing the goddamn light fixture up there." Schneider took one hand off his head and pointed up above the sink.

Conover tensed. "Easy, Fucking Schneider. Who told you to fix the light?"

"Who the hell do you think? The man who lives here. Dan Marlowe, that's who."

This was not looking good.

"Ahhh, for Chrissake," Fucking Schneider said, dropping his hands down to his sides. "He told me a couple of months ago to fix it. I'm just gettin' around to it now. I'm a busy man, you know. I'm like a one-armed paperhanger. Especially now that it's summer."

"Why did you come in the window?"

"I ain't got a key and I know Dan keeps that window unlocked. I've used it before."

"How were you going to fix it with no tools?"

"I was going to use Dan's." He pointed to an open tool box on the floor. "I didn't bother bringing mine. It's an easy job."

A handyman, a stinking handyman. Conover lowered his weapon. "All right, fuc . . . uh, Schneider. Here's the story. I'm a police officer and a good friend of Dan's. He's had a few break-ins recently and he asked me to check the place every so often. When I saw you going through the window, you can imagine what I thought."

"Yeah, I can imagine, son," Schneider said. He grabbed his hat with both hands and adjusted it. "But you better be careful who the hell you're pointing that thing at from now on." He nodded at the Glock.

Good thing Bartolo wasn't here. No way would Conover's

partner listen to a lecture from a handyman. Somehow Bartolo would manage to find a way to intimidate the guy, shifting all the blame onto the handyman and then demanding not only his cooperation, but his silence too.

Conover took a deep breath. Now was not the time for bemoaning missing partners, especially when those partners got you into more trouble than they got you out of. "I'm hoping you'll keep our little encounter here quiet. Don't want to spook anyone. I'd still like to catch the creeps who've been breaking into Dan's place."

"I'll keep my mouth shut. For Dan," Schneider said pointedly. "Get on outta here now. I got a light to fix." Schneider waved his hand as if he were a king dismissing a subject.

Conover walked out of the cottage, surveyed the street in front of him, and headed back to his surveillance post to get his things. This wasn't getting him anywhere. He'd have to try something else. He hoped his next step wouldn't be as screwed up as this one. But the way things had been going, he knew that was a lot to hope for.

Chapter 29

DAN DRAGGED his feet off the beer crate and sat up, a move both his head and his body protested. He bent forward, resting his elbows on his knees and his forehead in his hands.

Boar's Head, Shamrock, cocaine.

He stared at the floor, thinking as hard as his aching head would let him think.

Boar's Head, Shamrock, cocaine.

Suddenly, Dan sat up. Shamrock never went anywhere except work and his room down on Ashworth Avenue. He certainly couldn't have hidden all those bags in his little room. Besides, that was the first place the cops and the smugglers would've tossed.

Which brought him right back to the High Tide. And if Shamrock had hidden the cocaine here at the High Tide, where the hell else could it be but in the one place no one ever wanted to go except Shamrock Kelly–the crawl space under the floor Dan was staring at right now. The crawl space was filthy and it stunk and you had to crawl on your hands and knees just to get around. Christ, Dan himself had only gone down there once or twice in all the time he'd owned the business. Dianne hadn't been down there at all. Every so often there'd been a drain backup or some other problem that had to be taken care of. The only one who'd take care of the problem–in fact, volunteer for the duty–was Shamrock Kelly. If he had the dope, the crawl space was the perfect place to hide it. The man came to work so late that even the drunks who splashed out after the bars closed were long gone. No one would've been around to see him hauling the bags from his car to the back door of the restaurant.

Dan eased himself out of the chair, locked the office door, and limped over to the access hatch in the far corner of the room. He grabbed the handle of the wooden trap door and opened it, then gently lowered himself the few feet to the cellar floor. It seemed to take years before he located the string for the single overhead light bulb and pulled, flooding the crawl space with light. And there they were. Against the back wall. Duffel bags stacked neatly one on top of the other.

He crawled over on all fours. He opened the zipper on the closest bag, took one look at the kilos inside, and zipped the bag closed. Then he retraced his steps, unlocked the office door, and sat back in the chair.

Now what? Hand the stuff over to the two state cops and try to convince them that he had nothing to do with its theft and the murders? That the coke just happened to be hidden all this time in the cellar of this restaurant, right below his feet? He almost didn't believe it himself. Even when they had the coke, they'd probably still make life hell for him. Big time.

Besides, he had the smuggler to worry about. How could you protect your family from people like that? In the long run you couldn't.

And Peralta? Dan had to handle him, but that could come later. He owed the man.

So it wasn't hard for Dan to see that handing the stuff over to the smuggler was what he had to do. At least that would keep his family alive. The rest he'd deal with when the time came.

Unfortunately, he'd experienced firsthand what coke could do. His stomach backed up into his throat when he thought about releasing all that shit on the streets. But his children's lives were at stake. His first obligation was to them.

The beating he'd taken must have rattled his brains a bit, because as he sat there on the chair all banged up, his feet up on the empty beer case again, an idea gelled in Dan's head: ask the smuggler for money to get the coke back. Crazy? Maybe. But if this worked, he could use the money to buy back the High Tide or open a new bar. And when his wife saw that he was getting it together again, he might win his family back. It was worth a shot, especially since it was the only shot he had.

Sure the smuggler would probably try to kill Dan before handing over the money, but they'd probably try to kill him anyway.

He'd have to come back tonight after the restaurant was closed and move the coke, but now he had some arrangements to make. Dan got out of the chair, walked out of the office, and right out the High Tides' back door. Outside it was late afternoon and Ocean Boulevard was crowded with people and cars. All the noise made his head throb. His body ached and he had a limp, but he moved along at a good clip.

The first thing Dan did when he got back to the cottage was pull the shotgun out from under his bed and sit down in his chair. He snugged the shotgun in his lap like a child's security blanket, called the beeper number the smuggler had given him, and punched in his phone number. He sat there waiting for the return call, surprised that he felt fairly calm. In about ten minutes the phone rang. On the fourth ring he answered it, told the man on the other end he'd found the missing coke, then listened to the rant.

"Listen, you cocksucker. If you don't hand over my fuckin' product, I'll come over there and cut your cock off and shove it in your mouth."

Dan didn't feel so calm anymore. He squeezed the

shotgun grip and took a deep breath. When the voice on the other end stopped yelling for a moment, Dan told him what he wanted and how he wanted it done. And even though his voice was shaking, he got it all out. And that was something.

Chapter 30

"WE'RE HERE, Boss."

Dominic looked out the Lincoln's window. They were
in a parking lot, one of a couple dozen cars. Outside a
few people walked through the heavy drizzle, heading
towards and then disappearing around, a large gray
bathhouse.

"Don't look like a famous beach. Talkin' Beach–bah.
Whoever named the place was dumb as a post."

"Singing Beach, Boss," Jorge answered, speaking very
slowly, like he was talking to a child. "Singing Beach."

"Singin', Talkin', who gives a fuck?" Dominic shrugged.
"It's a stupid name for a beach. Why the fuck they call it
that anyway?"

"I heard it sings like Sinatra," Sal piped in. No one even
chuckled.

"It's because of the sand," Jorge explained. "It makes

a noise when you walk on it. Kind of like a squeaking sound."

"Ahhh, I don't believe that," Dominic said. How the hell did the kid know something like that? Dominic had lived around Boston his whole damn life and he'd never heard of a beach that could sing. Yet the kid–smartass that he was–knew all about it.

But that was one of the reasons he was going to leave the kid in charge of the business when he went south anyway. The kid had a good head on his shoulders. Knew stuff that would keep him ahead of the boys. And those smarts were going to keep Dominic comfortable in Florida, real nice-like.

A carrot-topped teenager with a black windbreaker sporting the words "Parking Attendant" walked up to the driver's side window. Sal lowered the window.

"Sir, you need a parking sticker to park here." Carrot-Top's eyes were locked on two young cuties sauntering by.

"Kid, look at me," Sal said. The kid slowly turned, an insolent look in his eyes.

"Get the fuck outta here." Sal tapped the pistol tucked under his coat. Carrot-Top blinked twice, then headed back to his booth.

Jorge turned in his seat to look at Dominic. "There wouldn't be any parking except for this rain. It's usually packed this time of year. Our meet guy must've checked the forecast."

"So, he's smart. We're smarter," Dominic said. He'd

spent enough time thinking through all the ifs, ands, and buts on the drive over. There was two hundred grand in the trunk, compensation for the sleazebag who'd ripped off his product.

Some punk steals his–Dominic Carpucci's–product and then demands that he buy it back? Wasn't going to happen. He still didn't have a plan, but that didn't matter. He was real close now. So close he could almost smell his product. Time to go get it back.

Dominic opened his door and slid out into the rain. "Let's go see if we can make some dreams come true."

A puzzled expression flashed across Jorge's face. Surprised at the statement or the fact Dominic had opened his own door? Either way, it was good to keep the kid on his toes.   Dominic chuckled to himself as the look disappeared.

"Sure, Boss," Jorge said. "Whatever you say."

Chapter 31

DAN WASN'T EXACTLY sure why the hell he'd suggested Singing Beach as a location to meet, except that it was the only place where he might have a chance to pull this deal off without the smuggler being able to get his hands on him. He'd listened to the weather, knew it wouldn't be crowded. He felt comfortable near the ocean, but it couldn't be Hampton. Too many familiar faces around. And he knew Singing Beach pretty well.

Besides, if he hadn't said someplace fast, the guy with the dirty mouth would've come up with a location himself. Dan hadn't wanted that. He needed an extra day or two to transfer the cocaine and he wanted to pick a switch location where he was in control. He was going to call the shots on this. Otherwise, he wouldn't have a prayer of coming out of this little adventure alive.

He'd settled on asking for two hundred grand. Too

high and he wouldn't have a chance in hell of getting the money. Besides, he wasn't greedy. Two hundred grand along with some legitimate financing would be enough to get him back in the restaurant business.

He'd arrived forty-five minutes early, wanting to be in position before Garbage Mouth showed up. From his vantage point high up on the rocks at the north end of the beach Dan would be able to spot anyone approaching from the parking lot. Beside him, stuck between two rocks and within easy reach, was Betsy.

It was mid-morning with solid clouds overhead and a good drizzle. Not a beach day for sure, but a number of people, some with dogs, were still walking along the water's edge.

Dan stuck his thumb and forefinger into the change pocket of his Levi's. He could feel the key to the storage unit where he'd stashed the coke. Touching the key made him feel a bit better–or maybe it was the yellow valium he'd taken an hour ago.

Would the smuggler really hand over two hundred grand to get back his own cocaine?

The whole idea seemed a lot more farfetched now that it was about to go down. He wasn't sitting in his favorite chair back at the cottage. This was the real deal. And the more Dan thought about it, the more he figured he might not get out of this with his life, let alone the money. What the hell had he been thinking?

At the far end of the beach two men high-stepped across

the sand, heading straight toward him. Had to be him. Smuggler and Company. The pair didn't look like local Yankees, that was for damn sure. The first was medium height, suit, compact like a fireplug, walking like he meant business. Even at this distance, Dan could see the guy walking a step behind the first was all muscle. He was taller than the first guy and casually dressed. The tall guy was dark, Hispanic maybe, and he was carrying a very large gym bag in his right hand.

Dan didn't say a word as they trudged across the sand and finally reached the base of the rocks down below. The shorter one looked up at Dan, placed his foot on the rocks, and started to climb.

"That's close enough," Dan said, pitching his voice loud enough for them to hear.

The man hesitated, a frown on his wide face. "We're gonna talk like this? You up there and us down here? There's people around."

"There's nobody close enough to hear us," Dan answered. There were some people strolling along the beach, but not many. Only a few made it as far as the rocks, and the ones who did turned around and headed straight back without lingering.

"We'd still rather come up there and talk." The shorter guy sounded like he was used to giving orders–and having them followed.

"I'm sure you would," Dan called down. "But if you move one more foot, I'll be gone and so will your packages." He'd scoped out an escape route earlier that morning: through the bushes behind him, through the yard of one of the cliffside houses, and out to his car parked on the street. "You'll never see me or your stuff again."

"All right, all right," the shorter man said like he wasn't used to agreeing to someone else's demands. This guy must be the foul-mouthed jerk Dan had talked to on the phone.

"You've got the money?" Dan asked. His voice cracked. Not surprising, considering he could hardly breathe. He was amazed that he could talk at all.

"We got it. But we wanna get a look–see at our merchandise first."

They were trying to play him, Dan realized. Time to show these guys he wasn't messing around. This little deal meant too much and he wasn't going to blow it.

"You're not going to see anything." Dan's voice shook, but he didn't give a damn. "Not until I see what I want."

"Don't worry about it. Ya wanna see it, ya can see it."

The smuggler turned to the taller man–definitely Hispanic–and nodded. The Hispanic opened the gym bag and held it out so Dan could check out the contents. Even at this distance, it looked like real cash. But two hundred grand?

That's when Dan realized the shortcoming to his plan– how the hell could he tell how much money was in the bag from way up here? He wasn't an eagle. Still, it looked like a lot of money.

Maybe this was really going to work.

"See," the smuggler said. "That's yours. No problem. Now we're comin' up."

The smuggler stuck his foot back on the first rock.

"Don't make another move," Dan said. He reached over and curled his fingers around the stock of the shotgun, keeping his eyes glued on the two men below.

The smuggler blew his top. "Look, you fuckin' asshole. You gimme that stuff or you'll be eatin' your cock. And I mean now."

Dan didn't doubt for a second the guy would do it if he had the chance. The man was for real–a heavy. He took a deep breath. "This is the way we're playing it. I'm going to throw you a key. You're going to pick it up and walk away, leaving the bag behind."

"So you can rip me off again, motherfucker? Not fuckin' likely. You get the gym bag when I get my stuff, not before."

Dan slid Betsy from her hiding place and drew the shotgun close. He kept the barrel out of sight, but ready. Maybe this wasn't going to turn out like he'd hoped after all. Maybe, just maybe, Singing Beach was the last beach he'd ever see. And wasn't that a kick in the ass.

Chapter 32

DOMINIC HAD WANTED Sal to walk to the rocks with them, but Jorge had suggested that someone stay with the car, in case this joker they were meeting had a trick up his sleeve. That wasn't Jorge's real reason for wanting Sal to stay behind, but Dominic'd bought it and had told Sal to stay put.

Now the old man wouldn't shut up, just kept yelling and screaming and threatening the guy with their coke. Jorge shuffled his shoes back and forth in the sand, listening to it squeak. How the hell could the old man have been such a big wheel in Boston for so long and never have heard of this beach and its singing sand? Yeah, the old man wasn't an old-money Yankee like most of the local snobbery. But neither was he. Still, the old man could probably buy and sell a lot of these snobs. And if things went like Jorge planned, he'd be able to do the same someday.

The ocean was the color of black ice today and probably just as cold. Small waves slapped gently against the white sand. Rock formations at both ends of the beach enclosed it like parentheses. Some expensive homes, set back from the sand, ran the length of the beach. Other residences, situated high above on the rocks, faced out over the ocean. No wonder the old Yankee families had claimed this place for their own one hundred years ago.

He'd read somewhere that some of those original Boston Brahmins had made their dough in opium, and that was real encouraging. He could almost visualize one hundred years from now all the old-moneyed Yankees gone from this beautiful beach, replaced by rich Hispanic families. And one hundred years after that it would be said some of them had made their money in cocaine.

Jorge glanced again at the man up in the rocks. He had to hand it to the guy–no way they'd get up there before he made good with his escape. No dummy this one. Jorge lowered his gaze. Too bad he couldn't say the same thing about the old man in front of him. If he didn't watch carefully, the old guinea's stupid Italian temper would screw up everything.

All the old man cared about now was making enough dough so he could retire to Florida and either let a lucrative cocaine distributorship network die or hand it over to one of his young Italian punks. The punks that had done next to nothing for the organization while he, Jorge, had worked and sweated for years helping the old man run the business. And now to be cut out and left with nothing? No way. Not if he could help it.

The way Jorge had it figured whoever controlled the coke would be the man. The dealers–in fact, the whole organization Dominic had built up over the years–weren't particularly loyal. They'd buy from whoever had the coke. And they'd buy again and again and again. For years. Forever maybe.

And the suppliers? They'd sell to any reliable and trustworthy man they saw was able to move so much product. It was just business, just economics, nothing more. And whoever that man was would be the new boss.

Yep, the key to taking over the whole operation was that hundred kilos of coke.

Good thing this guy was smart. The old man would put a bullet in the guy's head as soon as he got a chance whether he had the coke with him or not. The old fool would fly into a rage and pull the trigger without thinking. They wouldn't get anywhere if the guy was dead and the coke wasn't with him.

Only one problem–the old man'd never give up two hundred dollars let alone two hundred grand. Stubborn fool. He'd hem and haw, charm and threaten, lie and exaggerate, anything, but there was no way he'd hand over the money. He wanted every stinking penny he could get his hands on. Well, that was all right if it was your own life you were going to fuck up, but this old man was about to take Jorge down with him.

Jorge glanced around. This end of the beach was empty except for their little party.

"Give the fucker one more peek." Dominic waved at Jorge to open the gym bag. As if the guy hadn't seen it the first time. Ridiculous.

"You see–I kept my word. Now you're gonna keep yours." Dominic moved forward for the umpteenth time.

"I told you before," said the guy on the rocks. "One more step and I'm gone."

The old man went completely bananas and started screaming every dirty epithet he could squeeze out of his mouth. Jorge wasn't surprised, just vaguely disappointed. Here was a man he'd looked up to at one time. A man he had truly admired and considered his boss. A man who had been very good at what he did. Who had been ruthless but smart–very smart–with business. A man Jorge had respected.

Those days were all over, and what was happening now proved it. If he waited any longer to make his move, there'd be nothing left to move.

The back of Dominic's neck flushed red, and his body stiffened with rage. He turned to Jorge. "We're gonna go up there and kill the cocksucker."

Dominic pulled a handgun out from under his suit jacket and turned back toward the guy up in the rocks.

At the same time Jorge opened the gym bag and removed a .22 hidden below a couple of layers of bills. He glanced up at the guy sitting on the rocks and saw what he was pretty sure was a shotgun nestled in his arms. That'd be fun, Jorge mused. Trying to take a guy with a shotgun sitting in the crow's nest.

Jorge removed a silencer from his pocket. He quickly attached it to the barrel of the .22. He glanced around; no one was near. The old man was moving, one foot up on a large rock getting ready to climb. No doubt now—the crazy old bastard had definitely lost it.

Jorge took two quick steps, right arm outstretched, gun in his hand, and when the barrel was just inches away from the back of Dominic's head, Jorge pulled the trigger quick three times. The shots sounded like loud farts, and Dominic Carpucci's skull had bullets bouncing around inside it as he went down, crumpling on the sand.

Jorge stared at Dominic's body for a long second. It had to be done; he'd had no choice. He glanced up at the man on the rocks. Making Swiss cheese out of a man's brains was easy. Getting back the coke might be a little more difficult.

Chapter 33

DAN HAD TO FIGHT to catch his breath. He swung the shotgun around so it was pointing at the Hispanic man down below. The barrel of the shotgun bobbed up and down. He clenched the stock tight, trying to squeeze the shakes from his hands. Would the Hispanic make a move? Or maybe even worse–would Dan have to use the shotgun?

Things were definitely not going as planned.

The Hispanic glanced around, unscrewed the silencer, put it back in his pocket, and tucked the gun somewhere in the back of his pants. "He was in the way of us making a deal, wasn't he?"

"Was he?" Dan kept Betsy pointed at the Hispanic.

"Of course he was." The man was real calm and confident, like he did this every day. "And you didn't see a thing either, did you?"

"Not a thing." There was something weird about how

this was unfolding. Here he was pointing a shotgun at a man who'd put his gun away and the guy was telling him what to say.

"He wasn't going to let you leave with the money, you know."

"What do you mean?"

"Simple. He was going to do to you what I just did to him."

What the Hispanic said blew away the valium in Dan's bloodstream.

The Hispanic pointed the toe of his shoe at the body on the sand. "He was lying to you all the way. He was going to kill you. I told him not to; he wouldn't listen. Like I said, he was in the way of us making a deal."

Dan stared at the Hispanic with the gym bag full of money. Maybe this man didn't realize that all Dan wanted was the money, nothing else. He wouldn't double-cross the guy, not with his family vulnerable. And he wanted no part of the cocaine. But he'd have to make this new guy believe it if Dan wanted to walk away from Singing Beach in one piece and with the money.

How do you tell someone you don't want something worth millions of dollars? How do you tell him—and get him to believe you—so he doesn't think it's a trick?

"I know it's the money you want," the man said, pointing at the bag on the sand. "Why would you have gone this way if it was anything else? All I want is the product."

"If I tell you where it is, you'll leave the bag?"

The Hispanic nodded. "Of course. Like you said–if I didn't, maybe you'd call the cops, have them get there before I do. I'm ninety percent sure your family means too much to you to try that little trick. And I'm willing to pay a security deposit for that ten percent I'm not sure sure about." He kicked sand at the gym bag. "Two hundred grand. All yours."

"How do you know I'd be telling the truth when I told you where it was?"

The Hispanic very serious now–no bullshit. "Because I'm telling you the truth . . . the money is yours. But I'm also telling you the truth when I tell you that if you try to screw me, I'll hunt you down and that'll be after I visit your family."

Dan took the key out of his pocket and tossed it. The Hispanic snatched the key hard with one hand.

"Safe and Sound Storage on Route One in Saugus," Dan said. "Storage room number's on the key." He gripped the shotgun hard, pointing it at the man below.

Nothing left to do now except pray the Hispanic walked away without the bag. If he didn't, Dan just might go crazy and blow the guy away. Without his restaurant and the chance it might've given him to win his family back, well, he might as well put the shotgun in his mouth right now.

Dan stared at the bag until his stomach tied itself into knots. Finally, the Hispanic flipped the key up in the air, caught it again, and turned to leave.

"What about him?"

The Hispanic jerked his chin at the body lying there with bullets in its head. "No one's going to cry over him, not even the cops. Although I'd advise you not to be here when they come." He hesitated, then added, "Kid." He smiled and walked away.

Dan hesitated for only a minute before scooting down the rocks and grabbing the blue gym bag. He forced his gaze away from the body as he hefted the bag in his right hand. Felt good, heavy. Then he bounded back up the rocks, grabbed the shotgun, and got the hell out of Dodge.

Chapter 34

BUZZ AND SKINNY MISSING their chance to grab Dan Marlowe at the fireworks show had turned out to be a blessing in disguise. The next day Buzz had been informed by one of his associates on the Drug Task Force that the state police had Marlowe under surveillance. The cop had told Buzz that the state police knew Marlowe didn't have the cocaine but might lead them to it. So Buzz had decided he'd be better off keeping a close tail on Carpucci and his crew. Carpucci would track down his coke, and when he did Buzz would be right there to steal it again.

This time they'd followed Carpucci right into the parking lot at Singing Beach in Manchester-by-the-Sea and now he and Skinny were sitting around, twiddling their thumbs, waiting. Again.

Buzz shoved the car door open. "Come on, we've waited long enough. This has to be it."

"You mean we're gonna take 'em here?" Skinny's tongue whipped around his lips. "There's people around." He tipped his head at the other cars scattered around the lot.

"If this is where we have to do it, then that's all there is to it." Buzz was out of the car now, leaning down and looking through the driver's side window at Skinny. "You saw that gym bag. They aren't doing calisthenics down there. Something's up. Now get your goddamn skinny little ass out of there."

"Sure, Buzz, sure." Skinny leapt out of the car, slamming the door behind him.

"Got your piece ready?"

Skinny reached into the pocket of his imitation brown leather jacket. "Sure. I got it."

"Let's go."

Buzz headed toward the beach. He didn't waste any time, crossing the parking lot in long strides that forced Skinny to do a weird little skip every so often to keep up.

They went around the far side of the bathhouse, staying out of sight of the driver still sitting in the Lincoln. A few steps later, Buzz and Skinny were standing on the sand. Buzz stopped for a minute and looked both ways to get his bearings. There was a sprinkling of people on the beach, some walking alone, some in couples, others with dogs. Most everyone was dressed in sweats and windbreakers, a fashion statement neither he nor Skinny lived up to.

"There's one of them." Skinny pointed down the beach to their left.

Buzz shoved Skinny's hand down. "I can see him, moron, you don't have to point." It wasn't like he could miss the guy. How many big spics wearing expensive clothes you got walking on a beach like this anyway? And this one was way down at the end of the beach, heading back this way. By himself.

Where the hell was Carpucci?

"Where's Carpucci?" Skinny asked, furrowing his eyebrow. "And where's the bag?"

"How do I know? Come on. Let's go get a look-see." He gave Skinny a little shove and the two of them, looking like some kind of Mutt-and-Jeff team, started trudging across the sand.

"Hey," Skinny said, hitting a real high note. "Ain't that cute?"

"Ain't . . . I mean . . . isn't what cute?" Buzz said, trying to keep his mind on what was at hand. Not an easy task what with Skinny's voice hitting the ceiling again and giving Buzz chills right up his spine and into his head. He wouldn't have to listen to that lousy voice too much longer. What a pleasant thought.

"The sand," Skinny answered. He was looking down with a look on his face like maybe some acid he took in '68 was kicking in again. "It's making a noise."

"It's squeaking. This is Singing Beach, Dumbo. The sand makes a squeaking noise when you walk on it, so they call it Singing Beach. Get it?"

"If it squeaks, why do they call it Singing Beach? Why not Squeaking Beach?"

For a moment, Buzz forgot about the spic. He stared at Skinny. No wonder everything on this scam had gone wrong right from the start. He must have had rocks in his head bringing a dimwit like Skinny in on a once-in-a-lifetime score like this. Too late to worry about that now.

"Will you just shut the fuck up." And Skinny did shut up–for all of five seconds.

"What do ya think is in the gym bag, Buzz?"

Buzz'd been mulling the same thing over in his head ever since he'd seen the spic remove it from the trunk. "It isn't jockstraps and deodorant, that's for shitting sure. It has to be cash. And if I'm right, then Carpucci's here to buy his own stuff back."

Skinny's eyes glazed. "You mean it's full of money?"

"That's exactly what I mean."

"How much, you think?" Skinny asked dreamily.

"How should I know, Birdbrain? I don't have x-ray eyes."

Buzz'd been involved in enough busts through the years where cash had been confiscated in everything from paper bags to varying size boxes to the inside of socks still on someone's feet. In other words, he had enough experience to make an educated guess. The way Buzz had it figured a big gym bag, like the one Carpucci's boy had been toting, could hold maybe a few hundred thousand in big bills. Hard to imagine a man with Carpucci's reputation handing over that kind of dough for his own merchandise.

The spic was getting closer to them now, and beyond him, where the beach ended at the rocks, Buzz could see the bag and something else just sitting there in the sand.

"Move," Buzz shoved Skinny forward. "We're going closer."

"He'll make us," Skinny whined.

And Buzz had to admit he was right again. The spic was going to pass within yards of them. He'd make the pair of them if Buzz didn't do something fast. He reached over, wrapped his arm around Skinny's thin waist, and pulled him close, using his other hand to force Skinny's head onto his shoulder.

"Hey! What the fuck?" Skinny jerked and pulled, trying to get out of Buzz's tight embrace.

"Shut up, you little asshole," Buzz said as he gave Skinny a hard noogie rub on his head. "Believe me, I don't like this any better than you. But Carpucci's boy won't look twice at a couple of queers strolling the beach." Buzz gave Skinny a good tug and they started moving in the direction of the rocks.

"Jesus, I hope nobody I know sees me," Skinny muttered as they walked, his head buried in Buzz's big shoulder, their arms around each other's waist, real romantic-like. Buzz pulled Skinny's head in even tighter to his shoulder and lowered his own head onto it. He veered them off a bit in the direction of the water. The spic still passed too close for Buzz's comfort, but if he took note of them he didn't show it.

"Sees you? For Chrissake, the only people that you know haven't been out of Charlestown in twenty years except to stickup a bank or go to the joint. Shut up so I can see what's going on." Now Buzz could see a man high up in the rocks and if he didn't have a shotgun in his hands, Buzz'd eat his hat. In the sand below him was the gym bag and . . . Jesus–a body!

Dominic Carpucci.

Buzz walked Skinny as close to the bag and the body as he dared before they turned and slowly headed back the way they'd come. The spic disappeared behind the bathhouse.

"What's happening?" Skinny mumbled, his head still plastered to Buzz's shoulder. "See anything?"

"Shut up." Buzz spun around and started heading back toward the rocks real slow, both of them hugging tight as lovers.

Skinny had a bird's eye view of the rocks now. "Carpucci! What's he doing on the sand?"

"He's not taking a nap, genius. The spic must've drilled him. Now shut up."

"He's getting away." Skinny suddenly pulled himself free from Buzz's love embrace. "He's got the money. What are we waiting for?"

Buzz had to decide. Fast. No way to know how much

was in the bag–fifty grand? Three hundred grand? Three hundred grand sure wasn't what it used to be. It wouldn't even come close to letting Buzz retire in comfort.

"What are we going to do? They're both gettin' away. Jesus, Buzz."

Buzz didn't need a scorecard to figure out where the spic was headed. He'd found the cocaine and was probably on his way to a hundred-kilo payday. A payday worth at least two and a half million uncut. Didn't need to be a math whiz to figure that one out.

"Come on," Buzz sprinted toward the bathhouse. "We have to get to the car before the spic takes off."

Skinny ran right behind him. "What about the bread?"

"Forget the bread, you dope. We're going for the main course."

Chapter 35

"WE'RE HERE," Sal said. He made a quick right at the Safe & Sound Storage sign and drove through the open gate in the chain link fence. "Which one do we want?"

"Just drive. I'll tell you when to stop." Jorge peered at the unit numbers as the Lincoln cruised between the corrugated steel buildings. He wiped his sweaty palms on his pants, pulled the storage unit key out of his suit pocket, and turned the key over in his hand. If those sweet little footballs weren't hiding behind Door #1 . . .

Jorge glanced again at the unit numbers. No use contemplating what he'd do to the guy if the coke wasn't in the unit like he'd promised. He'd take care of that if and when that time came.

"There it is," Jorge said. He jabbed his finger in the direction of one of the units. "That's the one we want. Pull right up in front of it and stay in the car."

He swallowed hard and took a deep breath before opening the car door. His entire future was riding on this gamble. He walked up to the door, fumbled with the key and padlock. After what seemed an eternity, the padlock clicked open. Jorge rolled up the overhead garage door, and stepped inside.

At first, it appeared the unit was empty. He clenched his teeth, refusing to accept what his eyes were trying to tell him. He found a string dangling close at hand and yanked hard. Overhead a single light bulb flared to life. His initial impression had been right–the storage unit was empty. Except for a pile of duffel bags stacked against the far wall.

His heart skipped a beat. This was it. His future.

For the first time since leaving the beach, Jorge allowed himself to really think about the street value of what he was about to unleash on his little corner of the world. Fifty of the keys out the door as is for $25,000 each, cash up front; twenty fronted to fast pays at $30,000 per; and the last thirty he'd whack up into forty and piece out for $35,000 each to the small potatoes people who took their sweet time to pay and bled the product dry to boot. Three and a quarter million–rock bottom. Made the two hundred grand he'd just given up seem like peanuts.

He walked over to the bags and opened one, half expecting to find someone's old gym socks. Instead, he found himself looking at neatly wrapped white bundles.

His cocaine. Still in their original Colombian wrappings.

Jorge smiled. This was just the beginning. With the kind of money he'd be raking in now everything would be wide open to him–both legitimate and illegitimate. First he'd plow the profits into lucrative real estate deals, nightclubs, and any cash business he could get his hands on. Maybe even bankroll other coke smugglers, so he was even farther away from the stuff. He could help out some fledgling Hispanic politicians he'd had an eye on, too. The same way the Italian, Irish, and Jewish gangsters had done it years ago. He'd help get some of his own kind elected, and in turn, they'd help him out. Soon he'd be so well connected and insulated that no one–not even the feds–would be able to touch him.

He walked out of the storage room like he was worth a million bucks. Outside the world looked brighter in spite of the drizzle. Sal was still sitting in the Lincoln, fingers tapping on the steering wheel. The big man wasn't the brightest bulb on the Christmas tree, but he'd been around long enough to realize what Jorge returning alone from the beach meant–and what might happen to him if he asked too many questions. He'd accepted the new change without saying a word. Jorge would make sure Sal was well rewarded. In fact, Jorge'd let a lot of money trickle down through the ranks. He wasn't stupid–that money would bring him respect and loyalty, two qualities he needed to realize his dreams.

Nice to stand here and realize he was now the one giving the orders. Never again would he have to take orders from guineas whose every other word was, "dem, dese, dose." And the *Eye*talians that worked for him would have to work harder than others to prove themselves, like he'd had to do all these years. The ones that proved themselves he'd use; the others would be history.

If he played his cards right, he could become the biggest coke dealer in Boston. New England, too. Maybe even the whole country. There'd never been a Hispanic godfather, at least not in the United States. But why not? If someone had the talent, the means, and the balls, the sky was the limit.

And when Helen's snotty parents got a glimpse at the magnitude of his new wealth, they'd change their tune. They'd welcome him as a son-in-law and with open arms too, just as if he were some kind of Spanish aristocrat. At least the old bag wouldn't be slamming the phone down on him anymore when he called, that was for sure.

Jorge went over to the Lincoln and waved at Sal to roll down the window. He gave a quick smile, feeling a sense of power flooding through his veins. "This is it, Sal. Come on and give me a hand."

"Sure." Sal climbed out of the car and together they headed into the storage unit, neither man aware of the four pairs of eyes watching them closely.

Two of those pairs of eyes belonged to Lieutenant John O'Brien and Inspector Carl Bumpers of the Saugus Police Department. The partners were sitting nearby in an unmarked car. They were on stakeout, looking for some B & E suspects who were using one of the storage rooms to stash loot. They'd been there quite a while and were just about to leave when two men had pulled up to one of the nearby units in a black Lincoln. Now they watched the men transfer duffel bags from the storage room to the Lincoln's trunk.

In a real hurry about something, O'Brien mused to himself. He was nearing retirement age and contrary to the popular trend, was not looking forward to retirement. Yeah, his hair'd gone gray and was a little thin in places, he had been forced to wear glasses when he couldn't pass the firearms test, and his belly stuck out enough to shake hands with the steering wheel, but his mind was still sharp. And that mind told O'Brien that something was not quite right about the guys tossing duffle bags into their trunk.

"Shit," Bumpers said, shaking his head. "They're not ours. Might as well head in and get our paperwork finished."

O'Brien glanced at his partner sitting in the passenger seat. Bumpers was young, black, and sharply dressed, a combination that never failed to amuse O'Brien. His own plainclothes "uniform" consisted of a navy sports coat that had fit nicely but now, because of his expanding girth, was two sizes too small; a white dress shirt; the same style tie he'd worn at his wedding eons ago; and black cotton slacks. Not to forget the white socks with black tie shoes.

"Hold on for a second. I'd like to see what this guy's up to."

"Up to?" Bumpers said, the annoyance in his voice growing. "They're loading stuff from a storage room. So what? That's what these places are for, aren't they? They're not our perps, I can tell you that."

"No, they're not." O'Brien would have to handle this carefully. He and Bumpers got along well, and he wanted to keep it that way. After all, he spent as much time with his partner every day as he did with his wife. And just like with a wife, it didn't pay to start trouble with a partner. "But that character got out of the car a little too fast. He's real anxious about something. Let's just see. I have a feeling."

"A feeling?" Bumpers asked skeptically. "Or is it because the man's Hispanic?"

"No, it's not because he's Hispanic, smartass," O'Brien said. "I told you, he was a little too anxious hopping out of that car. It doesn't hurt any to check it out. We got the time."

"I just don't think it's right, us watching this man because his skin's dark." Bumpers craned his neck and sat up straighter.

O'Brien's temperature raised a notch. This was the

second time today that Bumpers had accused him of being prejudiced. "Hey, am I the Lieutenant or are you?"

Bumpers turned his head to look out the passenger side window. "You are . . . Lieutenant."

"Good," O'Brien said emphatically. "And as the commanding officer of this here partnership, I say we hang around and keep an eye on these fellas a few minutes longer, and it isn't because one of them's Hispanic."

The two men threw what must've been their last load into the trunk. The guy who slammed the trunk shut was a big guy . . . period. Tough looking and definitely not Hispanic. Maybe Italian. If this guy wasn't a hood, then O'Brien would invest in a pair of those fag contact lenses his wife was always bugging him to get.

The men stood facing each other with the Hispanic chattering away.

"You think maybe that big guy had Granny's laundry stored in there?" O'Brien asked, glancing at Bumpers out of the corner of his eye.

"All right, all right." Bumpers nodded. "He does look a little shady."

"Thank you, Inspector."

They continued to watch as the two men stood there, the Hispanic still talking up a storm and moving his hands around like he was the Italian.

"What is it, John?" Bumpers asked, a bit more respect in his voice. "Pot?"

"Nah," O'Brien answered, shaking his head. "They're

not the type. Either of them."

"What do you want to do then?"

"We could pull them over." O'Brien held his breath for a second, pretty certain he knew what Bumpers would say to that one.

"No probable cause."

"Yeah, yeah."

The driver got behind the wheel and the Hispanic went back, closed the storage unit door, and locked it. He returned to the car, started to reach for the front passenger door, and hesitated. Then he took a step back, opened the rear door, and hopped in.

"What the hell was that all about?" O'Brien asked incredulously.

"That is strange." Bumpers shrugged.

"A little too strange for my blood," O'Brien said. "We'll do a routine stop on them. Hell with probable cause."

"Yeah, okay," Bumpers said, his voice tight and a half an octave higher than normal. The kid was nervous–or excited. Hard to tell which with this guy. O'Brien's gut was feeling a bit queasy at the thought of making the stop–that never changed. Out of the corner of his eye he saw Bumpers touch his weapon, then pull away, reassured the weapon was still in place.

Might turn out to be nothing. Then again, his gut was usually right, especially in matters of the darker kind. O'Brien started the engine and waited for the Lincoln to pull out.

Buzz had had no trouble following the black Lincoln from Singing Beach to the storage facility in Saugus–if he didn't count having to listen to Skinny's constant bitching about not going after the guy with the gym bag. Buzz had finally shut Skinny up with the threat of a smack in the mouth. It had worked–for a while.

When Buzz saw the Lincoln turn into the storage facility, he'd driven the car quickly through the open chain link fence, heading for the building adjacent to the one the Lincoln had disappeared behind. Now they were far enough back not to be noticed, but close enough to watch the spic and his goon load the trunk full of duffel bags. Then the spic hopped in back like he was John Gotti or something.

Buzz grinned. "Well, well. Didn't your mother ever tell you not to count your chickens before they hatched?" He reached forward and started the engine.

"He probably had a million bucks in that gym bag."

"If you say one more word about that guy and his gym bag, I'm gonna tear your fucking head off."

Skinny slipped a stick of gum out of his pocket, stuck the gum in his mouth, and chewed like a squirrel on speed.

"But how do you know . . .?"

Buzz cut him off. "What do you think is in those duffel bags they just threw in the trunk–living room furniture?"

"Wow! You think it's in the trunk, Buzz? Huh, huh?" Skinny was really working his gum now.

"Of course, lame brain. They don't look like they coach a youth hockey team, do they?"

"Nah, nah. I just was saying . . ." Skinny's voice slowed. "One hundred keys. 200 pounds. Jesus, that's a lot of coke."

"Your math's off," Buzz said, not taking his eyes off the Lincoln for a second. "More like 220 pounds. But you're right about it being a lot."

"Here they come! We gonna take 'em?"

Buzz could see the fear all over the thin man's face. Even if Skinny could handle what went down today, eventually he'd get jammed up on something and he'd flip like an acrobat.

A real lousy feeling flooded through Buzz. He and Skinny'd been through a lot together and that time was coming to an end. Buzz gave his head a little shake. He didn't have time to feel guilty about that now.

"No, not here. Someone might have seen us drive in. We'll follow them to wherever they're going to stash it. Then we take them."

"What if they lose us?" Skinny said, fear and excitement cranking his voice even higher.

"Jesus, will you lower your fucking voice. It's going right through me. We aren't going to lose them. That stuff isn't going anywhere except from their trunk into ours."

"Here they come," Skinny said again. The Lincoln drove right by them, the goon driving, the spic in back, both looking straight ahead. Buzz put the Sentra in drive . . .

"What the fuck?" A brown Ford blew by them only a few car lengths behind the Lincoln.

"Cops," Skinny shrieked. "I can tell by their bald heads."

"Motherfucker!" This couldn't be happening. Not when he was so close. Buzz banged the steering wheel with his fist so hard the whole car shook.

"What are we going to do?" Skinny whined.

"I don't know, but this isn't over yet." Buzz hit the gas and fell in line behind the unmarked cop car.

Chapter 36

THE LINCOLN HAD JUST passed through the front gate and was stopped waiting for the traffic on Route 1 to clear. Jorge glanced up and saw Sal looking at him in the rearview, his eyes big, puzzled, maybe even a little scared.

"I'm going to take care of you, Sal. A lot better than the old man did. You got my word on that. You're covered."

The big man's face relaxed. He was smart enough to know this little shakeup was as natural as the seasons. Just something that had to happen, like the sun coming up. "Sure, Jor . . . ah, Boss. Whatever you say."

That four letter word–Boss–sounded real nice. Made him feel like a damn peacock.

He'd just started to enjoy it when Sal shouted, "Fuck." The big man was checking something out behind them in the rearview mirror.

"What's the matter?" Jorge's muscles tensed.

"An unmarked comin' up right behind us."

"You sure?"

"I am now. He just put the flasher on."

Motherfucker! Jorge turned. Sure enough, a brown Ford was coming up on them, dashboard light flashing.

A setup. It had to be. They were watching that damn storage unit all the time.

Twenty years mandatory, no parole, flashed through his mind. Twenty lousy, stinking years behind bars. Minimum for the amount of coke they had in the trunk. That's if they didn't nail him for the carcass back on the beach.

No taking over the operation, no running the show, no becoming rich and powerful, no being the boss, and worst of all–no Helen. In twenty years he'd be an old man. Too old to start over again. Unless he wanted to go back to a street corner pushing grams and eight balls. He'd rather be dead. He had no other choice–it was all or nothing.

"Punch it, Sal."

Sal looked back over his right shoulder. "Why don't we just play it cool? Take our chances. Maybe it's nothing."

Jorge whipped out his .22, same one he did Dominic with. "Because it's a setup, you dumb bastard. I pick up all that coke and they just happen to be there? No way. It was either that shotgun punk or someone else. Either way, we're not sticking around to find out. Now get us out of here before I use this on you." Jorge kept the gun pointed right at the back of the driver's seat.

Sal's eyes widened. He turned around and stomped on the gas. The big car spun out onto Route 1, swerving around one car and just missing a collision with another. Jorge glanced behind them as the unmarked, light flashing, careened onto the highway right behind them.

"Move it, Sal, move it."

Sal was moving the Lincoln, good and fast, weaving drunkenly in and out of traffic, over in the passing lane, then back again. But the cocksucker behind was staying right with them. The cop behind the wheel was just as crazy as Sal. Suddenly, Jorge saw all his dreams, the dreams that had taken him this close to the top, going right down the tubes. Shit.

Jorge lowered the driver's side rear window, got up on his knees on the seat, stuck his gun out the window, and let a couple fly. The unmarked began swerving like crazy from the passing to the middle lane. Jorge couldn't tell if he'd hit anything, but from the way that car was swerving, he hadn't done any real damage. Couldn't really with this peashooter. Too bad he didn't have a larger caliber gun. He hung half his body out the window, holding the piece in one hand and the rear assist handle with the other, and when that unmarked pulled back into the passing lane behind them, he squeezed another one off. Jorge smiled as he saw spiderwebs spread across the unmarked's front window. The Ford swerved all over the damn highway, not a controlled swerve like when they'd been dodging bullets. Totally out of control like the driver was in trouble now.

Jorge smiled and pulled himself back in the car. "I nailed him. Let's go. We're home free."

Sal kept glancing up into the rearview. "I don't know about that, Jorge."

Jorge turned in his seat and saw the unmarked, its windshield cracked from the shot he'd just fired, right up on their bumper. He could even see the faces of the two crazy bastards inside.

"Jesus fuckin' Christ!" Sal yelled.

Jorge spun around. Traffic on the road ahead was stopped dead in its tracks.

"In the shopping center," Jorge shouted. "Quick."

Sal spun the wheel to the right, cutting off cars as he shot across the road and whipped into a large shopping center parking lot. Jorge saw the unmarked fly by them on the highway, brake lights flashing.

Jorge grinned like a maniac. They just might pull this off. "He can't get over. Punch it, Sal."

Sal hit the gas and the Lincoln shot forward. "Shit!"

Jorge grabbed for the seat just as the Lincoln slammed into the side of a car emerging from between the rows of parked cars. The impact hurled Jorge against the front seat. He struggled back into a sitting position and gripped the back of Sal's seat with his free hand. "Back up, back up. Get us out of here now."

Sal moved like a man in heavy water. He shook his head, shifted into reverse, and stepped on the gas. All too late. The unmarked, shot-up windshield and all, was blocking their way.

"Shit." Jorge pounded his gun hand on the top of the back seat. "Shit, shit, shit."

He glared out the back window at the two cops: a young black cop riding shotgun and an older white cop behind the wheel. The young cop was yelling at his partner. Jorge suddenly realized they could see the gun in his hand as he pounded the back of the seat.

"We give up. We give up. Please, don't shoot." Sal had both hands up, open wide and empty.

Like hell we give up. Fucking coward. As long as Jorge was alive, there was a chance he could fight his way out. If he couldn't fight his way out, his dreams would be over. nd without those dreams, he'd just as soon be over too.

Both cops piled out of the car. The black cop steadied his gun on the top of the unmarked's passenger door. A second later a bullet punched through the Lincoln's back window, stinging Jorge's face with invisible pieces of glass.

Jorge braced himself against the front seat and kicked out the rear window. Then he knelt on the backseat and fired at the black cop.

For the second time he found himself wishing he had a larger caliber gun–like his .44magnum. Then he could really do some damage.

Jorge caught a movement out of the corner of his eye–
the white cop running up quickly on the driver's side.
Just as Jorge was about to take out the approaching cop,
the black cop popped off another shot. Jorge spun around
and returned fire.

"Please don't shoot. I'm gonna throw my gun out. I
give up. I give up," Sal screamed, but not loud enough
to be heard outside the car. He reached inside his coat,
pulled out his gun.

Jorge fired again, and turned to his right long enough
to see the white cop point his pistol and Sal's big head
snap to the side from the force of the slug plowing into
his skull.

Jorge fired again. "Motherfuckers," he screamed. Pain
seared his left shoulder. "I'm the Boss. I'm the fuckin"
Boss."

He popped off a shot at the black cop and swung back
around to fire a shot at the white cop, only the white cop's
gun fired first, sending a bullet deep into Jorge's brain.

Lt. John O'Brien stood beside the Lincoln and took a deep
breath to slow the adrenalin surge. He kept his weapon
trained on the car's back seat. Out of the corner of his eye he
could see Bumpers coming up slowly from the unmarked,
his weapon extended.

Christ, Bumper was hit! He was bleeding heavily from a

wound on the left side of his neck.

"How bad is it?" O'Brien reached out and started to pull his partner's collar open. Bumpers pushed him away.

"I'm fine. I just . . . need . . . to catch my . . . breath." Bumper's skin color turned almost Caucasian and his knees buckled.

"Somebody call an ambulance!" O'Brien grabbed his partner and lowered him until he was sitting Indian-style on the asphalt with his back against an adjacent car.

Someone in the growing crowd of onlookers passed O'Brien a cloth. "Ambulance is on its way."

Someone else shouted, "Put pressure on it."

O'Brien tore open Bumper's collar. The wound was bad. Something serious had been hit. He glanced around, hoping to see the crowd parting to let an ambulance through. No such luck. He could hear the sirens off in the distance, but they didn't sound any closer than they had a minute ago.

O'Brien pressed the cloth tight over the wound with his right hand, shocked to feel blood pulsing beneath the cloth. It's all right, it's all right, he told himself, adjusting his hand so he didn't cut off Bumpers' air supply. It was just a small caliber wound; no one died from a small caliber wound.

That was a lie and O'Brien knew it. People died from small caliber wounds all the time. But those people weren't his partner.

Bumpers looked up, eyes glazed. He swallowed over

and over, like something was caught in his throat. "You were right, John. There was something going on. And it . . . it must've been something big."

"Yeah, sure. Something big," O'Brien answered. He cleared his throat and looked around again for the ambulance. What the hell was taking so long? "Don't try to talk."

"If I don't talk, I'll die." Bumpers smiled, his face still pale as a white man's. "It was something big, wasn't it?"

"Sure it was, Carl. It was something big." Warm blood ran between O'Brien's fingers. He had to press harder. Get the bleeding to stop. But all he could feel was that pulse pumping underneath his palm. If only it would stop for a minute, he thought, and then to his horror realized what that would mean.

"You were right from the beginning." Bumpers' eyelids drooped closed.

O'Brien's breath caught in his throat. He shook Bumpers' shoulder. "Right about what, son? Right about what?"

Bumpers' eyes flickered open. "You said something was going on. You were right. I guess there is something . . . something to say for intuition."

"Of course there is," O'Brien said. "I've tried to teach you that, son." Was it his imagination or was Bumpers' pulse slowing down? It just didn't feel like it was pumping as often or as strong as it had been.

Bumpers swallowed again. "Take a look, John. Please."

Someone stepped up beside him and took hold of the cloth pressed against Bumper's wound.   O'Brien hesitated for a moment, then stood. He made the few steps to the Lincoln, reached through the car's open driver's window, and removed the keys from the ignition without giving the dead bodies inside a glance. Like a man in a trance he walked to the rear of the car, opened the trunk, and unzipped one of the duffel bags. Quickly, he inverted the bag and dumped the contents into the trunk.

"Shit." O'Brien picked up one of the packages with his bloody hand as if it were nothing more than a loaf of bread and walked back to his partner. He knelt down beside Bumpers and held out the blood-smeared bundle.

Bumpers reached out and gently touched the kilo of cocaine with his finger as if it might be hot. "It figures," he said.

"Yeah, it sure does," O'Brien said.

Bumpers' head dropped and his body went limp.

O'Brien began to shiver and his vision darkened. He stood up slowly and walked back to the rear of the Lincoln just as an ambulance pulled into the parking lot. He hurled the bloody kilo of coke back into the trunk and slammed the trunk closed.

"Yeah, partner. It figures. It sure fucking figures."

Chapter 37

"IS . . . IS . . . IS IT OVER, Buzz? Huh? Is it over?"

Buzz couldn't believe it. His big dream had been this close, and he'd watched it die right there in front of him. And it had all happened in the time it took those two crazy cops to chase the spic and the goon from the storage joint to the shopping plaza. He could just about taste those piña coladas in Jamaica turning into 7 & 7's with a beer chaser at Duggan's Cafe. Shit. "Yeah, it's over."

"You sure?"

"Get up here, you fucking nitwit."

Skinny unrolled himself from under the dash and sat back in the shotgun seat. "What happened?"

"Nothing good."

Through the crowd that was slowly accumulating Buzz could still make out the two cops, one on the ground. Sirens sounded off in the distance. There had to be a way to salvage this mess. Buzz stared at the Lincoln and imagined the hundred beautiful, oval footballs in there. They'd be confiscated now. "Damn."

Skinny turned and looked at him with those sad, watery, junkie eyes. Even the thin man knew there wasn't any damn way to pull this thing out of the fire, not now. It was over, finished, and that's all she wrote.

"Damn," Buzz said again. Why the hell did this happen? he thought. I was this fucking close. Why?

"Well, there goes the coke," Skinny said, unwrapping a stick of gum and casually popping it into in his mouth.

The sirens were getting closer. Time to make tracks. But first there was one thing he had to do. He turned to Skinny and gave him a hard gangster smack upside the head with the back of his hand.

"Yowww," Skinny hollered, throwing his hands up over his face. "What the fuck did you do that for?"

"Because of that voice of yours, that's what for." Buzz felt real good–for half a second. Until Skinny looked over at him with those frightened eyes, like maybe he thought he was going to get pounded.

Skinny glanced around like he was trying to come up with something to keep Buzz from whacking him again. "I just thought of something."

"What?" Probably another dumb Skinny idea.

"Why don't we shake down the guy with the gym bag?"

Maybe it was the timing, maybe Buzz was that desperate, but Skinny's new idea didn't sound all that dumb. No, not dumb at all. Hell, he wouldn't be able to retire today like he'd hoped, that was for sure. But maybe someday. Until then a man had to make a living, didn't he? There was just one problem though. "Got any brilliant suggestions on how we're gonna find out who the hell that guy was?"

Buzz was really surprised when Skinny answered, "Only person it can be. The bartender–Dan Marlowe."

The thin man was right. Marlowe was the only one left in the picture. He must've buffaloed the staties. Either he'd had the cocaine all along or he'd latched onto it somewhere along the line. Buzz scratched his chin. "I wonder how much was in that bag?"

"Maybe a few hundred grand," Skinny said.

A few hundred grand. Not likely. But still, something– whatever that something was–had to be better than nothing. "All right, we'll give it a shot."

"You know what?" Skinny sounded almost cheery now.

"What?" Buzz was half afraid to ask. Getting more than one good idea out of Skinny was as likely as getting a good night's sleep.

"He'll be easy to handle. A lot easier than they would've been." Skinny nodded in the direction of the Lincoln.

"Yeah, I suppose you're right."

Buzz turned the Sentra around and drove out of the lot onto Route 1 just as an ambulance and what looked like every goddamn police car in creation began pulling in.

Chapter 38

WHEN HE GOT BACK to Hampton Beach, the first thing Dan did was shove the blue gym bag up into the small attic of his cottage. It would be safe there temporarily and he could figure out what to do with it later. Right now he had something else on his mind.

Revenge.

What he was contemplating was crazy. He could've chalked it up to some sort of delayed stress reaction from seeing brains blown out down on Singing Beach. But he'd been considering the same thing every day since the incident at Boar's Head. Only difference was that now he had the energy–and the attitude–to actually pull something off.

Look out Tony Peralta. Here comes Dan Marlowe.

It wasn't just because of the beating. It was more because of the feelings and thoughts that the coke he'd been forced to consume had awakened in him. They weren't good, those feelings. They hurt. And they'd keep on hurting for a long, long time. It was like dragging yourself through Hell, then making it out only to find someone on the outside who picked you up and dropped you back at the beginning again. A rotten thing to do to a man. Time to settle the score.

Dan waited until dark. Then he got out a gas can he kept under the cottage for the weed whacker, slipped on a pair of gloves, and filled six empty green Heineken bottles with the fluid. He stuffed a rag in the opening of each, then put the bottles in a six-pack holder. He took out a newly purchased .38 revolver and loaded the chambers. Then he looked up Peralta's phone number, dialed it, let it ring. When the answering machine picked up, he smiled. He was going to do this thing and he didn't feel a bit nervous. He stuck the gun in the back of his waistband, slipped on a light jacket, and carried the six-pack of Molotov cocktails out to the car.

Before he got in the driver's seat he looked up at the sky. It was a cloudless night, so clear it seemed like he could see every star that could possibly exist. The ocean thundered just over the dunes and a snap of salt hung in the air. It was the type of night that usually beckoned him out for a walk on the beach, but not tonight–he had something much more satisfying to do. He started the car and took off for Boar's Head.

Ocean Boulevard was a madhouse packed with

people and cars. Dan was immediately stuck in the traffic. He zigged around one car, zagged around another, then got stopped along with half a million other cars waiting for tourists to cross the boulevard. For some reason the traffic didn't bother him tonight. Maybe because he wasn't really in a rush. He'd never burned down a mansion after all, or even a small house for that matter. But he'd been brooding about what had happened to him ever since he woke up in the dumpster behind the High Tide. And he knew if he didn't take care of business tonight, he'd go right on brooding about it forever. That was for sure.

Traffic inched forward, carrying Dan along with it. He passed, in very slow succession, Buc's Lagoon, Le Bec Rouge Restaurant, and Blink's Fry Dough before getting stopped again.

He'd been wronged quite a few times in his life, like most people he guessed, and he'd let most of those incidents slide. Most of the time, the incident hadn't been worth risking any more trouble over. A few times he'd been just plain scared. But the incident up at the big house on Boar's Head was different. It wasn't going to leave him alone and it wasn't going to let him go. Unless he did something about it.

If he sat back now and did nothing, it would be like putting a big sign on his back that said, Kick Me, World. If the world didn't beat on him, Dan would do a pretty good job on himself.

He didn't have a choice. Not really.

And knowing that made him feel good–relieved–that it soon would be over.

When he'd finally made the short distance to the Casino, Dan broke free of traffic and headed north. A short time later he'd reached Boar's Head, a peninsula with a few dozen homes that jutted a hundred yards out into the Atlantic. He banged a right onto Boar's Head and drove up the slight incline until he was within a couple of houses of the mansion, about halfway up the peninsula.

He pulled over to the side and just sat there for a minute staring at the mansion. No lights, no sign anyone was home. Just looking at the monstrosity brought back painful memories. Dan shook his head. He couldn't take the chance of someone seeing him here and calling the cops, he had to move quickly.

Dan got out of his car and popped the trunk. He removed a large adhesive mailing label he'd brought from the cottage, tore off the backing, and stuck it on the license plate obscuring the figures. Then he pulled on the gloves, grabbed the six-pack of firebombs, closed the trunk, and started walking towards Tony Peralta's.

He stayed close to the houses on his right, out of the street lights. He didn't see anyone else out on foot; Boar's Head was good that way.

There was a large fence surrounding the mansion. Again, Dan lucked out. The main gate for cars was closed and locked, but the small gate for foot traffic was slightly ajar.

He pushed the gate open and walked through. No cars. No lights. No sign of life.

The building was an imposing sight in the dark. Because land was at a premium on Boar's Head even a mansion like Peralta's was on a small lot. That made the structure seem like it was right on top of him. He inched his way closer, gravel from the driveway crunching under his feet, until he could see that the two floors of the building facing him were covered with glass windows. Easy targets, but they weren't what he was looking for.

He skulked around the side of the building in the dark, watching his step carefully. He could see the Atlantic and the lights of the beach off to the south. When he turned back and looked at the mansion, there it was–the window that looked into the room where he'd been imprisoned. He wanted to make sure, so he walked up to the window, shaded his eyes, and peeked in. It was definitely the room– right down to the chair that the bastard had had him secured to. Dan moved back away from the building and placed the six-pack on the ground. He took out one of the bottles, lit the cloth wick with a lighter. He gazed at it for a second, then took two steps toward the house, and heaved the bottle with all his might. It felt like the best pitch he'd ever thrown; he knew it was good the instant it left his hand. The Molotov cocktail arced through the dark like a fireworks rocket and crashed through the glass. It exploded somewhere inside the room, against a floor or wall, he guessed. It wasn't a large explosion as far as noise goes but he could see the flames start to catch on something, so he was pleased. He grabbed another cocktail, lit it, and tossed that in too for good measure.

Dan walked quickly around the house and threw the last four firebombs through four different windows on a couple of different sides. Then he proceeded to get out of there. On his way past the first window, he noticed that the fire was picking up speed. The ground in that area was illuminated like it was daylight. He tucked the empty six pack container under his arm, went back through the gate, and walked to his car.

The road was one way, running up one side of the peninsula, around, and down the other side. When Dan pulled abreast of the burning building, the inside of his car was as bright as noon. He didn't notice any new activity from any of the other houses around. From the looks of it, it was going to be a big one, a real conflagration. Nice.

Just before pulling out onto Ocean Boulevard, Dan stopped the car and got out. He ripped the label off the license plate and threw the label, the empty six-pack, and the gloves into the trunk. He hopped back in the driver's seat, pulled out onto the main drag, banged a u-turn, and headed south toward the beach and home. He rolled down the window, took a deep breath of the sea air, and grinned like a little boy. Felt good too, not scared at all.

Dan turned on the radio in time to catch the afternoon bulletin. "Police shootout . . . three dead . . .

200 pounds of cocaine."

Not much time to think about it because seconds later, near the Ashworth Hotel, fire engines and police cars passed him going the other way. It looked like every piece of equipment on the beach was headed up there. Within a short time they'd be sending for help from all over the seacoast, after they saw how bad it was. But he also figured by then it'd be too late to save the mansion on Boar's Head. And damn if that thought didn't make him feel better than he already did.

At least until he got home and he could hear the phone ringing from the driveway. By the time he ran onto the porch, fumbled with his keys in the dark, and finally got inside to answer it, he was so out of breath all he could do was listen to the voice on the other end tell him what the speaker wanted and what was going to happen to Dan and his family if the caller didn't get what he wanted. It was déjà vu. And that made him feel not so good all over again.

Chapter 39

"THAT ROTTEN, FILTHY fed motherfucker," Tony said as he jumped in the driver's seat of the Jag. Wayne was in the passenger seat beside him, Rhonda in back. It was late night and they were in the parking lot of the North Hampton restaurant where they'd just had dinner and drinks. After leaving, Tony had used the outside pay phone and gotten some not-so-great news.

"What happened?" Wayne asked.

"Yeah, what's wrong, baby?" Rhonda leaned forward and stared quizzically at Tony.

The smell of her perfume distracted Tony, but tonight not even Rhonda's sweet perfume was enough to erase the conversation he'd just had. "What's wrong? What happened? I'll tell you what happened. That fed asked me a while ago to help him find the coke from the harbor. I couldn't help him and that skinny little fuck he hangs around with any more than I could help those two staties." He banged the steering wheel so hard it shook. "So, now he's going to cut me loose. Says he can't work with me anymore. That I'm on my own."

"What's that mean?" Rhonda asked, looking from Tony to Wayne and back again.

Tony shot her an angry look. "It means I won't have any protection with this asshole anymore. It means that any fucking rinky-dink local or state cop that wants to bust my chops can go ahead and do it now. He won't step in for me anymore. It's me against the world."

"He might be trying to rattle your cage, Boss," Wayne said as he drummed his fingers on the dashboard.

"Will you fucking stop that," Tony said irritably. "And if he's trying to shake me up, he's doing a good job. I got a good thing going here. I move what I want and no one looks at me twice. For years now, anyone got it in their head to give me grief, this asshole'd tell them to back off. And they would. Then I'd do the fed a little favor and go merrily on my way. I made money. He made busts. A real sweet deal." He shook his head. "Christ, I've been helping that cocksucker for years. I handed him some of the best busts he ever made. Isn't that right, Wayne?"

Wayne nodded. "That's for sure."

"You mean you won't be able to make any more money?" Rhonda sounded like a little girl who just found out she couldn't have ice cream on her birthday. "No more coke either?"

"Not unless I want to end up doing prison time. And I don't. I'm too good looking for that. All because of that goddamn rip-off. Now I'm getting screwed for something I didn't have anything to do with. That just isn't fair."

"We could keep trying to find the coke," Wayne said, but he didn't sound like he believed that would help. Then he perked up. "Maybe we could grab that Marlowe jerk again, have some more fun with him. Or maybe find somebody else . . ."

"Too late. It's all over. The fed said that the harbor coke was grabbed down in Massachusetts. So I guess because it wasn't his bust or something he's pissed and he's dumping me. Period. I don't know what the hell I'm going to do now."

Tony let out a long, deep breath. He stared out the windshield at the crowded parking lot and the traffic going by on Route 1. How the hell had it come to this, he wondered. Somebody kills a couple of boat people, nobodies, and snatches some coke. So what? What the hell did that have to do with him? He'd even done his best to help find the coke. And now that lousy fed was just going to walk away and leave him for the wolves. Local yokels and state cops who knew all about his cocaine business and had been dying to bust him for years, but couldn't even try because working for the fed made him bulletproof. Once those bastards heard he wasn't working with the fed anymore they'd be all over him like stink on shit. The only thing in doubt was who'd be the first to nail him. And with the weight he moved, shit, that could mean fifteen, twenty, maybe even thirty years mandatory. Tony shivered.

"Hey, Boss, you all right?" Wayne gave Tony a little shake on the arm.

"Yeah, yeah, yeah," Tony answered coming back to earth. "I'm fine. Just fucking fine."

"Maybe you could start over somewhere else," Wayne said. "Someplace they don't know us . . . err, you. You told me once you had a bundle stashed."

Christ! He'd been so shook up he'd completely forgotten about his stash! He'd stuck a safe in his bedroom walk-in closet years ago. He closed his eyes. Pictured the closet. Watched himself open the closet door, walk inside, and hit a concealed button, causing a large section of the far wall to slide aside. Inside that wall was the safe. And inside that safe was–$1,000,000 cash, give or take a few grand. Along with how much blow? He'd forgotten. Yeah, that would make a good start somewhere else.

Tony smiled. Suddenly the world didn't look like it was about to swallow him whole. He slapped Wayne on the shoulder. "You know, Wayne, you aren't as dumb as you look."

Wayne straightened up in his seat.

Rhonda started bouncing up and down in the back seat. Probably happy that her visions of having to return to hair styling school could be replaced with visions of lots of coke and money coming in. "You could sell the mansion, Tony. It must be worth a lot."

"Yeah, sure." Tony started the Jag and pulled out into the Route 1 traffic. "Maybe I . . ." Rhonda leaned forward again, staring. Wayne turned and joined in with his own stare. ". . . *we* need a change. Yeah, that might be a good idea."

They all laughed and Tony started talking about all the parts of the country he knew that were wide open, where he knew people, had connections. Where someone smart and flush like him could move in and just start right up, no problem.

No problem at all. Until they got to Route 1A, Ocean Boulevard. They were toodling along with all the windows down, surrounded by the nice aroma of the sea and– smoke?

"Hey, what's that?" Wayne asked. Ahead of them in the distance the sky was lit up like day, flames illuminating billowing clouds of smoke. There was a little intake of breath from Rhonda in the back. Tony floored the gas and the Jag sped up. No one spoke, at least out loud.

Please don't let it be. Please. The plea kept running round and round inside Tony's head. His stomach clenched like he'd just been gut punched as they got close enough to see that the fire was definitely on Boar's Head. The peninsula's main entrance was blocked off. Both sides of 1A were littered with cars pulled over and empty of people who'd gotten out for a closer look at whatever was burning.

Tony pulled the Jag into the parking lot at Little Jack's Seafood Restaurant and they all scrambled out. Tony's stomach flip-flopped as they hurried across 1A. With any luck he wouldn't know the people who lived in whatever the hell was burning.

"Hey, wait for me," Rhonda called. Tony couldn't stop now. Not until he knew for sure. He dodged around the police cars with Wayne close on his heels. Up ahead Tony could see flashing lights from the fire engines bouncing off houses.

He kept his mind focused on getting up the street, past the cops and gawkers coming back down the other way, not asking anyone what was burning, afraid of what they might say. Finally, he rounded the last corner . . .

"Oh, Jesus." Tony slowed down, walking like a zombie toward his burning mansion. Wayne walked beside him, his face lit up like a kid watching Fourth of July fireworks. Fucking pyromaniac.

Tony got close enough to feel the heat on his face before the cops stopped him. He stood, stunned, and stared at the smoldering remains of his home. There wasn't much left to look at–the walls had collapsed along with the second floor. Rhonda puffed up behind them as Tony pictured walking into the bedroom closet, releasing the false wall, opening the big safe, and looking at . . . a pile of goddamn ashes.

Wait a second! Hadn't it been a fireproof safe? Tony

asked himself. Of course it had. Only an imbecile would put in a safe that wasn't fireproof.

He tore his gaze away from the fire-ravaged building and studied the state police cruisers parked nearby and what he recognized as statie unmarked cars too–he could spot them a mile away.

And the men who belonged to those unmarked cars– he could spot them two miles away. They had on white short-sleeve shirts, guns on their hips, and buzz cuts. Five or six of them stood close to the house like vultures just waiting to sift through the ruins.

That sucker-punched feeling was back in full force.

"At least you can collect insurance," Wayne said.

"Yeah, insurance," Rhonda piped in, like that idea was a real stroke of genius.

Tony looked from Wayne to Rhonda and back again. Was it the flames making their eyes sparkle or the hope that they still had a chance to live the high life? "I don't have any insurance," Tony said. "It cost too much. Me being right on the cliff with the ocean and wind and hurricanes and everything. Just too much."

Apparently the flames hadn't put that sparkle in their eyes.

They watched what was left of the fire in silence. Until Tony noticed that the guys with the buzz haircuts were looking his way and talking amongst themselves. Once these guys were able to sift through what was left of his place, they'd find more than a few reasons to talk to him personally.

He'd had enough excitement for one day. "Let's go." Tony turned and began walking away. Wayne and Rhonda shuffled along behind.

"Well, you still got the Jag, Tony," Wayne said halfheartedly.

So he was Tony now. Amazing how fast a guy could tumble down in this world. Tony let it pass. What someone called him was the least of his troubles now.

"Yeah, the Jag," Rhonda said, her tone as flat as her hair, wet with the mist of the fire hoses.

"Yeah, I still got the Jag," Tony parroted as the three of them crossed 1A and headed for Little Jack's and the car. He started to tell them that there was only one month left on the lease, but stopped. If he lost Rhonda and Wayne, he'd be stuck with himself for company. Not a good option.

Chapter 40

RAY CONOVER had thought it was all over yesterday, but he couldn't have been more wrong. What with Carpucci found shot in the head down on that Massachusetts beach, and the drug dealer's associates killed in the shootout with the Saugus cops topped off with the hundred kilos being confiscated, he'd thought that was it. Just a little more digging and they'd find out those same men were responsible for the Hampton Harbor murders and that'd be that. He'd be able to tie up the whole episode nice and neat-like with ribbons and bows. At least that's what he'd thought . . . until Bartolo played him a tape of a call that had come over the tap on Dan Marlowe's phone line.

They'd just finished listening to that tape all over again. It was early morning and they were sitting in their unmarked unit in the Patriot's Corner strip mall parking lot on Ocean Boulevard. Conover was behind the wheel.

Bartolo sat shotgun with a small cassette player balanced on his knees.

"Bring the money in the gym bag, all of it," Bartolo said, staring down at the recorder in his lap. "What money? What gym bag?"

"Who the hell knows? It's got something to do with the coke, though. You can bet on that."

"Maybe Carpucci and his people didn't do the harbor hits after all."

That happened to be what Conover was thinking too. "Maybe. Maybe it was their load that got snatched and someone ransomed it back to them. How's that look?"

"Yeah, makes sense. At least it'd explain a gym bag full of money floating around. That'd mean Marlowe pulled the rip, sold Carpucci back his own coke, and now someone's shaking him down. Does that fly?"

"I don't see two murders fitting Dan Marlowe. How he got the coke, I don't know."

"What about whacking Carpucci? You see him doing that?"

"No. Had to be Carpucci's own men. The ones killed down in Saugus probably. Carpucci should've known better than to take chances, even with his own people. Too much powder involved."

"We still don't know who did the harbor murders. Or how Marlowe got the coke."

"We gotta lead on the guy who did the murders," Conover said. "Whoever is on that tape talking to Marlowe is the missing piece of this puzzle."

Neither man spoke for a minute. Finally Bartolo cleared his throat. "Would be nice to tie this thing up."

"Yeah. I'm ready for a little time off."

"You got that right."

Maybe Bartolo sounded a little too eager. Maybe he was burned out. Conover wasn't sure which, but something had his hackles raised. "How about we grab a beer when this is all over and celebrate?"

Usually the mention of beer put a smile on Bartolo's face. Not today. He just kept staring at that cassette player sitting in his lap. "A big gym bag could hold a lot of dough. It'd have to be a lot to buy back a boat load of coke, wouldn't it?"

Conover studied his partner's face. He hadn't liked what he'd just heard and he didn't like what he saw any better. Bartolo was suddenly sounding and looking like a taker. Or was it just his imagination?

Bartolo held the cassette player chest high with both hands. "Do you think Marlowe will actually show up at the jetty like this guy wants him to? Or will he try to pull something?"

"I think he'll show. He's not the type of guy to risk his family's safety."

Bartolo finally looked at Conover. "Then some bastard'll walk away with all that cash. We put a lot of work in on this, Ray. It's nobody's money. And that's who'd miss it. Nobody."

Conover was stunned–the man had come right out and said it. He turned toward Bartolo and leaned into his space. "Are you crazy? We're cops, and that's coke money. Get hold of yourself, man."

"Yeah, but you heard what he said." Bartolo sounded almost frantic now. "It's a gym bag full of money. Like you said, coke money. It belonged to Carpucci and he's dead. No one will miss it. We can grab it at the jetty and let Marlowe and whoever else shows up take a walk. Christ, they'll be glad to just get out of there without getting busted."

Conover looked hard at Bartolo. Was the man joking? Was he playing with a full deck? The answer to both questions was probably no. Bartolo might be serious, but he wasn't thinking this thing through. Whoever made that call to Dan Marlowe had already killed at least twice. They wouldn't just walk away from what they considered their money just because two state cops told them to. No way. These weren't kids you were telling to dump out their beers and head home. People like this, if you could call them people, wouldn't head home. They'd have to be taken care of along with Marlowe . . . what the hell was he thinking? Was he going crazy too?

Before he could decide whether to smack Bartolo upside the head or himself, his partner laughed. "Ray, Ray. For Chrissake, I'm kidding. Can't you take a fucking joke?"

It'd been no joke, Conover was sure. But he'd just scared

himself so much he was willing to let it go–for now. He turned back to watching the crowd meander in and out of the stores in the small shopping complex–laundromat, convenience store, surf board business, and coffee shop. Bartolo was still staring at the cassette player in his lap.

"We'll have to bring some others in on this," Conover said.

"And how are we going to tell them we found out about it?" Bartolo shot back. He set the cassette player on the seat between them. "With an illegal tap? We have to handle this ourselves, Ray."

Conover let out a sigh. Why the hell did he let himself get into this? "All right, all right."

"Good. I'm gonna grab a coffee. You want another?"

"Okay, but make mine decaf. I don't want to get any crankier than I already am."

As soon as Bartolo disappeared into the store, Conover listened to the tape again. The whole thing. And when he was done listening, he still couldn't figure out what the hell exactly was going on.

Bartolo returned with two cups of steaming coffee and a bagful of donuts a few minutes later. "What time is it?"

"A little after seven thirty," Conover said irritably. "Time to get moving." The meet was supposed to take place at eight. He and Bartolo needed to be in position before anything went down.

"Let's go then." Bartolo licked the last of the jelly off his fingers and wiped them with a scrunched-up napkin.

He dropped the napkin on the car floor and took a sip from the coffee cup he had resting on the dashboard.

"Let's walk." It was a weekday which meant there wouldn't be many cars in the state park. "We park over there, whoever's meeting Marlowe might make us."

"Okay, okay. We'll walk. Let's go."

Bartolo had a strange look on his face. Scared? Excited? Mad? Whatever it was, Conover didn't like it. Like maybe Bartolo knew something he didn't. That hackles-raised feeling slid down to his gut, settling in like an old friend. He'd had the feeling before–just before things turned sour.

"Remember, we agreed to take whoever shows up nice and easy if possible," Conover said, trying to diffuse some of the tension emanating from his partner. "Right?"

"Yeah, we did. Unless Marlowe or the other character tries to rabbit. Then it's up to us to stop the bastards. They're killers, for Chrissake."

Sounded like his partner was hoping they'd make a run for it. A good cop's nerves or was there more to it? That feeling in Conover's gut tightened, like radar going off. "Calm down, will you, Vinny?"

"I am calm." Bartolo massaged the gun in his shoulder holster.

Conover couldn't remember seeing Bartolo so nervous. Maybe it was because they'd never been so close to anything quite this big in their careers. But if that were so, then why did his inner radar just add another bleep to the screen?

"Come on. Let's go." Conover grabbed a pair of binoculars from the back seat as both men hopped out of the car and headed toward the state park.

It took them less than five minutes to reach the park. They walked across the unpaved lot to the sand dunes at the far end. Off to the right was the channel that flowed in from the ocean, under the bridge, and into Hampton Harbor. The men half crouched as they scrambled up a huge sand dune, Conover leading the way. When he reached the top of the dune, he knelt down and peered over the crest. The beach was almost deserted, with only a few early morning walkers and joggers scattered along the mile-long stretch.

Bartolo knelt beside him and looked around. "There they are." He pointed south.

Conover had already seen them—two men sitting on the jetty, just short of where the incoming tide stopped. He took a look through the binoculars. Those guys looked as out of place as snowmen sitting there. They had to be the ones meeting Marlowe.

"Where's fucking Marlowe?"

Conover glanced at his partner and almost dropped the binoculars. Bartolo's face was filled with pure fear. Conover started to say something, to make sure the man wasn't cracking, but something caught his eye. He scanned the beach with the binoculars and focused on a figure heading toward them from the opposite direction of the jetty. Someone carrying a gym bag.

"There he is," Conover said.

"Let me see." Bartolo snatched the binoculars and aimed them down the beach. He licked his lips, then licked them again.

For Christ's sake, what the hell's the matter with him? That funny feeling was going gangbusters, telling Conover that whatever was wrong with his partner, he was probably going to find out all about it and soon. Conover tugged the binoculars away from Bartolo and took another look at Marlowe.

"Come on," Bartolo said through gritted teeth. "Let's take them now."

Bartolo had a wild look in his eyes. He had his pistol in hand and was up on his hands and knees, ready to charge down the dune.

"Have you lost it?" Conover hissed as he reached over and grabbed his partner's arm. "Marlowe isn't even close yet."

"He'll bolt, I'm telling you. He won't get close to them." Bartolo tried to shake his arm free.

Conover held on tight. "Will you calm down. He is coming closer."

Bartolo's gun hand shook. Emotions flickered across his face faster than Conover could identify them. He'd stopped trying to free his arm, but Conover wasn't about to let go. He didn't have that funny feeling anymore–the inner radar had switched off. Didn't make him feel one bit better, because he finally realized what his intuition had been trying to tell him–Bartolo was going off the deep end. Too bad that intuition wasn't telling him what to do about it.

Conover turned the binoculars back to look at the two men sitting on the jetty. Whatever was about to go down wasn't going to be good.

Chapter 41

DAN SHOULD'VE known better right from the beginning. That money came from the same crummy merry-go-round that had screwed him up in the first place, the same shit that lost him his business and his family. He didn't need to be a Rhodes Scholar to know that the thing that'd almost destroyed him wasn't likely to be the thing to turn it all around.

He glanced at the two men waiting for him on the jetty. One of those jerks was a foulmouthed character who'd called Dan in the middle of the night, making demands and topping the demands off with threats. This new guy wanted the gym bag and what was in it.

That's when Dan decided that the only way this nightmare was ever going to end was if he put an end to it.

It was low tide and he had about a hundred yards to

go before he reached the jetty. It was a beautiful morning, one of those days you could actually see the Isle of Shoals twelve miles out, smell the salt air. There was a light breeze with a flock of squawking gulls circling overhead.

Out on the water a billowing sail caught his eye and he let himself dream for a moment that he was out there on that boat playing in the wind instead of walking toward the jetty and who knew what.

Dan glanced over his shoulder in the direction of Boar's Head and it actually took a few seconds before it dawned on him what was missing up there–Tony Peralta's mansion. There was just a big empty space like a jack-o'-lantern's smile where it used to be.

He'd taken care of that problem. He'd take care of this one, too.

Dan pressed his arm against the .38 tucked in his windbreaker pocket. He'd heard about the shootout on the radio. Two men and a cop dead, cocaine confiscated. At least the coke wouldn't be getting out on the street, that was something. But a cop dead? How responsible for that was he? That's what he'd been fretting over when he got the call.

Had to be a pal of the dead Hispanic. No one else knew he had the money.

The gym bag in his hand felt heavy, money heavy. Last night he'd realized that handing over two hundred grand wasn't going to protect anyone. Whoever was after the money couldn't let him leave this meet alive. No, the only way he was going to walk away from this was if he took action first. He had to take the chance; it was the only hope–for his family, for himself, for everybody.

Dan was about thirty feet away from the jetty when he stopped. He waited as the bigger of the two men, wearing a black leather car coat and sunglasses, got up and stepped forward. The other one, a skinny guy who looked like a real sleaze, followed close behind. Dan's heart lurched as the big man reached into the pocket of his coat. If a gun came out that fast, it'd queer everything. He wouldn't have a chance. His heart slowed a half beat when the big man's hand came out, flipped open what looked like a billfold, and flashed what looked like a badge.

"D.E.A., Marlowe. You're in deep shit here."

What the hell could he say? He'd never considered the whole thing might be a bust. Instead of worrying about shooting someone or being shot, he was suddenly in danger of going to prison.

"Put the bag down," D.E.A. said.

Dan slowly lowered the bag to the sand without saying a word.

"It's all there?"

Dan nodded.

"Come on, Buzz. Get the bag and let's get outta here," the skinny guy said in a whiney, high-pitched voice. He pulled at the big man's sleeve like a little kid. For a minute, it looked like the big man was going to clock the skinny guy. Instead, he shook his arm free. "Will you shut the fuck up before I give you one, too."

Give you one, too? Dan didn't like the sound of those words. If he bolted for the jetty, scrambled over the rocks, and dove into the ocean, would he make it? A more realistic question might be how many bullets would he have inside him before he hit the water and could he survive? But if this cop–if he was a cop– was going to shoot him, maybe Dan could get his gun out first.

He was just about to make his move when he saw two men running down the side of the dune. Both men had guns and they were headed straight towards him.

"Freeze. Police!" one of them shouted.

Dan didn't move. The skinny guy jumped behind the fed who spun around and pulled out a gun. He kept the gun at his side, waved the badge in the air. "Easy. I'm a federal agent."

The two men kept coming on fast, the one out in front screaming unintelligibly. The second man was shouting too. At the man in front of him?

As they got closer, Dan realized he knew these two crazies. Conover and Bartolo. The two state cops. Bartolo was out front, waving his gun like a madman.

"Look out. He's got a gun!" Bartolo shouted.

Out of the corner of his eye, Dan could see the fed waving his badge. Just then Bartolo fired two shots in quick succession. Both slugs caught the fed square in the chest, throwing him backwards into the skinny man's arms before he slid down onto the sand.

"Vinny, no!" Conover screamed.

Bartolo, teeth bared, swung the gun in Dan's direction. Dan didn't even have time to be scared. His whole body jerked when he heard the next gunshot, but he didn't fall. Instead, Bartolo collapsed like a sack of shit right at Dan's feet.

Conover stood just beyond Bartolo, his legs spread, his pistol still pointed at his downed partner. His face was as paper white as Dan imagined his probably was. One look at Conover's eyes told Dan he was going to live.

Dan took a deep breath and went over to the fed. He felt for a pulse.

Nothing. Conover did the same with Bartolo.

Looked like the cop was gone, too. The skinny guy just stood there whimpering and shaking like a leaf, a wet stain spreading down the front of his pants. No one moved as rusty red spread through the sand around the bodies.

Finally, Conover nodded at the blue gym bag. "How much is in there?"

"About a dozen."

"A dozen what?"

"Rocks."

"Where's the money?"

"What money?"

They both looked back at the bodies.

Dan could hear voices, like in a dream, coming closer.

Someone close by shouted. Sirens sounded off in the distance. The tide was coming in, waves lapping closer and closer to the bodies. He wondered briefly if maybe he should pull the bodies out of the way. After all, they were both cops.

Instead, he watched the water come in, turn red, and swirl back out to sea.

Epilogue

IT WAS A COUPLE OF weeks after the shootings at the jetty, the second Sunday in September and the last day of the Hampton Beach Seafood Festival. Dan never missed the Festival no matter what happened. It was his favorite weekend of the year. The crowd was the same size as the crowd on a hot summer Saturday in July, but the people weren't the same. Different people. New people. Good for people-watching people.

Ocean Boulevard was closed to traffic starting at H Street which was fine with him. A day like today was made for walking. When Dan reached the festival entrance, he held up his arm to show a volunteer the plastic wristband allowing him entrance and was waved through.

Nice to be able to strut down the middle of the boulevard without having to worry about being clipped by some joyriding kid. A lot of other people must have felt the same way because Ocean Boulevard was packed. The weather was picture perfect–endless blue sky mirrored by the ocean below, temperatures like a warm fall day, sun just warm enough to take the chill off the air. Most everyone was gorging on something. As people strolled by, Dan made a game out of telling what people were eating without even looking at them. The air was filled with the aromas of seafood of all kinds, sausage subs, BBQ chicken, chili, Chinese food, and other aromas he couldn't quite put a finger on.

Beyond the Chamber of Commerce building Dan could see more than a half dozen large tents set up in the street for the food purveyors. His copy of the Seafood Festival magazine told him there were about fifty seacoast restaurants participating this year, plus the usual Arts & Crafts tents, and the beer tent. There was also a lot of entertainment, just as there was every year.

Dan strolled along, checking out the food and weaving around people. The Seafood Festival drew a different kind of crowd than the beach got during summer weekends. The people here today were older. Made him feel almost young in comparison. And there were a lot more good-looking women in his age bracket too. Teenagers weren't the dominant age group on Ocean Boulevard. At least not this weekend.

Dan rounded the last tent and started down the other side with the ocean on his left. When he got to Tent #4 he stopped at the High Tide's tables. He hadn't worked at the restaurant since just before the incident at the jetty. Dianne was there, wearing a large white chef's hat and apron and overseeing a big pot of clam chowder along with a display filled with fat lobster rolls.

Dianne looked up from stirring the chowder, caught his eye, and smiled. She grabbed two lobster rolls and handed them across the table. When he offered money, she reached over, took his hand, and pulled him close.

"Dan, what we talked about?" she said in his ear. "You managing the Tide?   Maybe buying it back eventually? You decide anything?"

Dan shook his head. "To tell you the truth, Dianne, I don't feel up to being the boss of anything right now. Not even the Tide. Thanks though."

Dianne smiled and nodded. "Just remember–another summer like this, and I might end up in a looney bin and it'll be your fault."

A tall man behind Dan yelled for lobster rolls. Dianne squeezed Dan's hand, pulled away slowly, and got back to business. Dan watched her for a moment, then turned and walked away.

He headed for the gray railing that ran the length of the beach, looking for a spot free of people where he could stand and demolish the lobster rolls. The Hampton Police were pushing fried clams at their stand. A couple of cops watched him pass by. He had no idea how they felt about what had transpired on the beach recently and he didn't really care.

He finally found a little free space on the railing to lean his butt against, a spot just opposite Tent #3, the Gladys and Louie Pub. He had no idea who Gladys and Louie were, probably fictional. The smell of fresh beer wasn't though. He recognized one of the kitchen people from the High Tide checking ID's at the Pub's entrance. She looked up, saw Dan, and jokingly called to him that she was going to check his ID if he tried to come in. He smiled and gave her a wave in return. It was good to see some people were acting, or at least trying to act, as if nothing unusual had happened to him recently.

As Dan munched on one of the rolls he started to wonder again if he'd done the right thing–walking down to the jetty like he was on a Sunday stroll. The media had played the incident up big. No surprise there.

The whole story had come out: how the fed, Buzz Craven, had ripped off a load of cocaine belonging to Boston mobster Dominic Carpucci, and murdered the two men transporting the coke; how Shamrock Kelly had seen Craven and his associate stash the coke in a local cottage, then broken in and transferred it to the High Tide cellar where Dan had eventually found it; how Jorge Rivera, a Carpucci lieutenant, had killed Carpucci in an attempt to take over Carpucci's racket only to be killed himself by police who confiscated the cocaine; how Vincent Bartolo, the state cop, apparently went loopy with the thought of all that coke and money floating around and had to be shot dead like a mad dog, but not before he killed the fed and gave Dan a quick mental review of his own life.

What surprised Dan the most was that Ray Conover hadn't even tried to whitewash what his partner had done down there at the jetty. He'd told it straight, even on TV when a camera crew had caught up with him although he didn't look any too happy about it. He'd looked like he had the weight of the world on his shoulders. But still, he'd told it straight and Dan had to admire the man for that.

He'd even backed Dan up when D. E. A. agents and another bunch from the Attorney General's office had questioned him. Although Dan wasn't sure he'd actually needed the help. It seemed that everyone wanted to bury the case as fast as possible and get it off the front pages. Dan had been informed that no charges would be brought against him and that had been that. Within days, the Attorney General held a press conference saying that the investigation was complete, and he was satisfied that all guilty parties had been accounted for in what he called, "this unfortunate incident." What the Attorney General implied though, and what the media and public loved, was that all the bad guys had killed each other off and gotten their just rewards.

Dan glanced to his right as a group of people walked down one of the concrete stairways onto the sand.

"Which way is it?" one of them asked. A man pointed south towards the jetty. The spot had become a real tourist attraction. Hopefully, the attraction would die off. The beach there was a favorite spot to a lot of people, himself included. Christ, the people who lived in that area might forgive him for being involved in this whole mess, but they'd never forgive him if that end of the beach became a little Graceland.

Dan was swallowing the last bite of his second lobster roll when Ray Conover suddenly materialized out of the crowd and walked up to him. Conover was dressed in jeans and a t-shirt, something Dan had never seen him in before.

He squeezed in beside Dan and hopped up on the railing. For a while neither of them said anything.

"Looks a lot different without the mansion there anymore." Conover nodded toward Boar's Head.

Dan looked at the empty space sitting high on the cliffs. "Yeah, it does. But I'm getting used to it."

"Peralta probably isn't." Conover kicked his feet against the lower rail. "He wouldn't have been able to enjoy it much longer anyhow. I heard he's going to be indicted on some serious drug charges soon."

"Too bad," Dan said, not even trying to hide the sarcasm.

"Yeah, isn't it."

"What about Shamrock?"

"I don't think they'll bother charging him. No one can prove that he actually had the coke in his possession. Besides, what happened to him was probably punishment enough."

"I know he's well on his way to becoming a Hampton Beach legend."

"Yeah. They got Peralta's hammerhead gorilla for assault plus dope. Heavy record. He'll be decrepit by the time he gets out."

"The skinny guy? Halliday?"

"There wasn't anyone left for him to give up, but they still had to slap him to shut him up. He told the Buzz and Skinny story from beginning to end, over and over and over again."

Both men sat there for a few minutes watching people stuff their faces as they passed by. For some reason, none of that food smelled as good to Dan as it had a bit earlier.

He wanted to say something to Conover, but he wasn't sure exactly what or how. He hadn't seen the man in person since the day at the jetty and had no idea how Conover felt about what went down. Only one way to find out. "I want to thank you for what you did at the jetty."

"I had to do it." Conover stared straight ahead, although Dan got the feeling he wasn't really looking at anything or anyone. "I didn't have much of a choice."

"What do you mean?"

"I'd known for a while that something was wrong with my partner, but I'd never thought it was serious. It may sound a bit naive. The way the news puts it all together, cops crack every day. Maybe they do, but I'm telling you I didn't see it coming."

Conover let out a deep sigh. "Vinny Bartolo? He was like my brother, we worked so close for so long. When Vinny started acting strange, I just figured it was Vinny kidding around or something. Later, I thought it was the stress from the job and that it would pass. You have to remember–he was like my flesh and blood. I never really believed that Vinny could go bad. Not until he swung that gun on you. Christ, if he hadn't done that, he probably could've gotten away with telling me he shot Craven because he thought he was going to shoot us. I probably would've bought it. That's how much I believed in the guy. But when I saw you just standing there and Vinny drawing down on you, I knew the truth in a heartbeat. So I killed him. I have to live with that. And no, you don't owe me any thanks. Like I said, I had to do it. It's not something I want or deserve thanks for."

For a moment the only sounds were the waves against the sand, people passing by, and gulls squawking overhead.

"You must've heard about that Boston lawyer setting up a trust fund for Shamrock Kelly's rehab," Conover finally said. "Expensive. It'll be a long haul."

"Yeah."

"Anonymous donor, I heard. Strange though."

"Yeah?"

"There were big donations to funds for the families of

Vinny Bartolo and Bumpers, the Saugus cop, too. All anonymous."

"Oh yeah?"

"Yeah. For shits and giggles, I poked around a little. Seems the same lawyer that set up the Kelly trust also fronted for the Bartolo and Bumpers donations."

"Hmm."

"The whole ball of wax ended up being around a couple hundred grand. Should do a lot of good."

The loudspeakers squawked, announcing discounted foods at various booths. Every year, near the end of the festival, any purveyor with food still left dropped the price, hoping to dump any excess offerings before the crowd departed so they didn't get stuck with it.

Dan looked at Conover. "A lot of people got hurt." And he suddenly got a string of unpleasant visuals, one right after the other.

"Yeah, they did, but that doesn't surprise me," Conover said bitterly. "All that coke and money. It did its dirty work on all of them. Most people don't stand a chance with that crap. They don't know what they're getting into until it's too late."

Dan could attest to that. Surprised him that Conover could see the big picture. Not everyone did. The big picture wasn't something Dan dared to dwell on. If he thought about that shit too long, he'd scare himself good. He'd come close–too close. Only an ironic twist of fate had allowed him to extricate himself from what had taken all those others down. He would think about it someday, couldn't escape that. But it wouldn't be today.

"And that means my partner and Bumpers died for nothing," Conover said bitterly.

"They all died for nothing." Dan sounded just as bitter, even to himself.

"Yeah, but the others were punks and scumbags." Conover turned and stared at Dan.

Dan stared right back, thinking of Shamrock in the ice machine, Captain McGee and his crewman, McGee's brother, and himself even, how close he'd come. And others he'd known too, other times, other places. They weren't all punks and scumbags. "I know some damn good people that shit has brought down."

That was all they said about it. They weren't going to change each other's minds. Seemed Conover knew that too.

"I've put in for retirement."

Didn't surprise Dan. He kind of felt like he'd retire too–if he could. "What are you going to do with yourself?"

"Try to find something I enjoy doing for a change, like I did with police work a long time ago."

Dan understood completely. Even though Conover sounded discouraged, like Dan had felt himself for a long time now, the man would bounce back. At least Dan hoped he would.

"Maybe I'll move down here to the beach like you. That must be the life." Conover smiled wistfully.

Dan didn't answer that. The man had saved his life, after all. Why spoil his illusion? Instead, he just nodded.

Conover hopped off the railing and extended his hand. "Good luck, Dan."

Dan studied Conover's face as he shook his hand. The man looked older than the first time Dan had seen him. More tired. Kind of like Dan felt every day when he looked in the mirror. "Take care of yourself, Ray."

Conover turned and walked away, disappearing into the dwindling crowd. It was past six and the tents were closing. The Seafood Festival was over for another year.

A heavy feeling came over Dan, the slight depression he got every year at this time. And that down feeling got him thinking in a direction he didn't want to go–cocaine. He tried to get rid of the thought before it grew into something strong and demanding and the only way to do that was to swap the thought out with something just as strong. He started thinking about his family, a process that had always helped in the past. This time, though, it was a little different. This time he knew if he didn't get his family back, he'd be lucky to make it through another Hampton Beach winter.

Because there was nothing as lonely and desolate as a summer resort in winter.

Hampton Beach was no exception.

The setting sun draped red wisps across the horizon. The day and the summer were both over. You couldn't stop the sun from going down and the seasons from changing, just like you couldn't stop death from knocking at your door when it was your turn.

Dan Marlowe dragged himself off the railing and headed down Ocean Boulevard, past the High Tide Restaurant toward his part of Hampton Beach and home.

About The Author

JED POWER is a Hampton Beach, NH-based writer and author of numerous short stories. Boss is his first foray into the crime novel world. The second novel in the Dan Marlowe crime series, *Hampton Beach Homicide*, will be published in the fall of 2012.

Find out more at www.darkjettypublishing.com.

Made in the USA
Middletown, DE
24 June 2019